TOWN AND GOWN

JOHN HIDEN

Indigo Dreams Publishing

First Edition: TOWN AND GOWN

First published in Great Britain in 2012 by:
Indigo Dreams Publishing Ltd
132 Hinckley Road
Stoney Stanton
Leics
LE9 4LN
www.indigodreams.co.uk

ISBN 978-1-907401-63-3

British Library Cataloguing in Publication Data. A CIP record for this book can be obtained from the British Library.

Designed and typeset in Minion Pro by Indigo Dreams.
Cover design by Dru Marland: drusilla.marland@btopenworld.com

Printed and bound in Great Britain by: The Russell Press Ltd. www.russellpress.com on FSC paper and board sourced from sustainable forests

The objections which are urged with reason against State education do not apply to the enforcement of education by the State, but to the State's taking upon itself to direct that education, which is a totally different thing.

John Stuart Mill, *On Liberty*

-

Previous Publications:

Solely authored books:

The Weimar Republic, Longman, 1974. 2nd revised edition 1996
Germany and Europe, Longman, 1977. 2nd revised edition 1993
The Baltic states and Weimar Ostpolitik, C.U.P., 1987. Paperback
edition, 2002
*Republican and Fascist Germany. Themes and Variations on the
History of Weimar and the Third Reich,* Longman, 1996
Defender of Minorities: Paul Schiemann 1876-1944, Hurst, 2004.
(Winner of Biennial Book Prize of the American Association for
the Advancement of Baltic Studies)

Jointly authored books

Explaining Hitler's Germany. Historians and the Third Reich
(with J. Farquharson), Batsford 1983 2nd revised edition 1989
*The Baltic Nations and Europe. Estonia, Latvia and Lithuania in
the 20h Century* (with P. Salmon), Longman, 1991. 2nd revised
edition, 1994
East meets West: Policies for a Common European Home (with
K. Featherstone), Fabian Pamphlet, 1991
Neighbours or Enemies? Germans, the Baltic and Beyond (with
M. Housden), Rodopi, Amsterdam, New York, 2008
*Ethnic Diversity and the Nation State. National Cultural
Autonomy Revisited* (with David Smith), Routledge, 2012.
Foreword by former education minister Charles Clarke.

Jointly edited books

The Baltic States in International Relations between the Wars, (with A. Loit) University of Stockholm, 1988
Contact or Isolation? Soviet-Western Relations in the Inter-War Period (with A Loit) University of Stockholm, 1991
Scandinavia and the Baltic States - 9 volumes of documents from the confidential print of the foreign office (with P. Salmon), University of America, 1997
The Baltic and the Outbreak of the Second World War (with T. Lane), C.U.P. 1992
The Baltic Question during the Cold War (with D. Smith, V. Made), Routledge, 2008. Paperback edition, 2009

Translations

The Hitler State, Longman, 1981. Martin Broszat's classic account of the Third Reich, *Der Staat Hitlers*.

For Juliet

TOWN AND GOWN

Chapter One

Friday afternoon. Sitting in Varne's Jaguar by the traffic lights Albert Burkit turned up the stereo to nearly full volume. He waited for the band's introduction to finish before singing alongside the clarinet's statement of the theme.

"A tinkling piano in the next apartment," he bellowed. "A telephone that rings but who's to answer?"

He adjusted the pitch downwards.

"The winds of March that make my heart a dancer."

Something made him glance to his left where a middle aged woman in a mini was staring at him through her open car window. He nodded as the lights changed, letting her move ahead where the road narrowed beyond the junction.

Examining his watch Albert saw that he had thirty minutes to spare. He glanced in his driving mirror, stroked the stubble on his chin with the back of his hand and smoothed back his hair.

Turning into a lane on his left he pulled up two hundred yards farther on beside a row of terraced houses. One of them he now owned. It had seen better days, he had to admit. He fastened the middle button of his suit and sauntered up to the front door, where he pulled a small red notebook from his inside pocket and leafed through its pages.

"Mr. Fellows," he muttered, "two weeks behind."

Instead of using his own keys he knocked on the door. A thin young man wearing glasses opened it. He had a book in his hand and looked irritated.

"You're not Mr. Fellows." Albert stated."

The man's expression brightened. "Ah, our landlord," he said. As he closed his book Albert glanced at the title, *Language,*

Truth and Logic.

"Any good, that book?" He asked.

"Depends what you mean by good. It's supposed to be a classic."

Albert raised an eyebrow. "Mr. Fellows then, is he in?"

"Should be, shall I fetch him for you?"

"I'll just pop in to see him. You get back to your classic."

It was cool inside. Albert watched the man go upstairs before moving silently towards the back of the house. Thick embossed wallpaper lined the gloomy narrow corridor. Might need a quick paint job fairly soon, Albert thought. He approached a badly chipped door on his left at the end of the passage. It opened suddenly and Fellows came out with a towel over his shoulder, making Albert think of a rabbit caught in headlights.

"Mr. Burkit!" the man said, "I was going to contact you."

"I don't doubt it Mr. Fellows," Albert answered, walking his tenant backwards. "Tidy, at least," he commented, glancing round the sparsely furnished room. He indicated a chair by a large square table near the window. Fellows sat down.

"This," Albert went on, "is my little red book." He opened it and held the page out. "Basically, we need to put something in this column."

Fellows shrugged his shoulders. "I'm broke, completely, I really am."

Albert stared intently as the silence lengthened. Fellows relented.

"OK, as it happens I have just had a cheque. I can give you something but I need to buy a few essentials."

"Show me," Albert said, holding out his hand.

Fellows went to a bookcase near the door and brought back a cheque. Albert examined it carefully. He looked up and

14

smiled.

"This will do nicely. It covers what you owe me plus another few weeks. By then you'll be off to your parents for the hols. Stick this in your bank pronto and meanwhile give me one of your cheques."

"But I've got to eat!"

"Get another loan. That's what banks are for."

He watched the student return to the book case for his cheque book. "You don't look too good, Mr. Fellows. You should go out more."

Fellows sat down resignedly and picked up a biro.

"Alright, alright, just make it out for what you owe me. But," Albert narrowed his eyes, "start thinking about the next instalment as soon as you can." He smiled inwardly. Two weeks' rent was all he had come for but a shake- up would do his tenant no harm.

"Off to your shower then," he said, nodding at the towel still draped over the student's shoulder. "Be seeing you."

Just as Albert opened the front door the man who had let him in reappeared.

"Find Mr. Fellows did you? Actually," he paused. "I need to have a word with you about the sink in my room."

"Is it blocked?"

"Not really, but the smell sometimes is quite bad."

"Drains," said Albert. "Often the case with these older terraced houses. Give the council people a bell in the first place. See what they have to say. OK?"

Back in the car he jotted down the title of the student's book before driving past the playing fields at the back of the campus and on to the main road. He turned left through the front gates of the University, ignoring the 5 miles per hour signs en route to the staff car park. He reached this just as a battered

Mercedes came out through the exit, leaving a vacant space barely fifty feet away. Without hesitation Albert ignored the large "No entry" sign and slid the Jaguar into the empty slot. Only after locking the door did he notice the white estate car that had pulled up behind him. Its wispily haired driver was half out of the car and gesticulating angrily.

"I say," the man called out, "have you got a parking permit?"

Albert pointed at the sign in the estate car's window informing the world that there was a small person on board. "That you?" he asked.

Eleanor Varne, daughter of Albert's employer, stood at the top of a flight of steps leading up to the Arts building. She looked put out, he thought. But then she often did. Her pale skin and straight blonde hair made her look severe at the best of times. Smart, no doubt, but cold was how Albert would have described her, if asked. Good looking too, certainly.

"Sorry I'm late," he said, "you know what it's like here. I had to drive round for quite a while before I found a space."

Eleanor nodded disinterestedly. Nothing was said on the way back to the car. As usual on the odd occasion when Albert was asked to pick her up she sat in the front passenger seat next to him. She pushed her hands through her hair and sighed.

"Good lesson, was it?" Albert asked, as he backed the car out and moved towards the exit.

"It gets harder to study as you get older, so I'm told. And German is a bugger to master."

"I'm not sure that twenty-six counts as old exactly," Albert said politely.

Without apparent effort he nosed the car into the heavy

traffic streaming past the university entrance gates. It would take about twenty minutes at this time of the afternoon to reach Varne's house. With luck they should miss the school rush. That gave him time to get back to his flat for a bath before going into town for a meal and a film.

Ahead of him was a large roundabout. Over it loomed a building that stubbornly retained the appearance of the cinema it had once been, despite sporting the logo and trappings of a well known supermarket chain. He took the second exit and drove along a dual carriageway towards the village of Wilmington, on the outskirts of which was Varne's substantial home. He longed to switch on the stereo but that could wait.

"By the way," Eleanor suddenly said, "I'll probably need you again next week. "I plan to ask this tutor of mine for a drink to see if he wants to help us out with some Germans coming to see my father. When you drop me off you can give him the once over. You know my father values your impressions."

To Albert her tone implied her father's opinions were not hers.

"Right you are," he said. "Let me know when I'm wanted to see this, what's his name?"

"Farnham," Eleanor said, taking out a packet of cigarettes. "Eric Farnham."

The person in question leafed through his diary for the month of June. The pages were reassuringly blank, except for two dates pencilled in as "Examination." Even those were prefaced by question marks. He looked up to find Wallace Kingsly, Professor of Linguistics and chair person of the department, gazing expectantly at the assembled staff. Henry Helm, also a Professor, finished examining his own notebook. His pale complexion, dark

17

hair and prominent nose belied his fifty-nine years.

Kingsly's face, of sun-like hue beneath a frothy cloud of grey hair, turned towards Eric, who once more consulted his agenda for the rest of the term.

"Tuesday at two should be fine," he said, taking care to sound surprised at the unexpected gap in his working week.

"We need a meeting amongst ourselves at some point before the external examiner arrives on the Wednesday of that week," Kingsly announced for the second time.

"I have a session at two with some students," Peter Everton chipped in. "Two-thirty five any use?"

Henry Helm listened impassively to the outcome of Kingsly's attempt to arrange for a provisional review of final examination marks. He leaned forward in his chair.

"Why don't we say after the Board of Studies meeting on Monday, that is the sixth of June?"

His intervention settled the matter. All present relaxed while the sequel to Kingsly's request for any other business got underway. A numb sensation in one of Eric's legs brought unwillingly to mind an article he had read on deep vein thrombosis. He caught sight of Alan Branch briefly miming raising a glass to his lips and signalled agreement.

It was almost five o' clock. The late afternoon sun shone through the medieval-styled arched windows on to a long polished table. A map of Germany provided the backdrop to the six of his colleagues opposite, facing the window. The remaining four members of the German department, excluding Henry and Kingsly at each end of the table, were arrayed on either side of Eric's chair. White painted walls reflected heat as well as light. The air was stale. Margaret had firmly shut the windows to spare staff the noise of traffic from the main road.

"That should give us a chance to think about Peter's plans

18

for changing our examination procedures," she ca

For reasons unclear to Eric her rem
colleagues laugh as they gathered belongings and
The smell of fresh perfume in the corridor alerte
presence of the departmental secretary, Angela.

"Message for you, Eric," she called out. "A Ms. Varne
wants her tutorial to be next Tuesday if that's o.k."

Eric thanked her, briefly pushing aside the listlessness that
overcame him during staff meetings. Now then, young Farnham,
he quietly intoned on the way back to his office, sonorously
stretching out the last word of his query, what did you expect
from Aarkardeemia?

"Talking to yourself again?"

Eric was startled to hear Alan Branch just behind him. The
passageway in which the two of them stood continued the faux
medieval style of the building by being long, narrow and low.
Tiny windows with deep sills resembled the slits used by archers
in old castle walls. Down below Eric glimpsed Kingsly, his
current favourite for an arrow in the back, billowing towards the
common room.

"Alan, sorry, didn't hear you." Eric answered, remaining
near the window and gazing at the road in the near distance. The
city's distinctive blue buses threw up clouds of dust and shook
the branches of the trees as they passed the main gate. It looked
hotter than ever. Thinly frocked girls were much in evidence. The
bicycle traffic was building to its early evening crescendo.

"Good news," Alan said, clapping Eric on the shoulder.
"I've put you down for a staff versus student five a side football
match in the gym."

"Christ, during the summer term?" Eric asked.

Alan laughed, displaying small, even white teeth.

"The current student representative is keen, so it's soccer

ing."

Eric, careful of his physical regime in the thirty second year of life, grunted and went into his tiny office. Alan followed him. Opposite the doorway a window looking over the central courtyard was framed on both sides by crammed book cases. A desk between them was littered with untidy stacks of paper.

"Shouldn't be too strenuous," Alan commented. He replaced a book that he had picked up, throwing a disbelieving glance at the piled up papers on Eric's desk. "Make a note of the date."

Eric did so using a blank sheet of paper and placed it on his computer keyboard. "Come on, let's have this drink," he said, throwing the papers from the staff meeting into a random section of his filing cabinet and slamming the draw home with satisfying force.

Albert stood by the kitchen sink while Terry Varne sipped his coffee. Through the window Frank the gardener could be seen, hoeing what looked to be an immaculate flower bed. From the sitting room came the sound of a Hoover as Elsie the cleaner went about her rites. Mrs. Varne was arranging flowers in the dining room. Only Terry Varne was at rest.

"Help yourself to a coffee," he said, indicating a large silver jug.

"Not at the moment Mr. Varne," Albert answered. He had discovered the joys of espresso on a visit to Italy and the habit had stuck.

"I was talking on the 'phone to a business contact of mine," Varne unexpectedly stated. "Happened to mention he saw the Jag parked in Inkers Lane."

"Mate of mine lives there," Albert replied casually. He

20

looked directly at Varne. "It was on the way to pick up Eleanor so I dropped in for a chat."

"Bit of a rough area that, lad. Watch the car. Mostly students and drop outs. Ripe for development, those old terraces," Varne mused. "What with the university being so near…" He stopped abruptly.

Albert watched Varne closely as the latter put his cup down and eased his bulk back from the table. The city was a small place. Albert had heard rumours too. He made a mental note to be more careful where he parked the car in future.

Varne moved towards the sink with his empty cup, the top of his head roughly level with Albert's shoulder. He rapped on the window. When the gardener looked up Varne pointed vigorously to the far end of the flower bed where a garden cane had fallen to the ground. Frank looked towards it, waved and resumed hoeing.

"Don't know what I pay them for," Varne muttered. His small eyes focused once more on Albert.

"Shouldn't you be getting to the station soon?"

"No problem. A taxi will be here in a few minutes."

"Back to work," Varne stated. "Monday mornings," he growled, shaking his head as he went through the back door towards his office, a low brick building at the end of the garden. Albert watched his boss pick his way carefully across an expanse of unnaturally green grass via a series of inlaid paving stones and grinned. He picked up his overnight bag near the front door and went outside to wait for the taxi. It came on time, carefully executing a turn on the expanse of gravel. On the way to the station the driver stopped to allow a sizeable crowd exiting the campus to cross the road. Most of it made its way towards the pub on the opposite side. When do they do any work, Albert wondered.

21

Barely two hundred yards away Eric Farnham was listening to a student reading an essay. "Thank you, Andrew," he said when the speaker finished, "some useful points there, I think."

There were three other people present, two of them bearded. Eric glanced down at his half open desk draw where a row of labelled black and white passport sized portraits glared up at him.

"Any reactions, Alan?" He asked.

Alan James acknowledged that the essay seemed interesting. His companion, Nigel Hodges, continued to stare at a copy of the paper he had just listened to but said nothing.

"Well," Barbara Parker began, "what Andrew was saying about the historical background to Goethe's work seemed to me muddled. In my opinion...."

A welcome sense of relief overcame Eric at the anticipated intervention from a shapely, bespectacled girl, leaning forward with a business like air. Most of his colleagues these days fed course handouts through the photocopying machine until it became white hot but Eric's teaching entailed minimal preparation. It relied on raising the occasional question in a suitably speculative tone of voice and with appropriate facial expression, if and when discussion faltered. He rubbed his scalp gently, speculating on a link between headaches and thinning hair.

"Any value," he asked when Ms Parker was momentarily silenced by an interruption from Alan, "in comparing Goethe with, oh, let's say, a more modern writer?"

The conversation flickered back into life and Eric risked another quick look at the sheet of paper on his lap. It concerned the application of numerical grades in examinations, thrust into his hand by Peter Everton that very morning. At least it threw light on the laughter at the end of the staff meeting.

The 'phone rang and he picked it up, gesturing to those present to carry on.

"Eric, are you busy?" It was Clara's voice.

"Well, I'm in the middle of a tutorial."

"I'll be quick," she said, "I can't make it for lunch tomorrow."

"Oh," Eric said flatly.

"Come off it!" Clara's voice rose and then dropped to a lower tone. "It's Peter. He wants me to fetch some notes from his parents' house for him, over in York. He says he *has* to have them." Eric frowned at the telephone.

"Notes?" he echoed.

"I can't explain now. I have to go along to the school in a minute to see Ellis's teacher. Can we meet tonight after my evening class? In the *Duke's Head* at Cottingly, half-nine?"

"Right," Eric said and put the receiver down, aware of Barbara Parker's glasses glinting in his direction.

Some fifteen minutes later the tutorial petered out. After outlining tasks for the following week and mentioning a book or two Eric joined the on-the-hour traffic of students and lecturers. Almost immediately he was confronted by Daniel White. True to habit the latter seemed astonished at the physical presence of one of his colleagues on a normal working day.

"*Hello* there, Eric!" he called out.

"Morning, Daniel."

Eric's mind was still on what Clara Everton had just said on the telephone so he experienced a slight shock when Daniel mentioned her husband's name.

"What?" he asked abruptly.

"Peter's scheme," Daniel repeated.

23

The two of them passed the last of the sunken green lawns and went from the bright sunshine into the shadowed coolness of the building housing the Senior Common Room.

"To be honest Daniel, I've barely glanced at it. Is it any good?"

Standing alongside Eric in the staff lavatory Daniel eventually committed himself to the extent of saying that the scheme seemed involved.

"Confusing?" Eric suggested.

"Possibly. Complicated, anyway."

Their respective faces stared back from the mirror above the wash basins. Daniel's was round and cheerful. Eric examined his own heavy jaw and dark, tired-looking eyes. The water was barely warm and the cheap paper towel disintegrated immediately on contact with moisture. More evidence of economies could be found in the Senior Common Room in the shape of a steel coffee urn. It substituted for the cheerful lady who had served drinks up until a few weeks ago. Daniel put money in the box for two coffees before promptly accepting the coins Eric offered for his own drink. They sat at one of the low tables near the window.

"Kingsly seems quite keen on Peter's suggested changes," Daniel observed.

And that, Eric thought, should nicely guarantee Henry Helm's opposition. He said nothing of this to Daniel, aware of the latter's unease at the mere suggestion of departmental friction. Daniel had barely touched his coffee before catching sight of the Professor of English on the other side of the large room.

"Need to have a quick word with Philip," Daniel said apologetically, "must dash."

His short, dark-suited figure circumvented tables and

chairs before hailing the Professor on a rising note. Eric grinned to himself and picked up the *Times*, an unusual achievement on a busy Monday morning. The "Public Appointments" section had its habitual air of brevity. Next he turned to the weekly letters. As if in a film close-up, the name Everton stood out from the page. The missive was short and Peter had given his home address rather than that of the University.

"Sir, your recent correspondence on the financial strains facing universities appears to be premised on the notion that such institutions are of intrinsic value to the community at large. Why then the persistent calls to make them more 'relevant?' Many lecturers have difficulty in identifying, let alone pursuing relevant ends. Before claiming to 'examine' undergraduates, academics surely need stringently to investigate their own aims and methods."

Eric read the letter through twice in gleeful disbelief, tinged with a curious sense of envy. He wondered what Clara had made of it.

Chapter Two

The following morning Eric sat in his office waiting for the Varne woman. It was another glorious day and he had opened the window to let the smoke out. He kept thinking of what Clara Everton had told him in the pub the night before, about her long drive to fetch from her father-in-law's house the dog-eared lecture notes that Peter had insisted he urgently needed for his class on Friday.

Eric stubbed out his cigarette and turned with a new eye to the proposed marking system. Peter had unearthed results for finals examination papers for the preceding six years (why six? Eric wondered) and converted the lettered marks of every single student to numbers. Table after table was appended, decorated here and there with asterisks referring to short sentences of explanation in the footnotes.

Eric acknowledged the obvious link between an A grade and a figure of seventy-five percent, as well as that between thirty percent and a failed D, a mark Margaret liked to refer to as a flash of Delta. As to the intricate calculations proposed by Peter to convert into numbers the less clear cut alphabetical marks between these two extremes Eric could only gaze in wonder.

A knock on the door brought him back to reality. He thrust Peter's scheme into its blue folder and buried it beneath a pile of books.

"Come in," he called.

A medium sized blonde entered carrying an expensive leather executive case. Her skin was smooth and tightly drawn over her cheek bones. Until she smiled briefly her face had a petulant, not to say disdainful look.

"Sit down, Ms. Varne," he said, half rising, aware from

bitter experience of the sloping ceiling of his office. Involuntarily he glanced down as she crossed ample but finely shaped legs. As far as he could tell without reaching out to stroke it her fawn coloured summer suit was made of silk. A rich fragrance filled the air.

"Christ, it's hot in here isn't it?" She said in a clear, loud voice.

When she bent forward to open the case her straight hair slipped forward from her shoulders. Slyly Eric watched her movements as she straightened up.

"There," she said," Another piece for you to look at."

He took the sheet of paper from her outstretched hand and handed back in return the previous week's exercise, now corrected. Her hands, he noticed, were small when compared with her otherwise generous proportions. At a rough guess the collection of bracelets dangling from her wrist barely exceeded his salary.

"Your last piece of work was quite good," he said, with a degree of honesty. "One or two minor slips, the odd careless use of the indefinite article."

"We mustn't have that, must we," she answered with the briefest of smiles.

Again, Eric found little evidence on this, her third tutorial that she was over anxious to become fluent in German. As if parrying this thought she announced, "My father is keen for me to carry on, if that's still all right with you?" Another smile, showing widely spaced front teeth.

"No problem on my side," Eric responded truthfully.

He moved a chair next to hers and they went through his hand written corrections together. The room seemed to grow even hotter. From time to time she turned towards Eric to acknowledge his comments. The allotted half hour passed more quickly than he would have liked. By the time he had explained in detail his comments on her translation exercise it was mid-day.

"Well, Ms. Varne," he said," I think that's about all we can do for now."

She smiled again, this time with studied brilliance. Reluctantly Eric returned to his chair on the other side of the desk.

"Thank you, *Dr* Farnham!" she said. He looked up in surprise.

"Well, what should I call you?" he asked.

"Eleanor, perhaps?"

She shrugged as she spoke and opened her handbag to produce a packet of cigarettes. Why not, he thought, when she offered him one. He lit both cigarettes with a match from his paper clip tray. For some reason he could think of nothing to say and the silence lengthened. He began to feel an obscure resentment mingled with a desire to prolong the moment. She sighed and blew out a cloud of smoke before standing up abruptly.

"Same time, same place next week?" she asked.

Eric half rose once more but she gestured quickly.

"No need to see me out."

She picked up her things and opened the door. On the threshold she paused.

"Actually, I have a business proposition to put to you. Perhaps we could meet for a drink in the week?" She came back towards his desk. "Here's a card with my home number on it. "Bye, *doctor.*"

Eric was both pleased and irritated that her path crossed that of Margaret Allen, who now entered his room. Pleased because Margaret was obviously curious about the attractive and well heeled young woman, irritated at having to postpone thinking about the unexpected ending to his tutorial. He slipped Eleanor Varne's card under some blotting paper, as if saving a last square of chocolate for later consumption.

"I haven't seen her before have I?" Margaret frowned.

"Not one of ours Margaret, I'm afraid."

She continued to stare expectantly. He gave in.

"Private tuition, not one of our regular students," he said shortly.

Margaret's visit was rare in itself. Eric guessed rightly that it portended more tedious departmental jockeying and waited for her to speak. Her lips pursed at regular intervals, as if worked by an inner clock and her tortoiseshell glasses glinted beneath a grey fringe. Not for the first time he made an effort to think more kindly of her. She was, he knew, fifty-five. Months of speculation about voluntary retirement and what the Vice Chancellor called rationalisation had given staff a rabid interest in scanning the landscape to identify candidates for either fate.

"Look, Eric, I'll come to the point. I have a class in a few minutes." He waited for her to resume after another pause, "What do you make of Peter's scheme?"

"It's interesting, Margaret," he responded cautiously."

"Good. I was hoping that you would be open-minded."

Eric shifted uncomfortably. "Margaret, what does Henry Helm think of all this?"

She frowned again, the ensuing silence long enough to make Eric consider leaving the room.

"Since he is not in the chair this session it does not matter quite so much. Er, in the sense that he, well, he won't um actually, one would imagine, lead the discussion. He certainly doesn't appear to be overly enthusiastic about the proposed changes," Margaret added, startling Eric with an unwonted directness.

"Ah, well," she finally said after a momentary silence, "I need to have a word with one or two more people."

No sooner had the door closed behind her than Eric realised she had said nothing about Peter Everton's letter to the *Times*. He dismissed the thought, retrieved the visiting card from beneath the blotting paper and sat looking at it.

Albert was in the Jaguar in front of Varne's house waiting for Eleanor. He knew from experience that she would be late. Varne had long since made plain that the same latitude was not extended to Albert. Not that Albert minded. He usually carried a book in his pocket, despite or, he often assured himself, because of leaving school at fifteen. His interest had been instantly captured by the opening words of the small volume he now held in his hands. Best of all he savoured the sentence at the end of the first paragraph.

"For if there are any questions which science leaves it to philosophy to answer, a straightforward process of elimination must lead to their discovery."

Albert had already committed the phrase to memory. He chuckled at the thought of repeating it to the tenant who had unwittingly introduced him to the book. The picture on the back cover showed a silver haired gent in a high backed chair, well stocked bookshelves in the background. Albert liked the look of A.J. Ayer. His expression suggested amused disbelief at the behaviour of the wider world, a sentiment with which Albert felt at one. He was especially pleased at the discovery in the preface that the philosopher was known to his friends as 'Freddy.' It somehow brought him nearer, Albert felt.

"The traditional disputes of philosophers are, for the most

30

part, as unwarranted as they are unfruitful," he read aloud, before hastily stuffing the book back into his pocket at the sight of Eleanor coming down the front steps of the house. Her dress looked good, Albert noticed.

"What have you been up to then?" Eleanor asked when she was seated and he had started the engine. He looked at her in surprise. She pointed to his pocket.

"Good book? Can I see it?"

Albert resignedly handed it to her. For a few moments they drove in silence.

"Who would have thought," she said, handing the book back to Albert, "a closet philosopher."

The indifference she conveyed with this remark stung Albert.

"I like to read a bit," was all he said.

"You know that pub on the corner, where the university road meets the main route into the city?" she asked. "Can't remember what it's called. It's by the traffic lights."

"The Falconers," Albert said shortly.

"Right, that's where we are going. I'm a bit late so step on it. Not that our Dr. Farnham is likely to leave before I get there."

If only, Albert thought.

Eric's attention was taken by the singer's bottom, framed in the triangle made by Alan's outstretched clarinet and arms. The pianist played a loud chord under the closing words of the song. Finally, the clarinet joined with a trill or two above a flurry of drums. All finished more or less together except for a last clash from the cymbal. Eric had the feeling, but was not sure, that this was intentional. Even so, the applause struck him as over enthusiastic.

Alan, clarinet under his arm, bowed, looking highly

pleased. His forehead shone with perspiration and his glasses glinted as he announced a short interval. Looking round at the faces Eric detected no overt hostility. Not that their expressions were all that clear. Despite the many lamps the light they cast was absorbed by the dark panelling of the walls and the clouds of tobacco smoke

Eric and Alan navigated their way from the raised stand in the corner through a sea of tables. Few of these had chairs, so that most drinkers were compelled to stand. A large archway led to a second room with neon lights and a long bar. Alan pushed past bodies holding the arm of the singer, a typist from the Department of Sociology called Edna. He nodded happily as the odd friend congratulated him but a large bearded youth wearing what looked like rompers clapped him on the back.

"Get Acker a beer, Susan," he called to a barmaid with stiff blonde hair and extraordinarily long eye lashes.

Eric could only guess at what Alan made of this remark. He had long been so bewitched by a legendary American clarinettist that he wore the same spectacles as those seen on photographs of said musician. There, Eric thought unkindly, the resemblance abruptly ended.

"Right then, Acker," the man said as he passed Alan a pint of beer, "I'll just have a chat with your singer." He pronounced 'singer' as two separate words. Edna disappeared behind a massive forearm. Alan held up his drink.

"Seems to have gone quite well, don't you think Eric?"

"You haven't been thrown out. Still, it's still only just nine o'clock."

"Actually, we hear the landlord might want us to play here more often."

Eric nodded absently. He felt hot and his jacket was growing heavier by the minute.

"Is she not here yet?" Alan asked.

"Well it will only be a flying visit."

As if on cue, Eleanor came through the door wearing a soft, dark coloured dress. To his surprise she was followed by a man of medium height, neatly dressed in a pin-striped suit. There was an air of suppressed menace about his well proportioned features that Eric could not at first account for. Then he realised that it had something to do with his curiously flat looking stare. After listening to Eleanor the man glanced briefly in Eric's direction, nodded and moved to the other room. Eleanor joined Eric and Alan.

"Sorry, I'm late," she said, "and I have to leave even earlier than I thought. We are due to collect my father from a business meeting."

She glanced at Alan and Eric hurriedly introduced him. To his relief Alan shortly afterwards made his excuses and went to the other room.

"What would you like to drink?" Eric asked her.

"It's being taken care of. Albert is getting it. He works for my father by the way."

Eric, thrust against Eleanor by a passing customer, experienced a brief resurgence of the irritation he had felt when she was in his office.

"Does this Albert chap usually drive you about?"

"Very rarely, as it happens, I have my own car of course. What is your point?"

"Nothing, really," he conceded.

"You're probably used to quizzing students," she said dismissively.

"Right," he said, catching sight of Albert carrying their drinks on a small tray. The man had little difficulty in moving through the crowded room, inclining his head slightly as each obstacle removed itself from his path before he joined Eleanor and Eric. He gave her a gin and tonic, took his own whisky and handed Eric a beer before putting the tray on a nearby table.

"Cheers, Mein Herr," said Albert.

Eleanor snorted at Eric's expression. There was silence for a few moments and Eric became aware that Albert was studying him closely.

"Well, this is all very jolly," Eric said."

Eleanor raised her eyes briefly towards the ceiling. Albert turned to her. "I see what you mean," he commented."

"Albert," Eleanor said quickly, placing a hand on his shoulder, "I'll join you shortly. Bring the car round and I'll be out in ten minutes."

Albert gave Eric a blank look, finished his whisky in one gulp and moved back through the crowd. Almost at once two drinkers stood up to leave and Eleanor promptly took one of the chairs. Eric sat beside her.

"Don't mind Albert," Eleanor said. "He doesn't come across too many lecturers."

"No, my fault. I probably sounded a bit offhand." He paused. "Now, what did you mean about a business proposition for me?"

"Could you," she said, placing a hand on his arm, "would you help us out for a few hours next week?"

"Us?"

"My father is looking for somebody to show a group of Germans around. I told him you might be interested. Oh, they all speak a fair bit of English but we think it would be nice if somebody who knew their language was on hand. We want to make a good impression."

"I doubt if I would be much use as, what a courier?"

"There you go again!"

34

He put his hand to his forehead "Right. So, what does your father do by the way?"

"He has various ventures," she said vaguely, waving a hand. "Of course, you would be paid if you could help us out."

"And Albert?" he asked. She smiled.

"He just came to check you out. You would be working with him if you are basically interested in the idea."

Eric saw Alan waving from the other side of the room and he held up an answering hand. "Well," he responded, "I don't think Albert took to me, do you?"

"Why, because you were dismissive of him? Look," she added, "I really have to go soon. Shall we make another effort? Perhaps go out for a meal?"

"That would be nice. At least you can tell your father you tried." He stood up with her, reluctant now for the conversation to end. "Shall I ring you?"

"No, we'll be in touch by the weekend. Think it over at least."

Eric felt and looked perplexed.

She scooped her bag from the table. "If Albert had taken a dislike to you...." She left the sentence unfinished, pecked him briefly on the cheek and left him standing between the tables.

"What did you make of him?" Eleanor asked Albert as they drove towards the city to pick up Terry Varne.

In the darkness of the car Albert smiled to himself. Recalling Varne's earlier reference to developments in Inkers Lane he concluded that no matter what he thought of this Farnham bloke, a contact in the university could be very handy.

"Big chap for a lecturer isn't he? Yeah, he'll do if he's willing."

Chapter Three

Eric arrived for lunch the next day to find an unusually crowded Senior Common Room. It dawned on him that he had never seen most of the people before, anywhere in the university. Alan was being served at the bar and Eric tapped him on the shoulder.

"I'll order one for you," Alan said. "You'll need a double today."

"Bad as that Alan?"

His colleague looked startled. "Checked your mail?" he asked. Eric shook his head. "Seen the morning papers?" Alan persisted.

"No, why?"

"The letter! It arrived today."

"Oh," Eric said, "I thought that was weeks away."

He looked about him more carefully. In the far corner of the room three classics lecturers were huddled together. They didn't look happy. A few tables beyond them sat a larger group. These at least Eric identified as historians.

"Not good for us?" Eric asked anxiously.

"Far worse than we thought," Alan said, "15 per cent cut."

"For the university as a whole? Not for our department surely?"

Again Alan studied him closely. Nearby a large, florid man with flowing grey hair guffawed loudly. Eric had a vague idea that he was a scientist of repute.

"Yes," Alan muttered, frowning, "he can afford to celebrate, look."

He handed over two sheets of paper stapled together. Eric glanced down at a series of bullet points summarising the deliberations of the University Grants Committee on his

36

university's future. "Physical sciences to expand," he read. Farther down there was a reference to classics being phased out. Art history, it was suggested, should be merged with a similar department at a university a mere seventy-five miles distant. He turned the page with trepidation. Under modern languages there was a reference to future diversification of the department's mission. Eric looked up from the text.

"No actual mention of job losses for us then," he said.

Alan gave a short laugh. "You think those on the hit list are going to give in without a battle? Did you take in that little sentence about our 'mission'? I think we can assume that life won't be improving. Probably means more service teaching for us, at the very least." He noticed Eric's puzzlement. "German for scientists, beginner's classes in French for humanities students, you name it. We can wave good bye to our small classes." Alan adjusted his glasses. "If you look again you'll notice that staff-student ratios are expected to rise dramatically."

Eric quietly absorbed the significance of this. As he did so two of the historians pushed past in the direction of the bar.

"All right for some," said one of them, a burly man with protruding teeth.

"Fred," Alan acknowledged the man.

"Bloody disgrace," Fred said, with genuine fury. When he was out of hearing Alan explained that the history department had been virtually condemned to closure. Privately Eric felt this took some pressure off him.

"What happens next?" he asked. Alan looked reflective.

"Nothing much, for the moment I imagine. The university has to consider the proposals, make its responses."

Eric tried to recall in more detail the procedures he had read about only cursorily months ago in the press.

"You and I *should* survive," Alan went on thoughtfully.

"Two or three of our colleagues might take early retirement." He shook his head. "Mind you, when the ball gets rolling there really is no telling what the outcome will be. We'll see wheeling and dealing on an epic scale, you can bet on it."

As if on cue Henry Helm appeared at Alan's elbow. Not one to waste words and to conversations what drought was to flowers, Henry said tersely, "I'm trying to fix a session for next week so that we can discuss the implications of the letter."

"Good idea," Eric said with what sincerity he could muster.

Henry smiled briefly and left as abruptly as he had arrived.

"How old is Helm?" Alan asked.

"Fifty-seven. I read the dust jacket of his book on German thinkers of the 1930s."

"Were there any?" Alan asked, completing their usual joke.

They pushed through the growing mob to return their glasses to the bar then made their way upstairs to the dining room. In it the aroma of fish vied with that of curry. The queue for lunch, contained between two rows of trestle-like tables, stretched back from a door at the far end of the room. On either side of the room were small round tables, already nearly full. Peter Everton was seated at one by the window with Daniel White. Two vacant chairs separated them.

Despite the warmth there was a generous sprinkling of woollen sports jackets and lounge suits. Someone was even sporting a thick roll-necked sweater. Above it, to Eric's surprise, floated not a sweltering red but a pale, thinly bearded face. Its lips moved in a manner suggesting meaningful talk. Eric gave the idea the benefit of the doubt.

When they reached the service counter he listened half-heartedly to Alan exchanging pleasantries with the ladies dishing out food. Emerging once more into the dining room after paying for their meals they took the chairs between Peter and Daniel. The latter was tackling a steamed pudding while Peter Everton spooned yoghurt with exaggerated care. His dark hair had a faintly unwashed look and his round even features were showing signs of tiredness.

"Well," Daniel exclaimed, "what about that letter!"

Eric foresaw this query recurring with nauseating frequency. He looked up from his chicken curry and was disconcerted to find Peter staring intently at him.

"I glanced at your scheme by the way, Peter," Eric observed, without having intended to. "Interesting."

Peter Everton leaned forward with a serious expression and asked, "We were speculating about what would happen if we were to lose our jobs. What would you do, Eric?"

"Me!" Eric said in mock horror, "only now about to end my probation, to 'cross the bar' as they say."

"Some have been known to get stuck at the bar," Alan piped up. The others joined in the laughter.

"Don't worry Eric," Daniel said, "you should squeeze through before things really get bad."

Even as he spoke Daniel looked anxious to be on the move. He left them with a brief apology and went off towards the collection point for empty trays. Alan glanced briefly at Eric before addressing Peter.

"Clara OK?" he asked tentatively, "and Ellis?"

"I should hope so," Peter retorted. "Why not? They have money, food and a place to live. What can I say? Ellis isn't home much, even though his 'A' levels are coming up."

Alan expressed sympathy and silence ensued. Peter stood up abruptly.

"Playing squash at half-past," was all he said before

marching off.

"That man will go into orbit one of these days," Alan commented.

The remark prompted Eric to tell him about the episode of Peter's lecture notes. During the ensuing gossip it became clear that Alan, inveterate *'Guardian'* reader, had also not yet read Peter's letter. More interestingly to Eric, on later reflection, Henry Helm had yet to pronounce on the subject.

Albert looked at the clock on the wall above the door and reluctantly closed his book. Rinsing out a coffee cup he wiped the area around the sink and made sure the cooker was switched off. He liked his kitchen and spent much time in it whenever he came back to the flat. The large square table at the centre of the room was surrounded by expensive fitted units. Highly polished wood had not been spared. Sometimes, idly looking at homes of the famous in Sunday magazines, Albert worried that the room was too neat. The odd plant had been added and most recently he had moved a few books from his lounge to a shelf near the cooker. Automatically he straightened his chair before checking that the door to the small back garden was locked.

In his bedroom he rummaged through a collection of ties and chose a pale blue one to go with his light grey suit. Varne was touchy about appearances at his pre-lunch drinks sessions for visitors. It was Albert's task on these rare occasions to ensure that all the guests had their glasses topped up. Not that he minded, particularly after realising how much information could be gleaned when wandering about with a tray. On this particular Sunday he was looking forward to seeing what Varne made of the Farnham character. He grinned at the thought of the lecturer turning up in the worn corduroy jacket and jeans that he had sported in the pub.

"Too much to hope for," he said aloud. Satisfied with his own appearance Albert picked up the car keys and left the flat.

Looking back at its solid front door and wide bay window always put him in good spirits. He'd heard that the flat above his own was coming on the market soon and he was definitely interested. The building was located on the edge of one of the city's parks and the area was looking up. What better investment, Albert mentally asked his long departed Mum, for the rental income from his house in Inkers Lane? On top of all that, he had discovered that a famous poet had lived and died only five doors away from his own. The man's name was already on the growing list of authors that Albert intended to read.

Eric walked slowly along a tree lined avenue looking for 'High Trees' before arriving at a broad, yellowish brick building of some ugliness sitting astride a wide arc of gravel. His general knowledge of cars was not extensive but he guessed the total cost of the dozen or so machines littering the driveway would fund several lectureships. He was hot and his reflection in the gleaming chrome bumpers surrounding him confirmed that his linen suit was indeed wrinkled.

The clinical neatness and symmetry of the building reminded him of a crematorium he had once been to. He knocked on the dark blue front door and was surprised to find it opened by Eleanor in person. She was wearing a sleeveless but expensive looking brown dress.

"Glad you could make it," she said.

"Sunday is not my busiest day," Eric lied, thinking of Clara's pleas to meet him for a mid-day drink.

"Did you bring your bathing things?"

41

Eric gestured at a plastic carrier bag he was holding. Privately, he had no intention of swimming. They passed through an enormous entrance hall with a domed glass roof and a balcony some fifteen feet above floor level. There was a strong smell of wax polish. The image of the crematorium was deepened by the clean white paint and the abundance of flowers in vases.

"Drink first, though, so follow me," Eleanor called over her shoulder.

Eric did as he was told, patting his hair surreptitiously as he passed an enormous mirror in the corridor leading from the entrance hall. They entered a room whose proportions suggested an airport lounge. Its furnishings, largely low slung and expensive leather chairs, were scattered in careful disarray. A series of sliding glass doors ran the length of the room, giving way to a covered pool at the far side of which Eric glimpsed lawns. There were also some indisputably tall trees in the distance. A corner of a tennis court showed between them.

Eric's impression on examining his immediate surroundings was that there were too many people in the room for the number of cars outside. His eyes met random, disinterested glances from those bothering to register his arrival. Eleanor had gone off somewhere and just as he was looking for a drink he turned to find Albert at his shoulder with a tray of glasses. Eric couldn't quite suppress a grin.

Albert gave him a warning look and handed over a heavy glass containing a generous looking measure of whisky before moving off.

Clutching his drink, Eric drifted towards the fringe of the nearest cluster of guests, where a small, red-faced man was holding forth. An exceptionally thin blonde woman clung to his arm. Then he caught sight of a group near the French windows, wearing fawn or pale blue light weight suits. Eric's feeling that these were the German visitors was confirmed by the accent with which one of the men greeted Eleanor. She was in the process of detaching from them a short, fat man in a dark blazer.

This must, Eric told himself, be the father, though the idea entailed a determined suspension of disbelief. No obvious similarities suggested themselves between putative parent and offspring. Whereas Eleanor swung smoothly across the expanse of deep, red-patterned carpet her companion contrived to keep upright in defiance of physical laws. His feet were small and from these sprouted short legs clothed in pale cotton slacks. Above these the large body made the buttoned blazer swell out. An electric blue silk tie and a snowy white shirt completed the outfit. Topping everything was a face capped by brown hair of a neatness and uniformity of colour suggesting a wig, an idea a disappointed Eric found on closer inspection to be mistaken.

"Daddy, this is Dr Farnham, Eric, that is."

Eric looked into watchful eyes set in soft, pink flesh on either side of a nose with a flattened tip. "Pleased to meet you. Good of you to ask me to your house," he said.

Varne said without ceremony, "You're here to talk business aren't you?"

At that point a heavy, dark-haired man with a great deal of gold in his teeth attempted to pass by and Eric risked a few pleasantries in German.

"Well, well," Varne said to his daughter after the man had left them, "I think he's trying to tell me something, don't you? Look, lad, you don't really want to swim do you? Any road, with your size and shape you'll make the guests feel threatened." He chuckled appreciatively at his own humour. A strong scent of aftershave wafted from him as he moved nearer and finally shook Eric's hand.

"Eleanor love, have some more drinks sent through to the

43

study. I'll borrow your man for a few minutes."

Eric followed Varne through the passageway to the front of the house. They turned off before reaching the domed entrance hall and doubled back along a corridor running parallel to the first to emerge in another large room. Two sofas faced each other in the centre of the carpet. There was a splendid fireplace, above which hung an oil painting of Eleanor. One wall was entirely taken up by an impressive glass book case. It contained directories, building trade manuals, some records and, in the middle section, an expensive looking collection of cut glass decanters. Sunlight streamed through large windows onto cream coloured walls.

Seated opposite Varne, Eric felt he had to make a conversational opening in the face of his host's impassive, somewhat fish-eyed gaze.

"I'm still not entirely sure what your business is," he said, "or where I fit in, if in fact I do."

"Cigar?" Varne responded. He got up like an old spaniel and waddled towards the book case, returning with a wooden box. When they were both puffing out clouds of fragrant smoke Varne spoke again.

"I've all sorts of interests. Started off in building. Still do that, you'll have seen my sign around the town. Did some at your university years ago. Nothing against them myself, universities I mean. Nor the students. Lecturers, well, I don't come across many in my line."

Eric waited.

"Then I started buying up old houses, including the furniture. Sold bits and pieces of this too, mostly in my wife's name of course. Now we've got contacts all over Europe looking out for buyers. Big thing about old English furniture over there."

"The Germans, are they here to buy?" Eric ventured.

Varne nodded.

"Some of that." He puffed his cigar again with an irritating air of deliberation. "But they like to get the feel of the place too, nose around a bit." He laughed again. "Eleanor had the idea of you helping to show them one or two places, talk in their own lingo if they feel like it. We need to make an impression, Eleanor has told you that."

Eric was mildly surprised to realise as he listened that the prospect of helping the Varnes was beginning to appeal, not least as a distraction from fretting over what might be happening at the university. There was a loud knock on the door and Albert came in.

"You'll be working with Albert," Varne said chuckling, "a foreigner like you, from London."

Albert gave no obvious sign of being surprised by the joke.

"No problem," he said, handing Eric a second large whisky. "With my brains and his brawn we can manage nicely."

"I'll take my drink through with me." Varne announced, pulling himself up again. He followed Albert to the door, where he paused to look back at Eric.

"You've my daughter to thank. She wants to have a chat with you by the way, so sit there and finish your drink."

The door slammed behind him but almost immediately re-opened to admit Eleanor.

"Made up your mind to join the firm?"

Why not, Eric thought, as she sat beside him and rested a hand lightly on his thigh.

Chapter Four

Eric normally enjoyed pacing the city's streets but Tuesday was humid enough to make him almost regret his decision to walk to the campus. Sooner or later he would meet the road snaking out from the town centre to the distant coast, a route eventually bisecting the avenue leading to the university buildings. Yet there were several different access points. Today, after meandering through red-brick terraces, he skirted the back of the old hospital and reached the city road just before the level crossing. Fifteen yards from the crossing gates was a Victorian pub where nightly singing took place.

He had just been reading an editorial about university spending cuts. Was it Immanuel Kant, Eric wondered, who had enjoyed a life-long, undeviating daily walk in his home town? It didn't seem so much to ask. He turned left at the traffic lights near the corner pub, forlorn in mid-morning, where Alan had played. It was cooler and altogether more comfortable in the shade of the trees lining both sides of the avenue.

Just past the bus depot Eric saw Wallace Kingsly a few yards ahead of him. Under its white hair Kingsly's skull contrived to suggest, by its shape, that its owner was leaning backwards. It added to the overall impression of complacency he exuded. Somehow sensing scrutiny Kingsly suddenly looked over his shoulder.

"Morning," Eric called. "I can't be late for the meeting now can I?"

Kingsly was dressed in a dark blue jacket and flannels. He barely concealed a quick survey of Eric's worn cotton jacket and open-necked sports shirt. "True," he agreed. Then his tone became suddenly confidential, as if the black painted railings looming on their right concealed eyes and ears. "As a matter of fact, Eric, I wanted to have a wee word with you. How are things in general?"

"Fine," Eric said, "apart from the news about the cuts."

"Not good," Kingsly agreed, "not good." He paused. "It's about your probation. Shouldn't be a problem for you but at times like this, well, who knows?"

The two of them passed under the branches overhanging the main gate. It was just after eleven o'clock. The changeover of lecture classes created a colourful scene. Kingsly looked furtively at several young women crossing his line of vision.

"You haven't published much, Eric, since your doctorate. Still, at least you finished that in reasonable time. Your teaching seems to be fairly satisfactory, so far as I can tell. A bit short on hours. I was thinking that if you pop into my office sometime we can throw a few ideas about for your interview."

Despite pronounced misgivings on this score Eric thanked Kingsly. On entering the Arts building the professor abruptly brought up the subject of the forthcoming and hastily convened meeting.

"We ought to look at the changes proposed by Peter Everton." Again he dropped his voice. "We've got a bit slack just lately. Some well thought out new guidelines could be no bad thing. Got to look, er, proactive."

Eric's mood dropped another notch at the mention of the dreaded 'p' word, spreading like a virus among staff. Ten minutes later he joined the rest of his colleagues in the seminar room, with its drab but comfortable armchairs. On a wooden sideboard affair stood paper cups, a jar of instant coffee and a steaming kettle. Eric never ceased to admire what intelligent people could do with these simple tools. There were wet spoons, remains of sugar clinging to them, not to mention blobs of milk and dried coffee powder on the table. Damp rings made by the cups spread like spores from this central infection. His fellow Germanists lounged in various postures at the low tables.

Eric chose the one vacant chair, bringing him unintentionally into proximity with Peter Everton. The latter frowned briefly before turning to address Daniel on his left. Across the room Alan, neatly attired in grey jacket and cords, was watching closely. There was no time for an exchange before Kingsly opened the meeting. The most notable absentee, Eric now saw, instantly recalling Henry's remarks about the need for precisely such a meeting, was Henry himself. Eric's interest in the proceedings quickened.

"I must apologize for calling you together at such *very* short notice," Kingsly began in measured tones, "but the suggestions for university cuts need prompt consideration by the department. If I could just briefly outline the points as they affect us."

He proceeded to remind his listeners at length of what most knew only too well about the detailed build up to the University Grants Committee's letter. Eric distanced himself from the proceedings by thinking of Eleanor but his attention was suddenly caught by Alan formally recording regret that, according to the secretary, Henry had not been informed of today's meeting. This interjection was met by a low murmuring.

Kingsly's facial hue deepened. "I did try to telephone Henry in London but with no luck. In any case this is in the nature of things a preliminary meeting. It seems sensible for us to consider, in general terms and as quickly as possible, our response to the cuts. Put down a marker, as it were. But please make a note of Dr Branch's point," he said to Angela, who duly recorded it in her notebook.

After further talk Kingsly secured a grudging endorsement

of a proposal to arrange a meeting with the Vice Chancellor of the university, when he would convey the department's hope that German studies would be maintained without substantial staff cuts or significant reduction in student numbers.

"After all," Kingsly observed, "this is no more than the UGC letter suggested. Now, is there any other business before we move on to look at Peter's proposals for reform?"

"Is there any real value in having that discussion at this particular meeting?"

The speaker was Jake Hunslett, a tall, anxious looking, prematurely grey man approaching forty. As usual Kingsly took comment from this quarter to be a direct criticism of himself.

"What do others think?" he asked the assembly at large.

Margaret broke the ensuing silence to remind her colleagues at length of the effort Peter had put into his proposed scheme. She finished by expressing her preference for an immediate preliminary discussion. That's that, Eric thought, well aware that the absence of a determined effort to prevent debate was as good as waving a red rag to a bull. Those present shuffled through papers to locate Peter's proposals and, in most cases, to read them for the first time. Peter's unexpectedly low-profile presentation of his scheme threatened to numb his audience into endorsing the whole package without further ado. At some point during the discussion and much to his own surprise, Eric felt compelled to speak.

"Kingsly," he asked, "are letters really so unhelpful, I mean to students? It strikes me that putting down a numerical grade by the side of an essay is just as much a rough and ready measure as any other symbol we might care to use."

He sensed at once from mutterings and movements about him that this proposition by no means commanded universal acceptance. "Look," he pushed on, "when numbers are recorded

49

on lists, totalled, divided and so forth, they seem to be invested with," he cast about for a suitable expression, "with pseudo objectivity. I make the point for the sake of argument," he finished lamely and said no more.

Before long Kingsly summarised the meeting, ticking off points like a judge considering objections at law only to dismiss them. Even so, when the vote was taken the closeness of the count prompted a second motion, calling for further consideration and consultation. Those who remained undecided accepted the exit route with alacrity. Kingsly was manifestly ruffled.

Eric stood up stiffly and saw immediately that Peter was also looking decidedly annoyed.

"Well done," he said to Erik, "thank you so much for your contribution." He shook his head and left the room.

"Look on the bright side," Alan said, overhearing the exchange, "on top of everything you've managed to upset the head of department. Still, it serves him right for upstaging Henry." He looked at Eric with mock surprise. "Don't tell me you hadn't realised that this was all set up by Kingsly *because* Henry was not contactable in London?"

Eric frowned. "Well, I did feel something was odd," he said.

"Henry and Kingsly are both in the age range for an offer of premature retirement, "Alan went on. "If Henry jumps there's less pressure on Kingsly to leave. Right?"

"But he can't think Henry will go willingly," Eric responded with incredulity.

"That's Kingsly for you," Alan sighed. "Obviously, he's keen to get his feet under the Vice Chancellor's table as quickly as possible. Think about it. He's bound to try to exploit his position as head of department to stop it rotating any further, if you take my drift."

"The rest of us would never agree to that!" Eric said.

Alan lowered his voice as they approached Daniel and Margaret who were in earnest conversation a few yards ahead. "Money, Eric, that's what it all comes down to. Your fellow teachers' interest, like yours, like mine, is to carry on drawing a salary. Whoever gets the chop, make sure it isn't you. Even if Kingsly is a no hoper against Henry he won't be convinced. He can make life more unpleasant just by trying."

Eric reflected with no enthusiasm on the possibility of mending fences by calling in on Kingsly soon.

"Now then," Alan said, rubbing his hands together, "tea at my place *after* that game you promised to play in.

Following the five-a-side clash Eric stood in the showers, bruised but at the same time relishing the memory of one or two of his own satisfactory fouls.

"Might be an idea to check up a bit on this Farnham. Get an idea of how he spends his time," Varne had said offhandedly to Albert that morning. "No need to make a meal of it."

Albert knew better. He was sitting in one of the firm's white vans fifty yards away from where he had watched Eric Farnham approach the shiny black front door of a terraced house in a street near the railway crossing. A slender woman opened it. She wore glasses that were too big for her face, Albert thought. Still, there was something about her that he liked. When the door had shut he turned his attention to the book resting on his knees. There was a poem in it about some bloke arriving by train along the coast. Albert could almost smell the sea air as he read it. He examined once more the anxious, bespectacled face on the front cover. Albert had to admit that it fell well short of A.J. Ayer's looks. Still, to think the poet had lived just up the road appealed no end. There were worse ways to spend time, Albert reflected, going back once more to the beginning of the poem.

"The thing about bridge," the woman distantly admired by Albert was telling Eric, "is that the more you play the more there is to it. If you play bridge well with someone, you can live with that person."

While speaking Suzi arranged an enormous bowl of fresh fruit with nervous movements of her hands. Eric knew she was annoyed by his presence but this didn't stop him enjoying the tea. Alan had forgotten that the date of the football match had already been marked out by Suzi for an evening of cards. Two of the teachers from the school where she taught on the other side of the city were due to arrive later. Not for the first time Eric speculated on whether Alan's tunnel like vision accounted for his success in the field of linguistics.

He observed Suzi and Alan, perched on the floral patterned sofa, her trim figure alongside his solid frame, her round lenses twinkling next to his horn-rimmed spectacles and wondered for the hundredth time why, despite appearing more married than the few actually married couples he knew, they refused to wed. Suzi reigned supreme in this fresh, carpeted flat in a large Victorian house, while Alan maintained a room a few houses along the road. How often he used it Eric knew not.

The sun was now below the horizon but its reflected rays came through the skylight, catching the coloured prints arranged by Suzi on the white-painted walls. Straw coloured matting on the floor reminded Eric of glimpses of basement rooms in London terraces.

"What time are Freda and Eric coming?" Alan asked for the second time. Suzi sighed.

"In about forty-five minutes," she said, her full red lips pouting. She glanced anxiously in Eric's direction once more. He fully intended to leave before seven but found it impossible to resist looking pointedly at the table in the corner, where glasses and bottles stood at the ready next to a various items of food covered by a fresh white tea towel. He was rewarded by a fleeting look of annoyance from Suzi.

The telephone rang loudly and she left to answer it in the small hallway adjoining the sitting room. Alan pushed the door to and turned up the volume on the stereo. Impossibly fast notes from a clarinet cascaded from the speaker. Suzi came back and said to Eric, "It's for you. Clara Everton."

No sooner had Eric closed the door behind him than he heard Suzi expostulating with Alan. He picked up the receiver.

"Eric, thank goodness I've got you. I found out from Jake that you had been seen leaving the university with Alan. I took a chance on you being with him at Suzi's for a while."

Eric took a deep breath, tracing the faintly patterned wallpaper near the 'phone with his forefinger.

"Have you seen Peter?" Her voice rose.

"Only at the meeting, why?"

"He must have come home first," Clara said. Sniffling sounds came down the line. "His brief case is here by the desk."

"Well," Eric began, ready with a few banalities about not worrying. Clara interrupted.

"Come round, Eric, please. I want to show you something. Ellis is out."

He hesitated. From the sitting room he could still hear Suzi's voice, punctuated by deeper, half-hearted rumblings from Alan. No more please, Eric sighed to himself, what with Kingsly's meeting, the cuts, bloody football, Suzi and now Clara, all in a day.

"Actually, I'm supposed to be meeting somebody later this evening," he told her. That was true at least, although he had yet to telephone Eleanor to finalise the arrangements.

"Just pop round, Eric, for a coffee or something."

He murmured assent and replaced the receiver. When he rejoined Alan and Suzi she was standing, hands on hips, at the centre of the carpet.

"Thanks for the tea Suzi, I have to go now. See you tomorrow Alan."

Eric walked down the wide flight of stairs to the ground floor. Just as he left a thin, spotty man and a short, dumpy woman came through the front entrance. He had little chance to relish Suzi's likely reaction to the early arrival of her guests since at that moment he saw a blue and yellow bus a hundred yards distant. Somehow he arrived at the bus stop before the driver could reasonably have been excused for overlooking him. The man retaliated by insisting on the exact fare being inserted into the machine to the left of his driving wheel. Eric did what he was told, went upstairs and slumped into an empty seat.

Albert, who had watched Eric sprinting along the road, had time to put his book face down on the passenger seat before starting the van and moving smoothly in pursuit.

"What's the hurry?" he wondered.

The bus eventually made a right turn into a long, straight road lined with shops, shortly after passing the city's overgrown and disused cemetery. Albert found himself asking how a cemetery could be said to be disused. Freddy would know, he thought. He slowed down to let the bus pull further ahead once he saw Eric stand to ring the bell. His quarry got off outside a fish and chip emporium, crossed the street and walked along a wide avenue at right angles to the bus route. Albert, with his eye for property, knew that most of the enormous Victorian dwelling houses had long been abandoned by the city's wealthy. He had also heard that they were now favoured homes of university lecturers and teachers.

"Can't be doing too badly," he thought.

Much the same idea struck Eric on strolling past an ornate and splendid fountain in the middle of a cross road linking the avenues before he turned into Peter's drive. A few yards away, across the street, were the gates to a private hospital made up of three of the original houses.

When Clara opened the door he was pleasantly surprised to see that she looked far from distraught. She had obviously had a shower, her hair still damp. He could smell soap when he brushed against her. Automatically, he checked Peter's progress in stripping the doors in the high, narrow hallway. The room into which he followed Clara looked as if it might have been close to full restoration at one stage. It was now slipping back, like an abandoned outpost. The arm chairs were grubby; papers were strewn on a coffee table; the curtains were badly drawn although, like the carpet, of good quality.

Clara collapsed onto a sofa and Eric sat next to her. He looked at her round, snub-nosed face and waited for her to speak.

"Sorry about the 'phone call," she said. There was a brief silence before she began talking in her characteristic clipped sentences. She had found a letter yesterday, from a student of Peter's. A girl, young. Actually, only twenty. Christ, they had been seeing each other for months. It wasn't, Clara assured Eric, that she hadn't half expected to find out something of the sort but it was still a shock.

Eric found himself looking anew at Peter's recent behaviour.

"Really, I suppose I am more worried *for* him," she went on, lighting a cigarette from the coffee table.

"What do you want me to do?" Eric asked. Then, "so were you surprised or not?"

"Yes and no. I rather got into the habit of not bothering all that much about what he did."

"So why bother now?" Eric queried.

"Not bothering," she said quietly, "is not quite the same as not caring, which is what you do so well Eric." To his alarm he saw tears forming. "Oh, I suppose we were just about finished in any case. Ellis is drifting off. It all seems inevitable. I just want it to be, well, neater, I suppose."

She sat up with determination. "Coffee, I think," she said, then paused. "What I really need is moral support. Perhaps you could just have a word with him, tell him to get in touch?"

Eric looked at her doubtfully but kept quiet. "I have a letter," Clara added, "which gives her address in town. I don't suppose he would be there."

Eric could see no obvious reason why not. He followed Clara through to the kitchen, puzzled at how she ever found anything among the packages and utensils resting on every surface.

"What are we actually aiming for Clara?"

"I suppose I just want to talk with him. No recriminations. I really think this is it."

Eric glanced down at the address Clara had written for him. It was in a street that he vaguely recognized. The name Kendall meant nothing but then he hardly ever remembered the names of students. He sipped his coffee seated at a table mellowed by use and plain dirt and experienced a rush of ennui.

Deciding on the spur of the moment after leaving the house not to keep his promise to telephone Eleanor, he walked back to his own flat.

Well, well, young Dr. Farnham, Albert chuckled, watching Eric hug the woman goodbye at the front door. He decided he'd seen enough of the man's day for now. No need to give Varne all the details, he told himself as he drove back to his own place.

Chapter Five

The following day Eric felt that anything would be better than going directly to the department. He sat on the edge of his bed for a few moments trying to remember where he had put the map of the city. It turned up near his dictionaries and he located the address that Clara had given him. It was roughly where he had thought it was. Pulling on jeans and a thin shirt he made his way to the bathroom on the landing below. The only other occupants using the room were the elderly violin teacher on the second level landing and the reclusive Mrs Dyson in the basement. As usual the sink looked grubby.

By the time he got back to his room, above that of the violinist, it was flooded with sunlight. He looked down at the busy main road below. An expensive looking car was parked directly outside the house.

In the ground floor kitchen, reserved by some quirk in the lease solely for the occupant of the attic room that Eric rented, he slumped at the table by the window. It looked out on to a walled back yard. His cup and dish were standing on last week's copy of the *Times Higher Education Supplement*.

He turned to the page containing the addictive "Don's Diary" column, in which a series of academics recorded their week's activities. Some recounted arrivals at conferences in distant lands while others reported delivering successful papers or inspiration for new books. The note of pretentious unreality never failed to cheer Eric up. In his room, pinned to his cupboard wall, was his own unpublished entry: "Monday: dug out last year's lecture notes for a Monday. Tuesday: thought how little Monday had differed from previous Mondays, or would differ from tomorrow. Wednesday: prognosis confirmed. Thursday:

had idea for book on entering the Senior Common Room. Friday: abandoned project on returning from adult education class."

He pushed the paper aside, took his crockery through to the scullery, and covered it in water. After fetching his briefcase and a linen jacket from his room he left the house. At the far end of the front garden path stood Albert.

"Morning," Albert called out.

"Come to see the other half?" Eric asked, preserving a healthy distance.

"Nice," said Albert, eyeing the front of the house. "Seen better days?"

"More or less," Eric answered. He watched the neatly suited figure carefully.

"Shall we go?" Albert asked, indicating the Jaguar. "Your flat mate is watching you." He gestured towards the ground floor window. Eric turned to see a curtain drop into place.

"Look, I'm sorry, I prefer walking. I have to call in somewhere on the way to the campus."

"Dr Farnham," Albert began and then shook his head. "No, Eric." He grinned. "I had a buzz from Ms. Varne. Asked me to remind you of the arrangements for Friday."

"I didn't know there were any definite plans," Eric said.

"There you are. If you had kept your promise to meet the lady last night she would have passed on the details in person. I'll give you a ride and explain on the way."

Eric sank into the passenger seat. Without fuss Albert executed a smart "U" turn. A few moments later the car ground to a halt behind a row of vehicles and bicycles at the closed gate of a level crossing. Albert turned the motor off.

"Haven't they heard of bridges up here?" He exclaimed.

"Aren't you forgetting the Humber?"

"True," Albert said, "very true. And so many cyclists to the square mile too!"

"Sounds as though this place is getting to you."

"No, not really. Look, about Friday, we're taking three of the German visitors to a couple of resorts. Bridlington, Scarborough. Day out by the sea, lunch, show them something of Varne enterprises."

"Friday?" Eric repeated. "I'll have to check my diary." He stopped as Albert wagged a finger.

"Your timetable has been checked. Looks as though Friday is your day off, or another of them," he laughed. "Nine-thirty a.m. sharp outside the Station Hotel."

"I don't recall specifically agreeing to anything!" Eric protested mildly.

"You do have a lot to learn," Albert stated.

The car moved forward slowly. Albert's driving style deterred the city's cyclists from their habitual kamikaze swerves. Eric savoured the scent of the car's interior and furtively examined the controls. A driver himself, he had yet to replace the modest ford he had smashed during an earlier trip to London. Like his writing, the lack of transport was something he would remedy, sooner or later.

"Where to?" Albert asked as they approached the traffic lights.

Why not, Eric thought. "Could you call in at Coltman Street?" he said, glancing down at Clara's note. "Do you know it?"

"Has a second hand shop on the corner, opposite a launderette?" Albert queried after a momentary pause.

"Could be. Number 15, please."

"On our way."

Albert changed lanes smoothly to go straight ahead at the

lights instead of turning left towards the university. A Rover driver, forced to brake hurriedly, reconsidered a half-formed gesture at the sight of Albert's brief nod. The latter grinned.

"How did you end up here?" Eric asked.

Albert looked momentarily irritated. "What's your excuse?" He relented suddenly. "I used to work in a garage in Harrow. Came across Varne after I fixed his car. Did some driving for him. He offered me a better job. What can I say?"

Eric contented himself with this laconic reply.

"Then, of course," Albert added, "I'd been reading those northern novelists."

They both laughed and almost missed Coltman Street. The road was narrow, lined on both sides by terraced houses with bright red steps and net curtains. Despite this the street had a lifeless air, as though barely warding off a terminal condition. The cars lining the road looked not so much parked as ready to leave. Number 15 was much like numbers 13 and 17 on either side of it. Its door was painted black, the red brick front wall was low and three windows faced towards the street. A narrow, arched tunnel went between numbers 15 and 17, presumably to a back yard.

"Now what?" Albert asked.

A good question, Eric thought. The improbable nature of his mission struck him more forcibly than ever. What could he say to the girl, assuming she was in?

"Get on then," Albert said.

Eric left the car, approached number 15 and knocked. He was startled when the door opened instantly. A youth of something over six feet filled the doorway. His black jeans, open shirt and unshaven, sullen expression to Eric's mind fitted the street perfectly.

"Is, er, Rachel Kendall in?" he ventured, feeling compelled

to add, absurdly, that he was from the university. "I don't suppose there's a chap here called Everton, is there, Mr?" Eric plunged on.

The man moved closer and placed a large hand on the wall alongside Eric's head.

"Johnson." He answered. "What do you want with my cousin?"

Eric heard a car door opening and closing "It's just that I," he began to explain, noticing how much nearer were Johnson's pitted chin and muddy brown eyes. The clicking of the latch on the gate was followed by Albert's voice.

"It is half-past, sir. We do have that appointment."

Johnson shifted his gaze like a bull finding a fresh target then pushed himself away from the wall. Eric stepped back.

"If you do see somebody called Peter Everton," he said quickly, "could you tell him to contact his home? Thank you."

Johnson said nothing as Eric followed Albert through the gate and closed it carefully. Albert pulled away from the kerb and turned the car round. Johnson was rooted to the same spot, staring at them as they drove past the house and back to the main road.

"Well, well," Albert said. "A close shave, I would say."

"I'm shaking!" Eric agreed.

"He's no bigger than you," Albert said, "but it's the attitude that counts. You need to watch yourself there." He guffawed loudly. "Who was that, another lecturer?"

Eric gave him a quick report on what was going on.

"And the girl's name?" Albert queried.

The car turned at the lights again and soon neared the university. It had its good points, the campus, Eric reflected, being on the whole a place where physical assault was unlikely.

"Rachel Kendall," Eric answered to Albert's question.

Albert repeated the name. "I wonder, I wonder," he mused.

Before Eric could respond he saw, first with apprehension then with pleasure, that Albert was driving the Jaguar through the main gates and was about to deposit him on the sacrosanct few square feet before the arts building reserved for VIPs. When the car came to a halt Albert motioned Eric to remain seated before getting out and walking round to open the passenger's door.

"I'll pick you up at the Station Hotel on Friday, Dr. Farnham," he said loudly.

"Thank you, Albert," Eric called back at the same volume, catching sight of Kingsly and Daniel a few yards distant. Their respective expressions showed bewilderment. Albert murmured quietly.

"I might be able to help you with the Kendall thing. Leave it with me."

Eric greeted his two colleagues cheerfully as he overtook them on the stairs but his sense of well being gave way to one of apprehension when he reached his office. Henry Helm was standing outside it.

"Morning, Henry."

"No wonder you didn't reply, Eric!" Henry said, brimming with energy.

"Profitable trip to London?" Eric enquired dutifully.

"Very satisfactory indeed! Did a spot of work on some private papers I've been planning to read for a very long time. Have you a moment?"

Henry followed Eric into his office and moved books from a chair before sitting on it.

"Pity you missed our meeting while you were in London," Eric ventured by way of something to say.

"Well, I was pleased to see that nothing hasty had been done about the suggested reforms." Henry smiled. His black hair, nodding head and prominent nose made Eric think of a blackbird.

"I really wanted a quick word with you about your teaching, Eric. Do you feel up to outlining a new course for our final year students? I know you've always been keen to have a shot at post-1815 German intellectuals."

Eric suppressed a grin at an image of said intellectuals lined against a wall. He had certainly once voiced interest in early German nationalists. The reasons for this, along with the interest itself, had faded. Nevertheless, he indicated assent.

"It would certainly strengthen your case," Henry said, "if you were to put something else on your C.V. when you go before the probation committee."

Eric glimpsed an unexpected escape route from Kingsly's patronage. "Hasn't the department set a limit to the number of options on offer at any given moment?"

"That is so," Henry confirmed, "but I might propose giving mine a rest. One doesn't like to get stale. I shall also need my energies to deal with our responses to the cuts."

"Won't others want a chance to put on a new course?"

"No doubt." said Henry, "no doubt. Yours, however, would be an entirely new subject. There *could* be a case for giving it priority. Besides," he added, raising his eyes to the ceiling, "Peter is about due to rest for a while, or I should say his course is."

Eric agreed to put down a few ideas for the next departmental meeting. After a moment Henry said, "Did Peter seem upset by the postponement of his suggested scheme for later discussion?"

"He wasn't too happy. Of course I haven't seen much of

him for a couple of days, so I can't say for certain what his thoughts are."

Henry shook his head as if in sorrow. Whatever he was about to say he changed his mind.

"By the way," he then asked, "how is your part-time tutoring coming along?"

Noticing Eric's surprise Henry smiled. "Outside contacts are important now. We need all the kudos we can get. As a matter of fact I'm putting together some preliminary ideas on part-time degrees for mature students. Your experience could be useful."

"Well," Eric said warily, "I haven't had that much experience, apart from the odd evening class and the occasional private tutee."

"It all adds up. We shall have to operate on a number of fronts. Flexible approaches," Henry intoned, "will be the key." He stood up and left the office.

Eric sat with his feet on his desk, running over his options. Joining the Helm camp, as he thought of it, would certainly release him from Kingsly's clutches. By the same token it would irritate some of his colleagues, Peter Everton in particular. The thought of Clara's husband brought him back to his brief encounter in Coltman Street. He sighed, thinking he might as well see what the file had on the Kendall student. He knew enough about history, a subject he heartily detested, to accept his allotted role in the small part of it embracing his current existence.

"He said what?" Albert put his beer glass down carefully on the long bar in the student union building. A week had passed and Eric repeated what he had overheard the German visitors saying outside the lavatory window during the seaside trip on the previous Friday.

"They were just joking about extras for themselves. No details."

Albert continued to stare at him. "It makes you wonder why they weren't more careful."

Eric had asked himself the same thing. Only one member of the group had been devoid of some knowledge of English, although all preferred conversing in their own language. The best he could come up with was that it was all too easy to make a careless remark abroad that might have been more diplomatically phrased at home. He said as much to Albert, adding, "Anyway, is it really that important? It isn't much to show for my day out."

"That's not for you to say, is it Eric," Eleanor interjected, rejoining them. "You were asked to keep your ears and eyes open."

"And what big ears he has," Albert added.

Eric felt well enough disposed with the world to put up with the exchange, largely because of Eleanor's pleased reception of the episode he had subsequently related to Albert at her insistence.

"See you later then," Eleanor informed Albert, who managed to look both cross and resigned within the space of a split second. He picked up his glass, winked at Eric and moved towards the dance floor.

"That's better," Eleanor said. "Shall we sit down?"

The drinking area where they looked for a seat was a vast, low-ceilinged room with a bar at one end. Small tables were scattered about the floor. The chairs were near enough to the ground to prompt the thought that a job lot of furniture had been hi-jacked en route to Japan. The occasion was the "Jazz in June" programme. It featured the university jazz orchestra, of which

Alan was inevitably a founder member. Last year, Eric recalled, an earlier concert had been entitled "Jazz in May". The dinner-jacketed staff-student band was partly obscured by a low dividing wall near which he and Eleanor commandeered two of the midget chairs. Some ten feet from them were three steps leading down to a polished floor, where the audience shuffled and gyrated before a stage. The open-plan complex resembled the set of a space ship in a long-running television series.

Eleanor placed her gin and tonic on the table and flopped nonchalantly backwards, showing smooth thighs. Her simple black dress and shiny black shoes gave her a brazen quality that Eric liked more than he cared to admit, all the more so in that there had been little direct contact with her after his visit to her home. He didn't count the trip to Scarborough. She had spent most of the day in the company of the smoothest of the German guests.

"Do you know," he said, "I think you may have upset Albert."

She shrugged and blew smoke out exaggeratedly, leaning her head back and exposing her throat.

"Did you get your money by the way?" she asked after a few seconds had passed. Eric had indeed received a small wad of ten pound notes from Albert on the Friday evening after they got back to the city. He said so. Eleanor crossed and uncrossed her legs. Eric risked placing a hand on one of her bare knees.

"Later, if you're a good boy."

"And Albert?" Eric asked, feeling suddenly warm.

"I came in my own car. He's here for the music as much as anything." She laughed. "You won't credit this, but he once confessed that he would quite like to have been a vocalist with a big band."

Eric found the idea oddly cheering. Loud applause

sounded from the dance floor as the band finished an energetic but mildly uncoordinated version of "In the mood".

"Tell me," he said, leaning forward, "why should it matter what this Klaus and his friends said?"

"Does it bother you?" she asked after a slight hesitation.

"Well, in the sense that I was there and reported back to base, as it were."

"And very grateful my father will be too, when he hears about it."

Eric felt a spasm of irritation but accepted the offer of a cigarette from Eleanor's packet and kept quiet.

"Look," she went on quickly, "times are hard, you should know that. My father can't afford to have his business interests undermined if he can help it. Every bit of info helps."

"What interests in particular are we talking of?" Eric persisted.

Eleanor frowned but whatever she was going to say was interrupted by an announcement of a short interval booming through the loudspeakers. It signalled a general movement towards the bar. Eric decided to wait for the first rush to die down before attempting to refill his own glass.

"You're right, of course," he said. "None of my concern. Forget it."

"Look," she leaned forward, "he has businesses, shops, amusement arcades and centres in various spots along the coast, well you must have got some idea from the trip but he also has property here in the town. Don't believe everything you read about competition. My father's thinks the best way to deal with it is to stop it happening in the first place. Especially in a city of this size. Not so much to go round."

Eric said nothing for a moment or two. "So these visitors,

what, your father warns them off?"

"Something like that," Eleanor agreed vaguely. "Shall we have another drink?"

On their way to the bar they were rejoined by Albert, who was looking flushed. "Nice band," he commented.

Even Eric had to admit that the band had not sounded a total disaster. It was surprising how many of the staff and students had turned up to hear it. Across the room he caught sight of Alan happily talking to a group. Suzi, visibly less contented, hovered at the edge.

Eleanor's casual remark about dealing with rivals reminded Eric of what was happening among the wheelers and dealers in his own world. True, he had yet to detect on campus the whiff of criminality in the air during his Friday visit to the seaside. Give it time, he thought.

By some immutable law his path and that of his companions converged with Alan's group, which had initiated its own drift towards the bar. Eric resigned himself to the meeting as Alan caught sight of Eleanor and waved.

"Let me buy you a drink," Albert called, taking Alan's arm. "Nice band."

His swarthy grin embraced Suzi too. She regarded Albert, Eric saw with interest, without her usual expression of polite but chilling indifference to strangers.

"And you darling?" Albert said, encompassing her briefly with his free arm. As usual he had prompt service and then stood drink in hand near Suzi. She smiled.

"I don't normally come to this jazz thing," Eric heard her saying, her glasses glinting in the light.

"I like your suit, suede isn't it?" Albert asked, running his hand lightly over her sleeve.

She giggled, unprecedented in Eric's experience. A frown

69

flitted across Alan's face like a small cloud. He turned his shiny visage and glasses towards Eleanor.

"I must say, I rather enjoyed your little band too," she told him. "How long have you been playing?"

Eric sighed inwardly. He had lost count of the times he had overheard Alan responding to the question. Eleanor appeared to be listening to his answer. Eric sipped his glass of beer and looked about him. Suzi laughed loudly and Albert barked in reply.

"Don't you ever want to play full time?" Eleanor was asking Alan.

At the latter's self-deprecating wave of the hand Eric fully switched off his attention. On the far side of the bar a movement of blonde hair caught his eye. He shifted his position slightly and realised that the girl, thin and with a firmly chiselled face, was talking animatedly to a head Eric recognized. It belonged to Peter Everton.

He excused himself to Eleanor but to his annoyance found it difficult to cover the dozen or so yards separating him from Peter. There was too much traffic to and from the bar. He watched his quarry walk towards the swing doors leading to the entrance hall and cloakrooms. Just as he was in hailing distance of them a thick-set man, empty glass in each hand, rose in front of him and Eric was shunted into a siding formed by two tables and several pairs of crossed legs. Even so, he called out to Peter. The latter turned round, located Eric gesturing in his direction and promptly disappeared with the girl through the doorway.

When Eric finally reached this he found the entrance hall in near darkness. More economies, he thought. Crossing to the men's lavatory he put his head inside the door. A cistern dripped noisily onto the wet floor. Apart from a few moths the room was empty and the doors of the cubicles open. For a moment he stood listening then heard a car door slam. He trotted to the arched exit to the car park at the rear of the building. Perversely, it was brilliantly illuminated, offering a fleeting glimpse of Peter's profile through the passenger window of a white mini as it accelerated past the steps.

When Eric got back to the dance the volume level would have done justice to a combined children's outing for the entire county. He felt hot and flustered. Eleanor was alone, more or less where she had been. From the direction of the dance floor came the sound of tuning up.

"Sorry Eleanor, another drink?" She shook her head.

"Home, James"

She held his arm as they left. For a few moments Eric again stood in the entrance hall outside the women's lavatory. For some reason he recalled a recent document from the staff of Social Studies about gender equality. It was directed at sensitising all academic staff. To what? Eric wondered. There had been no mention among the welter of terms about chairpersons and the like, of lavatories. Why not all enjoy the bleak standard of public sanitation to which the male sex seemed condemned?

When Eleanor emerged Eric happily accepted her invitation to drive. At night the campus was in deep shadow, lit only by the occasional lamp. He admired the glow from the subdued dashboard lighting as they drove towards the exit. The beam from the headlights made the leaves of the trees glow a brilliant green. Once they hit the main road. Eleanor rested her head on his shoulder.

"I hope Albert behaves himself," she said, yawning.

"I must say, he did seem to hit it off with Suzi."

"Is that her name?" Eleanor asked.

The car went smoothly towards the traffic lights, where Eric stopped carefully. The statutory police car was parked in a

71

side street but showed no great interest in him. It was not quite closing time. Near the crossing a thin, angular woman in an old raincoat was locked in a passionate embrace with a balding man sporting a large beard. Eleanor looked at them as though they were another species.

"Why did you dash off by the way?" She asked.

Eric told her briefly.

"How sordid," she said. "You're not going to bother to contact this Everton man are you? He'll turn up at work sooner or later." She yawned again.

I don't know," he said defensively, "I promised his wife. He probably won't be around much before the examiners' meeting and the usual end of year post-mortem. I can hardly lean over his shoulder and say, by the way your wife is anxious to see you."

"Of course you could," Eleanor replied in a drowsy voice. "Put your hand there," she added. After a while she told him to pull over.

Eric rapidly scanned the street in the mirror and turned into one of the darkened alleyways at the back of the terraces half a mile from his flat before switching off the engine. As far as he could see everything was deserted. When after several long minutes Eleanor sat up again and shook her hair Eric re-started the car and backed out. The rest of the short journey passed in silence.

"Are you coming in?" He asked when they arrived at the flat.

She shook her head. "I'm tired." She grinned. "Too much of a good thing is bad for you."

"Speak for yourself. Shall I see you next week?"

"Can't say. Might be away in London for a day or so."

She leaned across and kissed him briefly. He got out and

stood on the pavement. Her movement sliding across to the driver's seat made him feel the week would be a long one.

"Oh, I nearly forgot," she said. "Albert gave me a note for you."

She unclasped her bag and handed him a folded sheet of paper. He opened it and read the terse scrawl. "Try a village called Barmton outside the city. The Kendall girl uses a friend's cottage there." The note was signed with a flowery "A." A telephone number, presumably Albert's, was added. Eleanor watched him reading the note.

"Do you actually intend to go to this place? Oh, yes," she added to Eric's look of surprise. "Albert told me something of what's going on."

"I might try to drive out there in the week, if I can get hold of a car," he said neutrally.

Indoors, he made himself a coffee and carried it up to his room. He sat in his armchair by the open window and listened for a moment to the sounds of revellers floating up from below, not feeling remotely tired. Putting his half-empty cup on the floor he selected a warmer coat and set out on a fast walk to Clara's house. At least, he told himself, he had some sort of excuse to call in.

Chapter Six

On the Monday following the dance the *Times* printed the reply Eric had been looking for. It was signed, "Helm, Professor of German." Henry made no specific reference to Peter's letter but mildly rebuked those who felt the urge to criticise colleagues publicly during a very trying period. However, he saw this as symptomatic of a general decline in morale among educationists. He closed with the hope that things would improve once university staff forged more outside links and reduced their dependence on government. Not, Henry concluded, that he blamed the government.

Eric put the paper down with a sense of disappointment. The placatory tone of Henry's letter, added to a conjunction of small episodes, fuelled the mild paranoia he had felt since arriving at the university an hour earlier. The first had been the discovery of the minutes of the recent staff meeting in his pigeon hole, the edited version of his small contribution making him appear a pillar of reaction. The second was the discovery that despite his recent talk with Henry no item concerning new courses had been tabled for the Wednesday departmental session. This was scheduled for immediately after the examiners final meeting.

Eric examined the agenda more carefully and frowned at item five, "Staff-student ratios." Then he hurriedly pushed the document aside, thinking it wouldn't be long before he began filing minutes of staff meetings and avidly researching past resolutions. From there it would be a perilously short step to saying, "Mr Chairman" or even, he shuddered, "on a point of order."

He picked up the *Times* again. On second reading it

seemed as though Helm was more concerned than angered by Peter Everton's behaviour. That seemed Clara's response too, never mind her husband's selfishness. The thought reminded Eric of his own promise to approach Peter on her behalf. Well, he could soon get that over with during the examiners meeting, despite what he had told Eleanor. He was startled by a loud knocking on the door. Alan came in carrying a folder and looking unusually subdued.

"The run of finals marks," he said, placing the folder on Eric's desk.

"Sit down," Eric said pleasantly.

His colleague did so but with an air of suppressed irritation.

"Eric," Alan said suddenly, "that person who came with you to the dance on Friday, do you know where he lives?" His accent broadened as he spoke and his glasses reflected light from the window. The effect was both comic and menacing.

"I take it you mean Albert. I have no idea. Why?"

Alan leaned forward and spoke quietly.

"Because he went off with Suzi at some point after the invitation waltz, that's why. I was concentrating on reading the music. I never even noticed them leaving the dance floor. Next thing you know, she calls at my place the following morning to collect a few things. She needs some time to think, can you believe it!"

"I'm sorry, Alan," Eric said, with some difficulty.

Alan stared bleakly at him. "That's good to know. So, his address?"

"As I say, I'm not sure. Somewhere near the park, I believe."

Alan slapped a hand on the desk. "That woman you're going about with must have an idea. Doesn't he work for her

75

father?"

"What exactly have you got in mind Alan? Suzi is her own woman. I can see it now," irritation impelled Eric to add, "ageing clarinettist, forward slash lecturer tackles local hood. Promising embouchure ruined."

Alan looked set to implode with fury. Instead, he fell back into his chair, red-faced but somehow deflated.

"Right," he said, "I admit it does seem a bit daft, all this. Suzi's not married to me. Still, we've been together for, well, I feel I must do something."

"I could get Albert's address for you," Eric said, relenting, "but I'm not sure what good it would do. Can you honestly see someone like Suzi planning to move in permanently with Albert?"

Alan said nothing. Eventually Eric felt compelled to say, "I'll find out what I can for you." Wild horses could not stop him, he thought. Alan stood up slowly.

"No, best to let things take their course. I haven't been thinking clearly. It's got bugger all to do with you, I can see that. In a city this small I'm bound to come across Suzi and your friend Albert sooner or later, I imagine."

"He's not as genial as he looks, Alan. And he's hardly what you could call a friend of mine."

Alan shrugged. Then, almost as an after thought, handed Eric another sheet of paper. "Nearly forgot," he muttered. "I have to collect timetable details for the review of departmental teaching coming up. Put down your teaching hours on this, student numbers and so on, what year they are in. Let me have it back, soon as possible."

Eric took the paper in much the way he imagined a debtor receiving a writ of summons. "Teaching hours?" he asked apprehensively.

"Kingsly wants the figures to hand to throw around at the next faculty meeting. Things are warming up fast." Alan returned to something like his normal self at the prospect.

"Alan," Eric began but decided under the circumstances not to ask if there was any news about new courses. "Never mind," he finished lamely as Alan paused at the door, looking absurdly neat with his scrubbed face, tweed jacket and sensible shoes.

Eric sat thinking for a while and then opted for a direct approach. He was quickly passed into Henry's office by Angela, after the statutory buzzing of the intercom and a brief exchange between secretary and professor, the tinny sounds from the speaker making a descant to the bass of the actual voice behind the thin office partition.

Henry sat at his desk in a coloured shirt and slacks. The term was not yet over but he unfailingly marked the end of formal teaching by donning casual garb. His room was lined with packed book shelves. On the huge desk was a manuscript that Henry was clearly proof reading. A pile of volumes for reviewing sat at his left elbow. Eric could also see a batch of letters and memos in the professor's neat hand in the filing tray, ready for Angela. Did the man actually sleep, Eric wondered.

"Have a seat," Henry said affably. "What can I do for you?"

Eric still found Henry's habit of peering at him over his thick rimmed glasses disconcerting. "I wondered, well, I happened to glance at the agenda for the meeting on Wednesday and I saw no mention of new courses."

Henry waited in silence but smiled encouragingly.

"In the light of what you were saying the other day I half expected a discussion of the whole thing at the staff meeting."

Henry gave what Eric could only think of as a pitying smirk. "No real urgency, Eric," he said, his voice rising as if in surprise.

Why then, Eric wanted to ask, had Henry brought the matter up in the first place.

As if the question had been voiced Henry said, "I meant you to be *thinking* about it, Eric, turning things over in your mind, getting a few book titles together. In the last resort, there couldn't be much change before next year, could there? These things take time."

"Yes," Eric conceded. "Still, I had the impression you were expecting a formal proposal of some sort imminently."

"Well, no real harm in getting something on paper if you can find the time," Henry conceded neutrally. "It can always be slipped in under any other business."

He shot a glance upwards and picked up his pen. Eric left the room.

"That was quick," Angela said.

Eric nodded. As he turned to leave her office the door swung open with some force. Kingsly entered, his face burning above a stiff white collar. He smiled fulsomely at Angela, whose glance slid away almost at once.

"Eric," he asked, "have you got the date yet? For your interview?"

"Not yet, Kingsly."

"Really? I should check your post if I were you."

He turned towards Angela and stood as near to her as he could while he went through the papers he wanted typing. Eric closed the door on her long suffering expression.

In short order two other doors opened along the corridor. From one issued Daniel White, from the other Peter Everton. Eric barely acknowledged Daniel's half formed smile of welcome and managed to catch up with Peter before the latter had gone far. The pair of them moved briskly in silence, competitors in a walk round the departmental circuit.

"Clara," Eric ventured.

"Enough!" said Peter almost at the same instant. The two of them paused, glaring at one another as they approached the stairway.

"Peter," Eric said, dropping his voice suddenly until a passing group of students had moved off, "can't you get in touch with Clara? She's worried sick."

"What exactly has it got to do with you?" Peter asked. "You must have enough worries of your own. Tell Clara I will be in touch soon, when I'm ready," he added, before heading off downstairs.

Eric got back to his room feeling distinctly the worse for wear. Whatever happened, he decided, it would do no harm to sketch out a new course. Another thought struck him and he rummaged in his wastepaper bin. There, screwed up with the most recent university *News letter* was the note to which Kingsly had referred. It briefly told Eric where and when to be present on the coming Friday.

The time and date, set out in black and white, set him back for a moment but for almost an hour he worked at producing an outline for a new course. The first draft was unconvincing; too detailed in parts, hopelessly oblique in others. In the end he opted for a terse statement of intent, hinting at intellectual weight but offering promise of entertainment. His desk now resembled the sorting office of the GPO before sorting. In disbelief he took in the five cigarette stubs in his ashtray. The room was blue with smoke. The 'phone trilled loudly as he clipped his notes together.

"Hello," he said shortly into the receiver.

"Eric, Eleanor here. Are you free or are you busy looking up a student's dress."

"Oddly enough I am alone in my office at the moment. If

you care to drop in and arrange yourself over my filing cabinet we can carry on where we never quite started."

A snort came from the receiver. "Are you doing anything this evening?"

"I could well be," he answered. "I thought you were away for a while."

"Came back earlier than expected. Well, are you free?"

"Ok, yes".

"Good. This girl friend of your colleague's, I thought you might like a lift out there. It will be a nice change from the city."

Eric frowned at the telephone. "Look, don't feel you have to."

Eleanor laughed. "Pick you up at your flat. Half-past seven or so. Bye."

"Wait a moment!" Eric's voice rose but the line clicked and the dialling tone sounded. He left his notes for Angela in the main office and decided on the spur of the moment to pick up the latest gossip on the cuts. He was discovering a gloomy satisfaction from exchanges with colleagues on the subject. It was almost as if, Eric realised as he strolled towards the Senior Common Room in the sunshine, joining in speculation about the university's future offered some protection against nasty things happening to him personally.

"I had a feeling this would be fun," Eleanor said.

They were seated in a small pub. Eleanor had wanted to go to the lavatory but after stopping refreshment had seemed in order. She emptied peanuts into her hand from a plastic bag only to nibble them in twos and threes.

"This Kendall girl has nothing to do with your father's set up herself?" Eric asked.

She shook her head. "Of course not."

In the far corner of the bar two locals were playing at a pool table, making frequent glances in their direction.

"Kendall, the father, the business rival, doesn't seem that much of a problem, well from what you've said so far."

"Oh, free competition again?" Her widely spaced teeth showed between red lips. "Money, there is an awful lot of it involved. There's a chance for a big development if we can get hold of this particular piece of land."

"But how does dishing up dirt on the daughter help? Who the hell cares what a student of twenty does, even if it is with one of her teachers?"

"Well, information, you know the saying, is gold. Besides you'd be amazed at what a dim view some of our city councillors take of loose morals. Those little men in shiny suits have a say in planning applications and my father has friends there. In fact," she added, picking up her drink, "he's even been talking about the university."

"In what way?" Eric asked with awakened interest.

"Well, if this deal comes off, he thinks there might be extra money through a joint application with the University for European Development Funds. I'm not entirely sure exactly what he has in mind yet," Eleanor added quickly, draining her glass.

"Could you," Eric said casually, "find out more about his plans?"

Eleanor grinned and picked up her keys. "I hadn't put you down for someone interested in campus politics."

Outside the sky was dull red in the fading light. They climbed into the car. On the far side of the car park Eric saw a white van back out of its space. He glanced at the houses they were passing on both sides of the road. The buildings were pretty, despite their forlorn air. Within minutes they were driving

81

through a village virtually identical to the one they had just left. Another pub and church completed the resemblance. A bearded man leant on a fork in a wild looking vegetable patch and gazed longingly after them.

"I wonder if they ever go to the wrong village by mistake," Eric speculated.

"Would it do you any good, Eric, if I found out more about my father's plans?"

His thoughts on this score were interrupted by Eleanor sounding the horn. A dog raced back to the grass verge.

"It wouldn't do any harm, I suppose. Do you know if your father has actually approached anybody at the university?"

"Not yet or at least not that I know of. Perhaps I'll get him to talk to you about it," she laughed.

For the moment he was content to watch the road unwinding. The countryside and hedges were still visible but lights would be needed soon. He noticed that Eleanor was looking repeatedly in her rear mirror, not, he had observed, a habit of hers.

"Anything wrong?" He asked, turning round. A fair way behind he could see a white van.

"Could that be following us?" she asked.

"Must be all sorts of cars on this road."

"Yes, but I think it was behind when we left town and we did stop for ten minutes or so after all."

"Come to think of it, there was a white van in the pub car park," he told her.

"This is vaguely exciting," she said.

They were approaching a sign assuring them that Barmton was three miles distant when the road began a series of looping bends. On the second of these Eleanor swung sharply through a gateway on the left. Almost immediately the car came to rest behind a large hedge. She switched off the engine. Outside, leaves rustled and warm air came through the window, mingled with wood smoke. Eric felt a sharp sensation of pleasure.

"You don't honestly think we are being followed?"

There came the sound of an engine. Not long afterwards a second, less noisy car passed.

"Not really but does it matter. You're enjoying this aren't you?"

Eric admitted as much but was having difficulty suppressing the image of their last encounter in a car. Eleanor switched on the ignition.

It was virtually dark by the time their headlights picked up the sign directing them down a narrow road towards the village where Albert suspected Peter and his girl friend might be. Eleanor and Eric passed the silent black outline of a church before coming to the first of a row of houses on their left, a quarter of a mile further on. There were no street lights. A second group of dwellings, this time on their right, gave way to a pub. Seconds later the car nosed through a gateway leading to a caravan park at the cliff top.

They turned round on a large gravelled space. The sea sounded above the engine as it idled. Another vehicle was parked thirty yards away, its windows misted.

"Nice work if you can get it," Eric said, nodding in its direction.

"True, but we didn't drive up here to play about in the car did we?"

"Heaven forbid. So what do we do?"

"Drive back slowly looking more closely at the houses?"

Eric considered the suggestion. "Why not park at that pub and take a stroll instead. You often miss things from a car."

The outline and shape of the pub, from what Eric could

see on closer examination, were at odds with the character of the village. The large building was of a sort normally found on roundabouts in many provincial English towns. Square windows and ugly pillars before the door hinted at the neo-Odeon style. The strip lighting from what was obviously the public bar shone out onto an assortment of cars and motor bikes.

"Which way?" Eleanor asked, coming closer to him and slipping her arm through his.

"Towards the church seems appropriate."

They moved away from the glow of the pub and walked quietly along the narrow pavement in darkness. Eric was again struck by the absurdity of the evening and laughed when Eleanor thrust him into the drive of one of the houses as a car's headlights approached.

"Might as well enter into the spirit of it," she whispered. They turned to inspect the house behind them. It was a low bungalow. Through a kitchen window Eric caught sight of an old woman holding a kettle to a tap. They continued along the hedge towards the next house, a cottage showing a complete absence of life.

They next came to what looked like a ranch style fence, the building behind it much as Albert had described it to Erik.

"Listen," Eleanor suddenly hissed.

"Come off it," Eric remonstrated in a whisper, "we're the only ones daft enough to be wandering about at the back of nowhere."

The hedge alongside them rustled gently and Eleanor drew in her breath sharply as a figure materialised. Eric was relieved to find that it belonged to Albert

"Same again," Albert said curtly to the man with wispy

hair and fish-like eyes behind the bar.

Eric was grateful for his second whisky. He glanced uneasily towards the door. Loud voices of darts players came from the public bar, where a match was in progress. He preferred not to think of ways in which the public bar could be differentiated from the lounge in which they enjoyed the benefits of a savage neon light. The decor was one where brown had the upper hand.

"How did you persuade Eleanor to go back to town with Suzi?" he asked Albert. "She looked thoroughly put out when you suggested she leave."

Albert lit another cigarette and Eric accepted one. The smoke and the smell of beer, even the horrible lighting, felt an intrinsic part of his parallel life. He made up his mind there and then to flout the tacit no-smoking convention at the coming examiners' lunch on Wednesday.

"She was not happy," Albert confirmed. "I've slipped down a notch on the popularity scale there. Still, there is one thing about Eleanor: she likes to stay on the right side of her old man. I suggested he would definitely be put out by her little escapade tonight."

"He didn't know? " Eric asked.

"Not about *her* coming here."

It took a moment before Eric registered the implication of this remark.

"Do you mean to say that you told Varne *I* was coming out here? And by the way, how did you find out I would be here tonight?"

"Not so difficult, Watson. I overheard Eleanor offering to pick you up. Of course, I kept Varne informed about the student. Wait," he held up his hand to stall Eric's protest, "I do *work* for the man. I must say," he added reflectively, "Varne was very interested in this Johnson character. In fact," he shifted uncomfortably, "when he heard about your planned visit he made sure that said Johnson was informed."

Eric showed his astonishment. "I thought I was supposed to have been helpful to Varne enterprises?"

Albert patted him on the shoulder. "You don't think he really *likes* you? He humours his daughter but only up to a point. It will be a bonus for him if you get between Johnson and Kendall. By the way, those two seem definitely to be more than just cousins from my enquiries. Mind you, I didn't let on to Varne that I had found the address by then. Just gave him the name of the village. It was the least I could do for you."

"Thanks very much! So, that white van belonged to our friend Johnson?"

"Right in one, with yours truly behind the white van keeping an eye on things."

Eric felt uncomfortably warm and slightly queasy. "Hadn't we better be moving?" he asked.

Albert gave an evil looking grin. "Johnson got here just before you, thanks to your little diversion along the way. He probably turned his van round at that cliff top parking lot and I guess he's somewhere in the village, hoping you'll turn up."

"So, now that Eleanor's taken the car back he won't really have much of a clue where we are." Eric's relief was short-lived.

Albert studied him with interest. "I know he's not supremely intelligent in your book, but even he might put his head in the only building that's open in this hole, just to check on things. That's what I would do."

"I assume," Eric said, "that Varne will gratefully hear how you removed his daughter from a nasty situation but why are you still here with me?"

"Let's just say," Albert replied, "that I'm not as committed to the Varne kingdom as I used to be. What do you call it, you lecturers, re deployment? Don't look surprised young Eric. I've been reading up on these so-called cuts since I was told to look into you. Unlike your bunch I've got one or two irons of my own in the fire. I'm not waiting for Varne to boot me out." He chuckled. "I won't be getting the sort of handshake you layabouts will pick up."

"Hang on Albert," Eric retorted, drawn into the exchange in spite of the situation, "we're not sure how much we'll be given. I'm small fry don't forget. I haven't even crossed the bar."

"What's this crossing the bar stuff? Sounds more in my line," Albert commented.

Eric explained briefly about the rites of probation. Albert looked genuinely nonplussed.

"Pathetic," he pronounced finally. "And you worry about things like that?"

As he spoke he stared fixedly over Eric's shoulder through the window looking onto the car park. "Time to go I think," he said. "Leave the back way but let him see you first. Follow me when you get into the yard. I'll be waiting there. We need to be ready to deal with this creep."

"From behind, with a brick in our hands?"

"You're learning," Albert said curtly and exited via the door to the lavatories.

Standing alone, Eric thought, inconsequentially, that he had yet to quiz Albert about Suzi. Then the pub door opened. Johnson was wearing a donkey jacket, blue jeans and large boots. Eric pictured a lens zooming in on him as the newcomer examined the room and caught sight of him. Eric moved quickly.

The darkness outside engulfed him and for a moment he felt panic, wondering if Albert had already gone. Then his arm was gripped and they ran together, Albert's feet soundless, Eric realised, alongside his own clattering shoes. Within a minute or so they arrived once more at ranch-style fence. The house was still in darkness.

"Go up to the door and knock," Albert whispered. Quickly," he hissed as Eric hesitated.

Eric did as he was told. Albert disappeared behind the hedge. Eric lifted a brass knocker, gleaming dully even in the gloom. The sound of its fall was explosive in the night air. Its echo sounded faintly from the house wall on the opposite side of the road. The building still looked deserted, the windows a deeper shade against the dark stone.

All at once a porch light went on. The sound of a bolt scraping on rough stone was followed almost immediately by the heavy thud of Johnson's feet on the gravel of the cottage garden. Albert emerged from the shadows and gripped the newcomer's arm.

"Two of us," he warned, but at the same time punched Johnson hard on the nose. Blood streamed from it. Johnson gave a muffled cry and clapped his hand to his face just as the cottage door finally opened. Peter Everton peered out.

"For God's sake," he began.

"Look, Peter, I know this must," Eric began but Albert brushed past him.

"That," he said, pointing at Johnson, "could have been your colleague. On the other hand, it could have been you." Albert made the prospect sound a welcome one.

A breeze had sprung up from nowhere. Eric looked apprehensively at Johnson. As if reading his thoughts, Albert said, "He won't feel like another round just yet. I think I can persuade him to leave." He handed a handkerchief to Johnson, who glared back at him." And you ought to move too," he added in an aside to Peter.

"We'll be seeing each other again," Johnson snarled, looking at Eric rather than Albert. He walked slowly away.

Fewer than five minutes later Peter and the girl came out to their car. It shot through the gate and away, its engine quickly fading. Albert and Eric walked back to pick up the Jaguar, noticing that Johnson's white van was still in the pub car park.

"Cleaning himself up in the loo, I should think," Albert commented.

Eric was overwhelmed by a longing for the peace and quiet of his own room but Albert, like an over-active child, showed every sign of becoming livelier as the night lengthened.

"Well," he said when they finally left Barmton, "you'll have to come in and have a night cap, say hello to Suzi."

Chapter Seven

"So, the VC turned to the PVC and said, 'that depends on the UGC, surely.' And, of course, the PVC was caught out there wasn't he? So much for the SMG. Do you know, I can't see the Board wearing this one Eric."

Mercifully, Daniel's alphabetical stream dried up, allowing Eric to take a firmer grip on reality. The Vice-Chancellor and Pro Vice-Chancellor were easy enough, but the other initials, the ones following the University Grants Committee? They had a tantalising air of familiarity but their meaning eluded him.

A week had passed since the eventful night in Barmton. Eric was sitting with colleagues in a corner of the Senior Common Room. Sunlight streamed through the window. Conversation was animated, partly in expectation of a free lunch after a morning session grading the run of finals papers. Eric allowed his mind to slide over the list, the names of the candidates on the left hand side of the unfolding expanse of squared paper indicating the range of marks for each individual. He winced at the recollection of his own part in the charade. Like his colleagues, he had examined each case with an outward show of serious consideration. Looking around he noticed Henry Helm chatting genially to one of the external examiners, a desiccated man with thick glasses, busily clawing nuts from a nearby bowl. The statutory sherry was being consumed. An air of suppressed hysteria pervaded the room. Other departments had held meetings too, or else were just getting ready to have one. The day was marked if nothing else by the number of suits, collars and ties. External examiners, ranging from balding, be-spectacled composites to distinguished grey-haired, pink-faced figures were easy to pick out, being the centre of departmental knots, queen bees surrounded by their workers.

It was the turn of Eric's department for lunch. As its members prepared to move Margaret joined him. The noise in the dining room when they entered was considerable. The history table was in full swing, bottles of wine distinctly the worse for wear.

"Are we paying for our wine, do you know?" Margaret asked as she took in the spectacle of the historians.

Eric had read in one of the countless items passing across his desk on the subject of 'economies' that staff entertainment was to be drastically curtailed. Whether or not this included wine he wasn't sure. He remembered one piece about staff travel and another about heating and lighting. There had been something, too, about the library.

"Couldn't say offhand, Margaret," he answered.

Sitting next to her was, he accepted, unavoidable. It was either her or Kingsly, who was hovering nearby. Uneasily Eric looked across to see Peter Everton talking to Alan. Henry was stationed near them with the external, doubtless, Eric was sure, relishing the prospect of the afternoon session. The morning run through of marks had already slotted the no-problem cases into their categories ("Two upper second and five lower second marks. Two-two overall, agreed?") By lunch time four students whose results were problematic had been identified as candidates for a *viva*. Eric pictured these, far removed from the joys of the Senior Common Room. Later, after brief oral examinations, there would be a brisk session to tie up loose ends. After the posting of the examination results there would be the end of term staff meeting and last but not least, drinks with the final year students.

As if reading Eric's thoughts, Margaret observed that it was going to be a long afternoon. "At least Peter's project won't take up too long now," she commented.

Eric was puzzled. Jake, seated on Eric's left, said, "Haven't you heard? Apparently young Peter has been persuaded that his scheme needs some serious re-thinking. He was in Henry's room for a long time yesterday."

"The upshot is," Margaret put in, "that the whole thing is shelved for now."

"Just as well," Jake interjected in a lowered voice. "Peter has enough on his plate, what with one thing and another."

Eric thought of Johnson clutching his nose in Barmton but said nothing. When he looked along the table again he caught Peter's eye briefly. Eric felt heartily sick of the man and his problems and resolved to tell Clara as much, albeit from a safe distance. He helped himself to some wine as Jake turned towards Angela to exchange pleasantries and Margaret spoke across the table to Henry Helm.

Eric suddenly felt a surge of excitement at the memory of the previous week's journey back from the coast. Albert had driven out of Barmton at speed, the car's headlights picking out the black ribbon of road. As if viewing a home-movie winding back, Eric had watched the villages pass smartly by in reverse order.

"Yes," Albert had observed as they passed the pub where Eric had earlier sat with Eleanor, "I should be able to go in for a bit more private enterprise of my own shortly. That's what this government wants isn't it?"

Eric had been surprised to hear that Albert had invested in property on his own account and said as much.

"I'm still only a small time landlord. Don't tell me this is the end of our relationship," Albert had added, laughing loudly.

"I can't imagine Varne being all that pleased, from what little I've seen of him."

"Like I said, it's small stuff. Besides I haven't told him,

have I?"

"You can't make that much on rent can you? Property isn't that valuable up here in the first place?"

"True," Albert had agreed, "and these cuts you keep on about won't help either. Still, the students pay in advance."

"Don't they object when you put the rent up?"

"No complaints so far," Albert had grinned, his face caught by a passing headlight. "Keep this to yourself."

"Who would I tell?"

"Fair enough, but you are seeing to Varne's daughter. No morals. I wouldn't trust any kids of mine in your hands."

"Right Albert, I could learn a thing or two from you there."

"You seem to be enjoying yourself" Margaret said, bringing Eric sharply back to the present.

"Just thinking, Margaret," he answered vaguely. He saw that Henry and one of the external examiners had risen. They were due to start the first *viva*. Eric watched with fascination as Kingsly's face took on a purple colour matching the glass of wine in his hand. Just then the pudding arrived, tinned fruit with thin cream trickled from a jug.

"Is it," Jake sighed, "like this in the common rooms of Oxbridge?"

A quarter of an hour later they filed through with their coffees to the oddly named 'Writing Room,' where they would re-assemble after the *vivas* before plunging into their departmental meeting. The historians must have already wrapped their business up, Eric guessed, having seen two of them slipping into the nearby billiards room. He had briefly glimpsed the history professor bending over the green baize in fierce concentration before the door closed on muffled laughter.

No sooner had he picked up a coffee than the secretary to

the Senior Common Room came through asking for Dr Farnham.

"You are wanted on the telephone," she said once Eric had identified himself. He followed her ample, blue linen encased bottom to the reception desk. Eleanor's voice came down the line.

"I'm ringing from your room. Your secretary told me you were at lunch. Can you come over for a few minutes?" Eric glanced at his watch.

"Meet me in the student bar," he said, "I don't have too much time, OK?"

He emerged into strong sunlight. A flawless blue sky arched overhead. The lawns were littered with students, singly and in groups. He was aware of a ripple of interest from a knot of undergraduates in his own department. No doubt some would still misguidedly be expecting the call. *Viva voce*, he thought, a gem of a description for the stunned silences too often typical when 'borderline' cases had the chance, in Henry's words, to "talk themselves up."

As luck would have it, Eric met Eleanor immediately outside the entrance to the student's union. She smiled briefly and he took in with approval her pale blue cotton trousers and loose white linen coat over a dark tea shirt.

"Do you actually want a drink?" he asked, thinking of the students again.

She shook her head.

"Then let's go through and sit on the sports field. It should be empty. The entire final year seems to have camped out in front of the main buildings."

He was pleased to feel her arm slip through his as they walked along the narrow drive between the student's union building on one side and, on the other, the high sloping wall of

94

the new purpose-built theatre, erected in the distant days when universities had found favour. The field at the back was a rich green in colour and they sat on a bench beneath a row of trees.

"Look Eric, I 'm sorry I haven't been in touch since, well, you know."

"We've all been busy."

She accepted the reply as well meant and nodded. For a moment or two they watched a lone figure jogging on the far side of the field.

"I wanted to let you know that my father *is* thinking of some sort of deal with the university." She stopped. "It's been difficult at home. He was furious with me for going to Barmton. Wait, I told him it wasn't your idea. He's come round to thinking you might give him some help preparing a proposal to your council, or whatever it is, Senate, I don't know. He's expecting you for dinner tonight, as it happens."

"Do you know more about what he has in mind?"

"Well, he never gives 'owt for nowt, as he puts it." She shrugged. "I know he has been talking to his accountant about these so-called EU regional funds. Apparently," she went on, "there are European grants for various projects that might help regions in need of regeneration. We need to know more about how they work, why and when grants are dished out, that sort of thing..."

That explained it Eric thought. Invest a few thousand quid and hope for a lot more back. It rang a distant bell now. The last university *News Letter,* laden with self-advertising snippets unstintingly provided by fellow academics, had published a piece on such funding. It was in the context of a bid from the politics department – Eric made an effort to recall the title. Something, he thought, about the machine tool industry in its trans-national setting. He had trouble suppressing a grin at the thought of his

95

own intermittent research into the life and work of Goethe.

"Sounds interesting," he said neutrally.

"Sounds bloody boring!" Eleanor declaimed. "Still, it might be useful to you."

Eric agreed, almost at once mentally mapping out phrases about the need for someone with a 'European' background (i.e. a modern language) to be involved in any bid. For some reason he imagined Albert looking over his shoulder and saying, "Go for it my son!" The thought prompted a question.

"I take it you were angry with Albert the other night out at Barmton."

She scowled. "What happened after I left?"

Eric gave her the gist of it, omitting what Albert had told him in confidence. She stared in silence for a few seconds.

"Do you know, I'm beginning to think that Albert might admire you. Something seems to be going on. My father has suddenly got quite touchy about him too. "

They stood up as the jogger changed his lonely circuit and came in their direction. The bright green and yellow running gear, Eric saw, contained an old leathery body. It passed by glumly, eyes fixed ahead.

"I have to go now," Eric said, "or else I shall miss the summing up and the final verdicts." He explained what he meant. "By the way," he commented as they walked back towards the main buildings, "your interest in German seems to have dropped off recently."

"What about," she said, taking his hand, "making up for it by spending the weekend together? And don't forget," she finished, "dinner this evening, 8.15. Please don't be late. My father hates it."

The *vivas* were over by the time Eric rejoined his colleagues just as they were settling down to revisit their lists for the final decisions. Catching sight of Henry in the corner momentarily alone Eric joined him and lowered his voice.

"Henry, can I have a quick word with you before the staff meeting later?"

There were two pairs of cotton jeans hanging in the airing cupboard. Albert inspected them with a worried expression. They had been carefully ironed to offer smart creases to the outside world. No good being ungrateful he thought. He should have mentioned it to Suzi. But then he had never expected anybody to iron for him. He quickly re-folded the trousers from seam to seam prior to smoothing out the creases. After stashing the ironing board away he put the jeans in his wardrobe under a jacket.

When he went to the kitchen to make coffee he noticed that the contents of the large fruit bowl had been re-arranged. Apples, oranges and pears were neatly piled in their respective segments. He ran his eyes over the rest of the room and discovered the drying up cloth folded in four on the draining board. He picked it up, unfolded it and hung it back on the brass hook near the sink. At the sight of the cups grouped in different colours inside the glass fronted cabinet over the cooker all he could do was to laugh out loud.

He sipped his coffee and thought about Varne's earlier exchanges with him. Not much had been said but Albert sensed a new hostility. It had something to with the Barmton escapade, surely. Still, he couldn't help wondering if Varne had also found out about the terraced property on Inkers Lane.

Instead of washing his mug and putting it away Albert stood it in the centre of the kitchen table then carefully placed one of the bananas among the apples.

97

As he nosed the Jaguar out of the city towards Varne's place he went over his conversation with Eric Farnham on the drive back from Barmton. At one point he had expressed envy at the ability to speak in another language.

"Shouldn't be too impressed Albert," Eric had commented. "No matter how many languages you learn if you haven't much to say in any of them."

The remark had appealed to Albert. Recalling it made him feel cheerful.

"Well," Kingsly was saying, "this brings us to AOB. Next year's options. We, er", he shuffled through the papers on the table before him and finally picked up two closely typed pages. "We have a proposal before us for a new course to be taught by Dr Farnham. Would you like to speak to this, Eric?"

Eric glanced down at his own notes. "I think on the whole the outline you all have is self-explanatory." He paused. "I certainly don't want to take up too much time now but it seemed to me a good idea to put on a new subject. The department has a tradition of rotating options (Turnip Townsend, he thought). Mine is a topic which has not yet figured prominently in our programmes."

There was a movement from Peter Everton's end of the table.

"Some of you know," Eric continued resolutely, "that I have a research interest in early 19th century German intellectuals. Clearly, I value the prospect of relating this more closely to some of my teaching. Especially since," he added with a serious glance round the room, "we are likely to have to do more rather than less teaching after the cuts. And...."

"Mr Chairman, I have to say that I don't think this is the

best time to be introducing new courses." Alan spoke with emphasis. A few heads nodded sagely. "Can I suggest," he went on, "that we move directly to a motion on this? Something along the lines that the department considers it inappropriate to make changes in the timetable until the full effect of the cuts is clear."

There was every appearance, Eric thought bitterly, of spontaneous composition

"I can quite see Eric's point," Daniel piped up. "Personally, I think his topic would get takers but, well, this might not, as Alan said, be quite the right moment."

Kingsly agreed with Daniel. "Moreover," he pointed out, "if Eric's subject does come on stream then presumably one of the other option courses will have to be dropped. Any thoughts on this?"

"I can see why Eric wants to put an option on at the moment," Peter called out. "Let's face it, the teaching loads are going to be looked at very closely. I would normally be considering giving my 20th century German novelists a rest," Margaret tittered appreciatively, "but ..." he shrugged his shoulders.

"Any other comments?" Kingsly asked.

Eric looked at his assorted colleagues and felt they richly deserved what was coming to them, whatever it might be. Here was an occasion when silence was the perfect response; silence was all that was required to preserve the status quo; silence enabled his colleagues to keep a clear conscience without personally opposing the proposed new option.

"Why don't we," said a voice from the back of the room, "put on record our interest in Dr Farnham's proposal and minute our intention to incorporate it in future teaching programmes when the overall situation is clearer."

The suggestion came from Christopher Morton, a balding

linguistics lecturer in his thirties and yet master of the wording of resolutions. The assembled staff gratefully raised eyes from an examination of the document prepared by Eric. There were murmurs and more nodding of heads. Alan and Peter, Eric noticed, exchanged quick glances.

"Would you like formally to propose that motion?" Kingsly asked Morton, who gave his wolfish grin.

"One moment, Mr Chairman," Henry spoke from the depths of one of the few armchairs in the room. "There is, if I might say, an aspect of this problem we are in danger of overlooking." He hesitated and peered over his glasses. "It could surely be argued that this is the time less for cautious retrenchment than for showing evidence of our, er, um, continuing readiness to contemplate changes, innovations in teaching, new courses and so on. Is that not so?"

"Well," doubtfully from Kingsly.

"It is a *possibility* at least," Henry insisted. "You Peter, would be most affected by Eric's proposal because it happens to be your subject's turn to go into cold storage, hm? But," he gave a rictus of a grin and removed his glasses, "you yourself have implied elsewhere that change in universities is no bad thing, hm?"

Eric felt the instant change in the atmosphere. Clearly, he had been far from alone in puzzling over Henry's failure so far even indirectly to refer to the letter in the *Times*. More to the point, Henry's specific reference to Peter's option signalled to colleagues that they were not at risk from the proposed new subject on the table. Talk became animated.

"As we know," Daniel interjected, "Eric is just about to go through the procedure of having his post made permanent."

"Good point, Daniel," said Jake.

Kingsly, Eric saw from a furtive glance, was far from

happy. The former turned towards Peter and asked, "How does this strike you then?"

"How does what strike me?" Peter replied coldly, looking not at Kingsly but at Henry Helm.

"I was coming to that," the latter said. "I suggest that for now we simply list Eric's proposed topic as an additional option. There need be no formal notification of the students about next year's classes for another week at least. By then we shall know the outcome of Eric's interview. Subsequently I can have another meeting with him, as well as with Peter. Agreed?"

Eric noticed, even while savouring Henry's coup, that all tacitly accepted his own status would be resolved on Friday. The absurdity of the whole procedure of 'crossing the bar' struck him anew. He looked up to find Henry watching him intently. But for their earlier chat about Varne's idea the meeting might, Eric was sure, have ended very differently.

Discussion mutated into a formless and generalised exchange of ideas about the university's future. Eric realised, as he listened to Margaret, just how pre-occupied he had been with his own situation. He hadn't even considered the unpleasantness of drastic change for academics in their fifties and beyond.

"We don't," Margaret was saying," even know how much we will get if we opt for voluntary retirement. The papers had some figures last week. As I understand it, how much you are awarded depends to some extent not only on your status and career length but, er, on your future prospects." She paused and adjusted her glasses before continuing. "What worried me was the assumption, um, that a Professor of mediaeval history, for example, could expect to earn, um, several thousand pounds from consultancy."

A roar of laughter greeted this and the meeting broke up shortly afterwards. Along with others in the department, Eric sauntered back to one of the seminar rooms in the main building. It had been set aside by long established custom for sherry with the final year students. The campus was now almost emptied of life. Few other departments had arranged a staff meeting at the close of a day's examining. He glanced at his watch, wondering if there was time to complete the formalities of congratulating the students who turned up for sherry, before joining them for a proper drink in the pub. It was already 5.30. He could risk a quick one, he decided, and then go directly to Varne's.

"Glad to see you looking pleased with yourself, Eric."

Alan had fallen in alongside him. The two of them walked in silence for a few moments.

"Look, Eric," Alan went on, adjusting his glasses. "I should say sorry."

"No problem, Alan." Eric anticipated an apology for his colleague's unhelpful intervention about special subjects. He was wrong.

"Suzi really *surprised* me, you know?" Alan said. "I hadn't thought things through when I crashed into your office. I feel a bit of a fool."

"You'll have been able to practise more," Eric ventured.

Alan grinned. "You're not wrong! My tone, you should hear it. Plenty of long notes, d'you see?" He laughed again. "I must have given the neighbours hell for a couple of days. And," he lowered his voice," I've been looking into buying a sax."

Eric marvelled at human nature in general. They entered the building together and moved slowly up the stairs. For the first time he noticed Alan's clothes. A bright red tie rested on a grey corduroy shirt. The old Suzi would have killed off the combination at birth. He was wearing suede shoes too. An embryonic bohemian, Eric thought, decades after espresso bars had vanished.

102

"Tell you the truth," Alan whispered as they entered the room where the students were assembled, "Carol Barnes and I met up again, well actually a few weeks ago. She used to be one of my finals students two or three years back, remember? She's teaching at the High School."

The mystery of Alan's attire was solved at a stroke. "I'm delighted, Alan, really," Eric said.

He concentrated on the room. Several bottles of sherry stood near the blackboard. The more successful examinees could easily be picked out. They were anxious to grin and wave. Others, less fortunate, were huddled together. Not for the first time Eric failed to understand why his colleagues enjoyed this ritual. He armed himself with a dry sherry, doled out by Angela, and moved towards a corner. He was taken aback to find Peter joining him.

"You might well look worried," Peter said but to Eric's relief with an absence of overt hostility. "We need to talk..."

"Now?" Eric asked.

"Later, in the pub."

"Peter, I realise this sounds absurd, but the other night."

"Later," his colleague repeated.

Two students joined them and Peter drifted off.

A loud rapping on a desk top heralded the formal speech from Kingsly in his capacity as chairperson. He launched into a fulsome tribute to the students and to the "family" of the German department. The speech droned to an end in a ripple of applause. It was followed by a few toasts. Eric smiled insincerely in Kingsly's direction, reasoning that the latter's toothy grimace was no more heartfelt. Angela and the other secretaries began to collect the glasses. Very few people, Eric observed, had touched the piles of crisps and twiglets heaped on dishes near the windows.

At the pub Eric pushed himself through the melee of bodies. Smoke hung in blue clouds, pinned in mid-air by the shafts of late afternoon sunlight. The noise was approaching the pain threshold. A constant and indiscriminate hugging and kissing was in progress. Eric heard his own name yelled from one or two places. Shouted queries flew across the room about results. He managed to get a pint of beer and was almost instantly joined by Peter nursing, to Eric's surprise, a large whisky.

"Cured now, are we?" Peter asked.

"Meaning?"

"Of your concern for friends and colleagues."

"Fair comment, Peter. At least you managed to get away from Johnson. Best to keep your eye open though."

"Well, " Peter replied quickly, "you might well be higher up than me on his hit list after what happened in Barmton. And," he gave a sly grin, "I didn't hit him."

"Neither did I," Eric answered hotly.

"From where I was standing he didn't strike me as the sort of person who makes fine distinctions."

Eric tended to agree. Johnson would think twice about repaying Albert in kind but…He tuned in to Peter's voice again in time to catch the end of a sentence."

"….staying at another flat myself. Still, that's my problem."

"How is Clara," Eric asked weakly.

"Funnily enough, she seems quite calm," Peter said. "I saw her on Sunday. We've been drifting apart for years. To be honest, I felt I had to talk to her, even before you stuck your nose in."

In some way, Eric now realised, Peter had lost some of his tautness. Hadn't there been a *New Society* article recently about traumas giving greater strength to some types? At that moment Alan joined them. To Eric it seemed as good a time as any to mend another fence.

"About the teaching options," he ventured to Peter, "would you really object to resting yours?"

"Not keen on that," Peter said dismissively. "This is not the place to talk about our so-called professional life, if you don't mind."

"OK," Eric agreed. "Any more detailed news of the cuts?"

"There will be a key Board meeting scheduled for the afternoon of your interview on Friday, Eric," Alan interjected, well informed as ever. He pushed his glasses up his nose. "Sorry Peter, for talking shop but," he turned to Eric, "didn't our staff meeting strike you as a bit odd? I mean, has Henry given you any encouragement for your proposed new course?"

"Not really," Eric lied.

Peter looked about him with an absent minded air. "I'm off," he announced.

Eric, whose own glass was empty, asked, "Can I get you a last drink, Peter?"

"No, let me." Alan said and moved off before any protest could be made. Peter quickly tossed back his whisky.

"I just wanted to clear the air a bit," he confessed. "Oddly enough last Friday night's fracas helped me to straighten things out in my mind. Give Alan my apologies."

Eric watched his fellow teacher's stooped shoulders and small, neat head until he left the room. "He's still an odd bugger," he said to Alan, who had returned with a surplus drink. A passing student when offered the glass accepted it in a seamless movement with a brief, "cheers."

"I can't stay long either, Eric," Alan said. "Seeing Carol later. We're due at a cheese dip party."

"Fine," Eric responded. "I've promised to see someone in any case."

He only just resisted an urge to tell Alan about his coming

talk with Varne. In the same instant he realised how little time he had to make his dinner appointment punctually. As he stood outside the pub with Alan one of the city's blue buses loomed in the distance. Eric decided to take this and walk the final half mile rather than wait for a taxi.

"Best of luck on Friday if I don't see you before," Alan said, holding out his hand.

"Thanks a lot Alan, I'd almost forgotten."

Alan laughed. "Sure," he said. "Mind you, the university's new profile should be known by then, at least in draft. That'll put your worries into perspective."

Thank you and good night Eric thought. Even he had heard about the drafting of a procedure for rationalising resources. It was due for fuller discussion in the early part of the vacation. Departments were in the first instance to put forward proposals of their own for making savings. The idea nicely offset the effects of what little alcohol Eric had managed to put down. He glanced out of the window of the bus as it pulled away and saw Alan bending down at the window of the car that Peter's girl friend drove.

Chapter Eight

"Right, I've a better picture of what might need doing." Varne settled back in his chair as he spoke.

His wife reached across to remove his plate. Eric, surreptitiously examining her tightly curled hair and ample figure, still found it difficult to see how she and Varne had produced Eleanor.

"Of course," he said, leaning forward, " the university will need to have a detailed proposal from you setting out what you have in mind."

Varne nodded. "Always best to have it in writing, in my experience," he stated. His hand flapped in irritation as the sleeve of his wife's Spanish styled dress brushed his face.

"This is where I could help," Eric said. "In actually formulating the approach to the university."

"Then you give me a bill for writing down the ideas I come up with!" Varne exclaimed, taken with his own humour and looking for appreciation from his wife. She smiled briefly.

"There is something in that," Eric admitted. "Still, these days there are fairly rigid guidelines for funding bids. Forms are time consuming. Besides, I can draw on my own department's knowledge of European organizations. You're a business man," he added with a touch of inspiration, "you must appreciate that services have to be paid for."

He sighed inwardly. Varne knew damn well what he was doing. It would suit him for Eric to do most of the donkey work. Chances were that even if the scheme ever came to anything the university administration would soon push a lowly lecturer aside.

"I could just discuss your general intentions with my head of department," Eric offered. For the moment he didn't want to think of the crucifying tedium that would engulf him in the event of actually having to formulate a final bid.

Varne gave him a calculating look. "I've no objection to that. Bear in mind there's a lot more to be considered before taking any definite steps."

He looked hungrily at the door to the kitchen and poured Eric another glass of wine. Like the sherry before the meal and no doubt the liqueurs Eric anticipated afterwards, Varne drew attention to the quality and price of the beverage. It was as if he were locked in combat with invisible rivals, all of them waiting predatorily for the smallest sign of declining wealth.

Mrs.Varne came in carrying an enormous cream and chocolate concoction. Varne relaxed. Eric smiled towards Eleanor, who was helping her mother dish out, what was it, Eric wondered, the fourth, fifth course?

"From what I hear from Eleanor, the government has at last got round to sorting you lot out then, yes?"

"Well," Eric answered, trying to sound reasonable, "this is not the best time to make cuts. Not when more and more school leavers are being encouraged to get degrees."

"Hm!" Varne expostulated. "I've had students working for me in the holidays and half of them can't even spell properly!"

"Some, perhaps," Eric conceded, uncomfortably aware that many of his colleagues shared Varne's assessment.

"Nothing personal, lad," Varne swept on, "but a shake up would do your lot no harm if you ask me. Lecturers are only at the university half the time even in their so-called terms, never mind their holidays!"

"Teaching needs preparation though and so-called vacations are when we have to catch up with reading and research."

Varne snorted.

"Not everybody can be a successful business man,"

Eleanor interjected, to Varne's evident pleasure. "Even academics have their uses, as you well know."

"Very true," Belinda Varne interjected. "There are more things to life than making money dear, isn't that right Eric?"

In some way her intervention depressed Eric more profoundly than anything Varne had managed to come up with. At least he found universities a fitting object of venom. His wife's comment succeeded at a stroke in reducing the world of reason to the status of a hobby.

"Anyway," Varne conceded through a mouthful of food, "it won't do any harm if you let your managers, or whatever you call them, have some idea of what I have in mind. Many a bridge to cross before I get in to bed with your lot, though."

Hoping to keep Varne in comparatively good humour Eric asked what had become of the Germans he had helped chaperone recently. Varne said nothing until he had finished chewing.

"Shan't be doing business with them again. I've had my doubts about them for some time." He drifted into a private reverie and a few moments later rose heavily.

"Right," he said, "a few 'phone calls to see to."

He kissed Eleanor briefly, nodded to his wife and left the room with a promise to come back shortly for coffee.

"Why not take Eric for a stroll round the garden dear," Belinda Varne suggested, "it really is at its best at this time of year."

It looked good, Eric had to admit. Despite the fading light he could admire the impeccably straight lines made by the lawn mower and the carefully disordered riot of colours in the flower beds. In the distance, behind a hedge, was the fencing round the tennis court. A figure could be seen bending over the net as they drew nearer.

A few seconds later they moved behind a shed and were

momentarily out of sight of the house. Eleanor stopped and reached down with her hand. Eric gasped and leaned back against the wood. It smelled of fresh creosote. A few moments later, when their walk resumed, he felt irritable. It was as if he were some sort of pet, given periodic but not too extravagant treats. There was even a degree of absent-mindedness involved.

At that moment they drew level with the figure on the court. It proved to be Albert, looking hot and dishevelled, with shirt sleeves rolled up and hair awry. He had furled the net and was busy cranking it down.

"Albert," Eleanor called out, "don't forget to put the big roller away."

A savage twang came from the handle Albert was turning. When they were out of earshot of the court and on the way back to the house, an extravagantly lit showcase against a blue-black sky, Eleanor remarked casually that Albert was leaving. Eric was startled and said so.

"It's very sudden, I agree." she told him. "He's doing odds and ends for the rest of the month and then he's off. He's keeping the car, though."

On an impulse Eric knelt down as if to tie his shoelace.

"Catch you in a second," he said.

"I'll put the coffee on. After that home for you, Eric."

When she had disappeared he trotted back to the court. It was empty and the gate locked. "Albert," he called out, then felt his arm gripped hard.

"Lucky we met, Albert said quietly. "I've got plans that might interest you."

"What on earth is that supposed to mean and do let go of my arm, please."

Albert did so. "Look," he said, I'll ring to fix up a drink and we can have a talk, right?"

110

"Fine, let's do that but I'd better get back inside otherwise she might come to fetch me."

By the time he got back to the house Eleanor and her mother were seated in the kitchen drinking coffee. Eric was glad to see that Varne had not kept his promise to rejoin them and poured himself a cup from an expensive looking silver jug. The overhead strip light was guaranteed to bring out every blemish, no matter how small. Reflected in the long kitchen window the three of them looked ghoulish, eyes dark-socketed, noses moistly highlighted. Eric, puzzling over Albert's remark, half-heartedly took part in the small talk. Not much later Eleanor kissed him briefly in the doorway and he made his way towards the main road.

He looked back at the house and saw its outside lights abruptly switched off. For some reason he felt in high good humour. The feeling lasted until he reached the front door of his flat. He had already turned the key in the lock when he heard a sound behind him and was thrust violently into the hallway. Johnson, Eric saw, thinking inconsequentially how quiet it seemed inside the house. He looked at the worn carpeting, fading up into the darkness of the second floor landing. There was a letter addressed to him on the hall table.

"Look," he tried to speak calmly. Johnson bundled him against the hall table. The indignity of it made Eric angry. "Look," he tried again.

"No bodyguard tonight?" Johnson sneered. "Now, your friend, the one shacked up with my cousin. Where is he?"

"No idea," Eric felt breathless. He barely registered a distant thud but felt pain then sat down heavily, his eyes on a level with the hall stand. The letter was still there. He shook his head and Johnson came into clearer focus. Behind him a massive black man suddenly appeared.

111

"What are you doing?" he said to Johnson.

"This is private."

"Not now. Here is my sister's room and we want no trouble."

To Eric's relief Johnson dropped his shoulders and after a murderous glare slammed out through the front door.

"Thanks, whoever you are," Eric said quietly. He stood up with the aid of the hall stand and automatically pocketed the letter. The giant rested a hand on his shoulder.

"Best come in for a drink. My sister can clean your eye up, she's a nurse."

Eric had the urge to crawl into bed and put a pillow over his head but his weak protest was brushed aside. His saviour seated him in a deep, old leather armchair in an unbelievably cluttered room. Eric registered kaleidoscopic colours, as well as photographs standing on every conceivable surface. Three pink lamps threw pockets of light. A short black woman came from a curtained recess and smiled shyly.

"You poor man, Dr Farnham, you let Elvin here get you a drink while I look at your bruise."

"Please, don't go to any trouble," Eric said.

After a brief examination and a few dabs with damp cotton wool and lotion he was pronounced fine. Elvin placed a beaker in his hand.

"You got some nice friends," Elvin said, sinking into a settee. It squealed in helpless protest. Elvin's round head, with lidded eyes and a moustache, turned towards Eric.

"And you a university lecturer," he said, stressing the third syllable of the word 'university.' "Nice looking eye you're gonna have tomorrow," he added, laughing. "Hope you got nothing important on. No big lectures, right? Hey," he called out to his sister, "why don't we ask our lecturer to the party on Sunday?"

112

Eric accepted the invitation and even agreed to try to bring one or two friends with him. When he finally left the room he half expected to see Johnson lurking at the top of the stairs. Instead all was peaceful save for the faint sound of a radio coming from the half landing below his own. He threw open his window and sat in the dark listening to the street sounds. A cool breeze ruffled the curtains. Despite his aching head he grinned at the thought of Peter Everton opening his door, wherever he happened to be, and sooner or later finding Johnson standing there.

He got up and switched on the light to look at himself in the mirror. A dark red weal extended from just below his right eye almost to his mouth. It promised to be even more colourful by morning. Mercifully, he fell asleep quickly.

The ante-room to the council chamber or whatever it was called was a mere ten feet by twelve and lined with dark wood. There were four solid, high backed chairs. Eric faced a thick and imposing door with three steps leading up to it. From beyond this came the occasional scraping of chairs and a staccato laugh. A scream would help, he thought, to round out the image of an inquisition chamber. There was comfort in the thought that he was one of several cases going through the arcane procedure. He became aware that his companion, a man with a large round face adorned by thick glasses, was talking.

"It's nay credible is it? I mean, fwat aw we doon here?" Eric waited. "They dinna want to hear what you've got to say."

Eric looked more closely at the rumpled figure barely seated on the edge of his chair. The man pulled out a packet of cigarettes but immediately put them back in his pocket before examining with interest the highly coloured bruise on Eric's face.

"Heavy neet?" he asked.

At that moment the door opened. The secretary to the court came out with a balding young man who disappeared through the doorway leading to the street. Eric watched his fellow sufferer stand up and march towards his interview.

While awaiting his turn Eric fretted in his own mind about his brief chat with Henry earlier that day. The conversation had been remarkable for the total avoidance of two topics Eric had hoped would come up. Namely, encouragement to get something in motion on the Varne front and, secondly, the matter of the proposed new course. Now he was anxious.

He breathed deeply, as Alan had assured him musicians did before giving a performance. The action had the effect of inducing a feeling of tightness. He gently stroked the bruise on his cheek.

The chamber door swung open and the young Scot emerged. Whereas he had entered the room as if stiffened by wire he came out loosely and shambled past Eric, merely nodding. In a curious way the silent exchange brought some of Eric's confidence back.

He found the committee arranged in the classic horseshoe pattern calculated to put interviewees at an instant disadvantage. On the table before his chair was a plan showing the names of his inquisitors in the order in which they were seated. He politely surveyed the semi-circle like a camera taking a school photograph on the playing field. The chairman was large and looked affable; the Professor of Physics, judging by the plan. Just the chap, Eric imagined, to chair a meeting on the future of a linguist.

He eventually focused on the chairman and the two women flanking him.

"Shall we begin?" The chairman glanced round before

gesturing to the woman with a somewhat severe expression to begin.

"Good morning, Dr Farnham," she said. "I just want to ask if you have enjoyed the university since you joined us. Has it lived up to your expectations?"

"Well, Professor Bloom," Eric began, after a rapid glance at the seating plan. A frown crossed his inquisitor's face. "I have enjoyed the work. I did have the good fortune to teach, in the first few terms, a course related to my research interests. As you know," another quick turn of the head, "this makes for a more rewarding situation."

He wondered if he was going too far but the faces crumpled neither into laughter nor disbelief. A few of them even nodded. He continued along the same lines for a few minutes until, half way through detailing his plans for research in the coming summer, carefully tailored to his putative option, he realised abruptly why Bloom had frowned. She was not Bloom but Professor Frank. It was the sort of mistake Eric made when map-reading, looking for roads on the left that were actually on the right. The real Bloom, a large and shapely woman, was now regarding him with some interest, smoke curling through her blonde locks.

His brain remained in overdrive, looking for a way to redress his unintended slight to Frank (alias Bloom), so that only fragments of the chairman's speech penetrated. "Difficult time – efficiency bar – case like yours – normally straightforward." The use of the word "normally" roused Eric as the chink of a bottle might wake an alcoholic. He returned to full alert but the members of the committee appeared to have lost interest in him. Small wonder that so little sound had reached the outer chamber. Nothing much was being said.

"No, salary is the issue now," the real Bloom pronounced

with a disarming smile. The mention of "salary" instantly revived the attention of panel members.

"Yes," the chairman interjected, "a man of your experience could reckon on a few points up the scale. But we are under tremendous pressure from the government to cut costs."

A small, balding man further along the table, with a fringe of dyed hair surrounding his skull like a decorative frieze on a cake, leaned forward and rested the elbows of his fawn-coloured suit on the table. Hastily Eric worked out from the plan that this was probably the Professor of Politics. This time he said nothing and confined himself to waiting attentively. .

"No need to worry, Dr Farnham," the man said, "we seem to be more or less agreed that you should cross the bar, as it were. But," his high-pitched voice paused and he snickered, "there isn't much grass on the other side, green or otherwise." The comment went down well with his fellow panel members. Eric waited.

"Are you prepared," the speaker went on, "to remain on your present salary point when your tenure is formally confirmed?"

"To be perfectly honest," Eric began, "I suppose I had expected, had hoped." He tailed off, recalling a story he had once been told, about Royal Navy ratings being compelled to request punishment for any misdemeanours they had committed. "Might there be some reconsideration later, when things improve?" he asked.

"That is possible," the chairman countered, placing deliberate emphasis on the last word.

"To be honest," Professor Bloom intervened, "your record is quite reasonable but teaching hours and so on, well, let's say that you appear to have been luckier than some."

There was a rustle of papers round the table as the material relating to Eric's case was consulted.

116

"Well, there is this new course I mentioned."

"I wondered about that," said the man with the fringed hair, "only there doesn't seem to be any specific reference to it in your Professor's report. He couldn't manage to get to the meeting in person as you know."

Eric imagined Varne jeering and saying you should have got it in writing lad! The clock on the wall showed that time for lunch was approaching and the mood of indifference that Eric had sensed earlier among his inquisitors had deepened. He half feared being asked to take a salary cut. Nor could he see a way of bringing up the Varne project, clearly also absent from Henry's formal note to the committee.

"Well, Dr Farnham, if you have no more questions? Then, gentlemen, and of course ladies, we minute that Dr Farnham be allowed tenure and record our regret that for the time being the university is unable to recognize his contribution with the usual increased increments. Of course," he added, "with future funding cuts in the pipeline *nobody* is really secure."

There was a murmur of assent.

"Thank you again, Dr Farnham, and congratulations. Best wishes for the future."

Eric left the meeting with a truer understanding of the Scot's posture and made his way back to the department. It was still hot and the campus retained its deserted air. The brief lull before the profoundly deeper lethargy of the summer vacation was something Eric normally found congenial. Not today. On the way to his room he met Kingsly. A wave of bad breath assaulted him as they drew level.

"No problems with the interview?"

"Not really, Kingsly. Thanks all the same."

"Well done. I thought you would be fine but I did just wonder, what with the cuts."

Eric told him about the salary issue, trying not to notice a look of something like pleasure flitting across Kingsly's face. The latter reminded Eric for the third time in as many days to attend the graduation lunch, if not the degree ceremony.

Eric's brief glance into the general office confirmed that Angela was alone. He shut the door behind him. "Angela, has the list for next year's courses been typed yet?" he asked casually.

"Eric! Have you seen the letters that I have to get out for the new students? Then I've got the graduation lunch to arrange. I won't bore you with the timetables and incidentally you haven't replied to my note asking you to confirm your teaching hours. Then I have a third chapter of Henry's book to see to. Kingsly has also asked for some stuff to be prepared for our students in France next year."

"What have you got on after lunch then?"

They both laughed.

"I was wondering," Eric continued, "if Henry had put the list of option topics into the system yet."

"Don't you mean Alan? He's next year's co-ordinator, Eric."

Eric managed to suppress an expletive and Angela handed him a folder.

"Here, this is the stuff I'm working on. You can glance at it. I haven't had the chance to look through everything yet. I won't get round to dealing with it until tomorrow at this rate."

"Angela, what would we do without you?"

"A great deal less."

Eric sat on the edge of the window sill and opened the folder. A book list, a book review. He glanced at this out of habit. The piece described a work by a very prominent Germanist at a distinguished centre of learning. Fulsome praise, Eric saw at a glance. Perhaps the book really was that good he thought. Next came the course options list, where students were supposed to indicate their first, second and third choice. One title was heavily scored through.

"I'll just take a copy of this Angela," he called out, going into a small side room where the Xerox machine was before she could protest. He left a moment later and went to his own office to examine the photo copied sheet again. There was Henry's option on obscure Austrian dramatists (but it wasn't called that); Kingsly's from Goethe to Grass (Gunther) was present and correct. There were also the usual standbys. Then, after the heavily scored line through the brainchild of a certain Dr Farnham, there appeared a brand new combined option to be run by Drs Branch and Everton, a comparative study of West and East German novelists of the 1970s.

"The predictable little shits," Eric informed his room. There was a certain symmetry to it he had to admit. Petty minded but for all that effective, exposing his light teaching hours at the worst possible time. He had no cause to doubt the probation committee's sincerity in predicting insecurity all round. No wonder Peter and Alan in the pub had skirted smartly round the issue.

An idea struck him. Picking up the city telephone directory from a pile of old scripts he looked up Johnson's telephone number and made a note of it. Next he rummaged in the top drawer of his desk for the university handbook. Among other things it listed course regulations. There had to be something there about proper procedures and due notice before the launching of new teaching programmes. He tucked the blue volume under his arm and went to check his pigeon hole in the main entrance hall.

The university news letter reminded him of the crucial meeting to consider the latest plans for "rationalisation," scheduled for that very day by the university's *prominente*. He resolved to find out more detail from the common room at tea-time. To be forewarned, he intoned to himself, is to be forearmed.

Chapter Nine

Eric called in at Clara's on his way to meet Albert and was surprised to find that much of the house's surface dirt had been removed. He was received in a kitchen verging on the tidy. Of interest too, he felt, was the absence of any noticeable aura of uneasiness. A clear case of the resolutely independent female, he thought. He had to admit that not having Peter around was a persuasive argument for the feminist viewpoint. Clara's attitude towards Eric was one of calm detachment. It reminded him that she had either once functioned as, or at least taken part in, a course to become, a social worker. He nearly forgot in the middle of Clara's discourse on her husband's vanity that he had called in to borrow a spare gown for the graduation ceremony, just in case.

"We'll have a drink sometime?" Clara asked.

"Of course," he said and just as they were parting with promises to keep in touch, he asked if she would like to go to his neighbour's party.

When he arrived at the Station Hotel he found Albert seated in a far corner of the lounge. He immediately ordered a round of drinks on seeing Eric, who glanced round automatically for any sign of Johnson. At least the man had not called in on Clara, no doubt assuming Peter no longer lived with her. Eric was now convinced that Peter and the girl met in Alan's flat. It was, like a good mathematical model, too neat not to be true.

"Cheers," Albert said, holding up a generous glass of whisky. It struck Eric that Albert no longer looked as menacing as he once had. He examined the room with its red plush armchairs and crystal lights and found its air of genteel shabbiness agreeable. The potted plants were noticeably thicker near a small raised platform, on which stood an old piano and some assorted music stands. Albert was grinning broadly.

"You're beginning to look like one of us," he said, indicating Eric's bruised cheek. "Anyway," he continued, "let me tell you what I've been thinking. Firstly, you can guess that after what Varne heard he wants no more to do with our German visitors. But," he lowered his voice, "I've managed to make contact with one of them who is still interested in a foothold of some sort in the area. More to the point, he doesn't seem to mind upsetting Varne which of course makes two of us. Now," he grasped Eric's arm, "this is where you come in."

Several drinks later, in a relaxed glow, Eric discovered that the idea of helping Albert cultivate his own German connection was less implausible than he had thought on first hearing.

"I'll think about it, Albert. The trouble is that at the moment I don't really want to upset Varne." He decided to say nothing as yet about the possible funding bid and instead used the excuse that he might lose Eleanor as a tutee if Varne found out what was going on.

Albert leaned forward. "You might take this the wrong way," he said, "but I doubt that you are all that important in Varne's scheme of things. So, don't take too long to make up your mind."

"No," Eric said as Albert raised a hand to the waiter, "this must be my turn."

When the fresh drinks arrived he put a note into the waiter's hand and left the change where it was on the tray.

"Cheers! Eric made an effort to concentrate, trying to pick up a thread of an idea waggling at the edge of his consciousness. "Of course, I'm flattered Albert but there must be more suitable candidates." He noticed that his glass was inexplicably empty. Albert's round, moon-like face hovered before him.

122

"You're in the picture," Albert said, "fairly reliable and available."

"Everything has a cause, Albert. Even a brief acquaintance with history stops one from believing in pure chance."

"There you are then," Albert's face split in two. "I've never studied history."

To Eric the logic was impeccable. "Ah, I remember now!" he exclaimed and produced from his pocket the piece of paper on which he had written Johnson's telephone number. "See," he said, waving it, "not just chance. Connections. No such thing as accidents."

Albert looked nonplussed then again signalled the waiter. In no time a white-coated sleeve appeared at the edge of Eric's vision and the tray with his change still on it was replaced by one holding two more glasses.

"Telephone," he asked, "is there a telephone?"

"Drink up," Albert said, standing, "we'll find one on the way out."

There were evidently far more tables and chairs in the room than Eric had realised. The same could be said of the ferns. Soon he found himself next to Albert in a small 'phone booth in the foyer. He gestured at his paper and Albert dialled the number on it. Eric listened to the ringing and then a gruff voice answered.

"This wee gurlie yurr looking fer," Eric said. "Ye'll nay go furr wrawng if yous try Harold Street, number 5a. Reet?" He dropped the receiver before examining the wall of the booth more closely.

He awoke to a distant rattle of crockery and turned his head. A vice was applied to it and promptly tightened. There was a frilled quality at the edges of his vision. A window above his head let in daylight and a red curtain flapped. The breeze was important. Somehow he had to get nearer to it. The vice was momentarily released before being locked on again at a different point. A disgusting aroma of frying bacon hit him with almost physical force as he struggled into a sitting posture. He felt both hot and cold at the same time.

It seemed easier to move his entire body than just his head. Some Darwinian impulse allowed him to master this trick relatively quickly and he stood, carefully tilting his upper half so that his eyes could look down at the floor. He opted to leave his shoes where they were. Nearby was a convenient wall along which to move. With the additional aid of one or two items of furniture en route he arrived like an explorer in the doorway to the kitchen, where the smell of fried food stopped him in his tracks. Still, the fuzziness in his vision was fading. As long as he kept his eyeballs floating steadily forwards the generalised pain in his head was tolerable. He tried to ignore the sensations in his stomach but at least signals were beginning to arrive from the rest of his body.

"Well, well," Albert laughed. His round face was freshly shaven and he showed no signs of tiredness. Eric held up a hand in protest and lowered himself onto a wooden chair at a table covered in a yellow-checked cloth.

"Have I really been asleep all this time?" Eric asked.

The clock on the wall indicated ten-fifteen. He became aware that the kitchen was large and square, with a tall window letting in light from a leafy courtyard. Albert stood in front of a complex stove. Eric registered the statutory stripped pine. A disproportionately large bowl of fruit on the table reminded him, more clearly than anything else in the room, that Suzi was still, to use Albert's terminology, in the frame. Albert disappeared through another door to the right of the stove and Eric caught a glimpse of a long, narrow pantry.

"Well," Albert said, putting a brown loaf in front of Eric and deftly slicing it, "sleep came into it. There was a lot of talking too."

Eric looked at the bread and crumpled one of the slices, eating it in small balls. He fought back a wave of nausea. If it helped pregnant women, he thought, chewing slowly. Wasn't there something about tea too? As if reading his thoughts Albert crossed to the stove and came back with a large brown pot. He poured from it, raising and lowering the spout as he did so. Eric watched the brown bubbles attentively and the way in which the dollop of milk that Albert added spread slowly to colour the drink. He sipped it.

"Talk?" he queried.

"Words were used but whether you could say they made sense, well. I mean, you talked in sentences."

Albert's tone reminded Eric insistently of that favoured by linguistic philosophers.

"Can't remember much," he agreed. He picked up another ball of bread and thought there was something to this morning sickness treatment after all.

"Rationalisation mean anything?" Albert asked. Eric frowned. "Then there was crossing the bar, well, I know about that one of course."

"I talked about that?"

"In between some choice remarks about your colleagues," Albert said, sitting down opposite with a plate piled with eggs and bacon. Eric averted his eyes.

"Something about course options?" Albert added.

Eric looked up carefully and patiently explained to Albert about such things.

"You actually offered to do more teaching?" Albert said in

125

mock surprise.

"For good reason, Albert, not just for the sake of extra work."

"I can see that," Albert said shortly and listened closely as Eric went on. "Now, let me see if I've got this," he said eventually, pushing his empty plate aside. "You do six hours a week, actual teaching, that is. Then the government - is it the government? - starts worrying about the cost of education, at which point you come up with a saver by piling a whole two hours a week, on top of your six, making eight. Right? And they call us the criminal classes!"

"You can't just give lectures without a good deal of preparation," Eric said.

Albert guffawed. "So you work day and night for the first few weeks until your lectures are written and then...." He shook his head.

The two of them moved through to the lounge via a corridor which ran past an open bedroom door. Albert noticed Eric's quick glance at this.

"Suzi is in London, doing some shopping for a couple of days."

"Doesn't she work? I mean her term is still going on."

"Taken a bit of time off," Albert said shortly.

Eric chose not to pursue the matter. They sat in identical armchairs placed on a pale rug in a lounge with a large, small-paned bay window. Through it the tree-lined avenue could be seen. In each alcove to the side of the fireplace were book cases. Eric noticed with affection the rows of dark green-backed penguins. A large square coffee table provided one point of focus. Another was given by a big sofa beneath a standard lamp.

"I gather your mates are not up to much after all."

"Sorry?" Eric said.

"This Everton, the chap you mentioned on the telephone."

Eric continued to look blank and Albert enlightened him.

"That little bit of direct action sort of sets off your, what is it, legal approach?" Albert asked innocently.

"Legal?" Eric asked. "Oh, you must mean course regulations. Don't tell me I went on about those too?" Albert nodded with a weary expression.

Eric had decided that his best chance of frustrating Alan and Peter lay in persuading the Board of Studies that their proposed combined option constituted a radical departure from the norm, thus meriting prolonged, if not indefinite consideration. Failing that there was the timetable ploy. This at least was tried and tested and had the advantage of triggering off the conditioned reflexes of colleagues. Any reference to the complexities of timetabling changes was usually enough to sink most schemes put forward on merely educational grounds. Unless, it now struck him for the first time, the buggers could argue that their course could begin without the statutory notification because, in its essentials, it had already been functioning, as it were, in its constituent halves. He conveyed the gist of this to Albert, who laughed derisively.

"And the 'phone call?" he asked after a pause, "was that to soften them up or just an afterthought?"

Eric shrugged. "We'll see," he contented himself with saying.

Unbidden, his mind slipped back to the latest news about the university's plans for restructuring. It wasn't as if the mill owner had called him up to the big house and given it to him straight. Indeed, he had received token security only hours before discovering on Friday afternoon, from hasty exchanges in the common room, that his own department was now pencilled in for a staffing cut of 2.8%. There had also been talk of moving to a "steady state" situation.

"Steady state!" he exclaimed.

Albert paused in the act of putting his cup down and raised an eyebrow. Again Eric explained.

"Sounds like a downhill slide," Albert said dismissively.

Eric's initial response to the 'steady state' concept had been that it sounded vaguely re-assuring. Somehow, though, his twilight knowledge of the laws of physics linked the concept to some post-catastrophe condition of the planetary system. Or was it matter?

"What gets me Albert is the waste of time. I've been studying something or other for ever. Now, bang, sorry, we can't afford you. Run along and do something else."

"Yeah, "Albert answered bluntly. "Must get the housework finished."

"But really, you'd think...."

"Or looking at it another way," Albert interrupted irritably, "how have you lot managed to get away with it for so long?"

"There is that," Eric admitted. "Trouble is, some will go on getting away with it."

"It is not clear," Albert intoned, "why a man should be held responsible for an action which occurs by chance." He smirked at Eric's expression. "Mr Ayer said that. Look, nobody is interested in your problems. Take me. I've always had to live on my wits. Put something by, keep my eyes open." He patted Eric on the shoulder. "Now remember, Monday is the big day."

It took Eric a moment to realise that Albert was talking not of the graduation ceremony but of meeting his German contact.

"I can pick you up at the University later in the day. Meanwhile," Albert went on, stretching, "let's have the hair of the dog. Look on the bright side. Think what that sod Johnson might do to your mate now that you've given him an address."

There was definitely something catching about Albert, Eric had to admit.

When he opened his eyes on Sunday morning Eric saw that Eleanor was already up. His dressing gown had gone from the hook on the back of the door and there was a neat, silky pile of clothes on the table near the window. He stretched and listened to the rain, brought on by a sudden change in the wind on Saturday evening. It was still warm he noticed, after he crawled to the end of his bed to open the window. Outside the odd passer by scurried along with newspapers carefully shielded from the wet. Why, he wondered, did he still feel the urge to buy a Sunday paper? He had no immediate prospect of securing a country property, a car number from the extensive listed columns, nor yet an exotic holiday. He flopped back on the bed willing Eleanor to come back to his room, unreasonably becoming irritated after a few moments of waiting. He got up and pulled on a shirt and a pair of jeans. As he did so Eleanor returned carrying two mugs of tea.

"How do you live in that kitchen?" she asked, standing one of the mugs on his radio.

She sat on the bed and the dressing gown parted. The paleness beneath aroused Eric but Eleanor appeared to be absorbed by the view from the window. She glanced round.

"Why don't you put something on," she suggested, nodding at the turntable.

Eric obliged by putting on the Mozart clarinet concerto. He thought of Alan's incessant but only intermittently successful attempts to work through its well-known phrases.

"Where on earth were you all this time?"

She giggled. "Talking to a large black man in the corridor, about this party tonight." She looked at Eric. "You didn't tell me about it."

"I was going to, of course," he said. "You're welcome."

"There is a better recording of this piece," Eleanor observed. The rain hit the window with another gust of wind and the alarm clock went off.

"Ten o'clock, so that's when you get up."

Her back was still towards Eric and he picked up her empty cup. She moved to the armchair and turned round. "Come on then," she said.

"What do you mean?" Eric asked.

"This," Eleanor said and opened the dressing gown. He thought how well her skin looked against the dark brown corduroy upholstery. He could feel the breeze on his back from the open window and wondered what on earth they must look like from the road below. They sat on the end of the bed in silence afterwards until the record finished. He felt suddenly restless.

"Shall we go for a stroll?" he suggested.

"Any chance of a bath first?"

He went to the walk-in cupboard at the end of his room and picked up a comparatively clean towel from one of the shelves. He threw it to her and said, "Don't forget to lock the door!"

When she had gone he tidied up the bed and then went back to the cupboard. It contained a mirror with a light above it just inside the door. He made faces at himself as he combed his hair. Peter's gown hung on a hook and Eric tried it on, striking a few well-known academic poses.

The crossed-hands, genital protection stance recalled

130

Henry Helm, whereas Kingsly, who always lectured in his gown, favoured both hands grasping the garment at about chest level. Eric gathered up the end of his sleeves in both hands and shrugged the gown up above his shoulders, baring his front teeth. A sudden loud knock on the door made him hastily tear the garment off. He threw it to the back of the cupboard and opened the door to his room. Belinda Varne stood there in an expensive looking raincoat. Her round glasses shone.

"Is Eleanor here?" she demanded.

"Er, no," he said truthfully. "Look, I'm just about to go to the kitchen for a coffee, would you like one?"

He ushered her on to his small landing and they went downstairs. He was acutely aware of the sound of running water coming from the bathroom.

"It's a shocking day, Mrs. Varne," he called loudly, "isn't it?"

They went down another flight of stairs. Eric never failed to marvel at how the elegant staircase transcended what various landlords had done in the way of carpeting it. For a change there was no sound coming from the room at the front of the house. A pale light shone through the glass above the door to the street. They moved towards the kitchen at the back of the building.

"Sugar?" Eric asked when he had fetched cups through from the scullery to the kitchen table. She shook her head.

"This must seem a bit odd," she said. "I'm not checking on Eleanor you know. I just called in to have a quick word with you."

"How did you know where I lived?" Eric asked, shaking his head when he was offered a cigarette.

"Your address was on the 'phone pad." She blew smoke upwards with an air of distaste, as if it had nothing to do with her, turning her head to the side at the same time.

131

"I was driving by on my way to Church. That's where I told Terry I was going." She paused and Eric caught the distant sound of the bath being emptied.

"He's upset with you," she said abruptly. "He's in a very bad mood just now. It all seems a bit sudden."

"Do you mean he's angry with me or about Eleanor and me?"

"A bit of both, I think. He's always put out if he gets the idea that anything serious is going on with Eleanor. He can be very difficult."

"In what sense?"

"Well, there was a chap last year, an estate agent, lovely man. When Terry realised that he and Eleanor were sleeping together it was quite unpleasant at home."

"Someone locally?" Eric asked with interest.

She blew another cloud of smoke to the ceiling and looked thoughtful.

"Not any more. His office had a fire. He left the city not long after. I think he lost heart."

Eric distinctly heard the slam of the bathroom door and footsteps going upstairs. "Mrs. Varne, you surely don't mean..."

"Good heavens, I don't think Terry would go that far."

She didn't sound too sure, Eric thought. He was relieved to find that no more sounds came from the stairway.

"Even so," she went on, "I recognize the signs. He called you, no, I won't repeat it. He doesn't understand your life at all, you know. Clever, is Terry, but without much imagination. He's very different from Eleanor."

"I really don't see what I am supposed to do," Eric volunteered after a prolonged silence.

"No, it's silly really. I came on impulse. I should never have troubled you."

132

She put her cigarette packet back in the black leather handbag on her shoulder and stood up, glancing at her watch.

"I have to put in an appearance at the church now. Don't take this personally," she added, placing a hand on Eric's arm. "I think he's even more annoyed with Albert than he is with you."

He went out to the hallway with her. No sign of Eleanor lurking on the stairs.

"Perhaps things will blow over," Mrs. Varne said as she left.

He watched her go down the path to her car then he shut the door. In the silent, empty hallway the previous ten minutes or so assumed an air of total unreality. He shook his head and turned back. Eleanor stood on the stairs, shoeless but in her silk two-piece suit.

"Same old game," she said angrily. "She knocked on the door of the bloody bathroom. Must have been on the way up. I don't know what stopped me from calling out."

Eric looked puzzled. "Game?" he asked.

She shrugged and moved back up the stairs.

"What did she have to say to you," she called over her shoulder.

He told her as they went back to his room. It felt depressing sometimes, he thought, to be at the top of this house. He perched listlessly on the end of the bed.

"I thought your father was the difficult one."

"No. She's right about that. He'll be angry with you, particularly now that I've stayed the weekend."

Eric's spirits lifted a fraction at the implication that Eleanor was remaining for another night.

"She uses him as an excuse to nose about, you know," she went on. "She probably thinks you're not acceptable. Not 'good enough' for me. It's happened before. I think she sees me married to one of the chinless but well off farmers around the place. And she's bored out of her mind."

"A job?" Eric suggested. He was rewarded with a snort.

"Everybody knows my father in this place. He won't have his wife working. I sometimes think that she might go dotty in the end. Well, perhaps not while there's food about."

"The comfort of the carbohydrates?"

"Not eating, thinking about food. Reading about the stuff. All those menus to plan. My father is the one who likes the consumption bit. That's partly why the two of them get on."

He shrugged. "You could always leave home."

"And live in the style you're accustomed to? Believe me, I like the way I live. And I really do have more than a passing interest in my father's business you know."

She was tough enough, Eric thought wryly.

"What *are* you grinning at?" Eleanor demanded suddenly, startling him. "You're always doing it."

He could think of no suitable riposte and instead said resolutely, "Right, now for a walk."

She took her umbrella from the corner of the room and Eric pulled a wind cheater over his shirt. Outside it looked as though the sun was making an effort to break through the clouds but half-way towards the park the rain came back with a vengeance. As a result they ended up in a hotel bar. Thereafter the afternoon passed quickly enough. To Eric, with distant memories of eating roast beef to the sounds of 'Family Favourites', this was the best thing Sunday afternoons could do. He tried to recall what had depressed him most, the oily tones of the radio announcer wafting though the window of their suburban semi or the deadly quiet after the washing up. He mentioned his thoughts to Eleanor, who looked at him blankly.

"We always ate in the evening," she said dismissively.

"Your trouble, shall I tell you what your trouble is?"

Eric had the impression the question would be answered soon enough and smiled over Clara's head. They had been washed up in their corner as the party seethed about them. It was hot and Eric had already drunk more than he had planned. Recalling his all too recent evening with Albert he put his glass down carefully on a nearby shelf. There were others there, nestling between framed photographs of grinning black faces.

"You don't care about anybody," Clara said, her dark eyes fixed on him. She was serious, too, with the effort of containing drink, Eric thought.

"Clara. That's a bit steep isn't it?"

For a moment he thought she was angry but she shook her head. "Look at you. It's just an act. The reasonable, bloody academic. Don't you ever commit yourself?"

The music reached a new level of intensity as he opened his mouth to reply. "I suppose I can be annoying. I'm sorry."

"You don't think that at all," she glared. "You just say it."

He caught a glimpse of Eleanor through the doorway to the hall. The party had been allowed to spill out from the downstairs room, along the bottom corridor and into his own kitchen. The guests were a mixture of cheerful West Indians and mainly white students, some of whom he dimly recognized. There was a spattering of lecturers from the Art College and the College of Education. Most of these were, or appeared to be, talking with seriousness to a variety of listeners, captive like himself between groups of armchairs, sag-bags and dancers. He had already had a bruising encounter with a small, black-bearded, leather-jacketed art college lecturer, motivated it seemed to Eric by a mixture of glee at the looming university cuts and unspoken resentment that he was not himself part of the university.

135

"You're not even listening," Clara said resignedly.

She offered a cigarette and he took it. Leaning forward to have it lit he caught her familiar scent.

"I am listening but what can I say? I'm glad to see you and that you and Peter are at least in the same house, even for a while." Poor sods, he thought.

"And jolly convenient for you too," Clara said with something like a glimpse of her old self.

"Besides," Eric said, "your dress looks nice."

Clara looked pleased when she answered, "Oh, what's the use."

He felt relieved. It had been tricky earlier, on first seeing Clara with Peter, the latter's face marked with a heavy bruise on the right cheek. There had also been something odd about the way he was holding himself. Johnson had admirably fulfilled Eric's expectations. Not surprisingly, Eric felt when Clara told him, the Kendall girl had moved back with her cousin.

Eric touched Clara's arm and moved towards Eleanor, who was talking to a thin West Indian. The man grinned at her before sliding into the kitchen.

"Enjoying yourself?" Eric asked.

"Pleasant enough. And you? Was that one of your old girl friends?"

"I have known her," he said facetiously.

"She didn't look too happy, what have you done?"

He promptly told her about his recent prank at Peter Everton's expense. Her eyes sharpened at the mention of Johnson.

"Let me get this straight. At roughly the same time as we were prowling around your colleague's seaside hideaway you were seeing his wife?"

"It wasn't quite like that Eleanor."

136

They were separated briefly by a girl in search of a drink. Out of the corner of his eye Eric saw another couple go upstairs.

"And your friend the clarinet player? Wasn't this Everton chap staying in his flat?"

"I didn't like to ask about Alan," Eric said sheepishly.

"And I don't suppose you care, do you?"

"You should have a chat with Clara," he said wearily, "on the subject of my caring."

"Actually, I think you have been rather mean," she added, "and your Clara was probably right."

"Oh, come on," he laughed, putting his hand on her shoulder. "My two friends, as you call them, dropped me right in it."

He found himself explaining yet again the intricacies of departmental jockeying to an outsider. "Anyway," he concluded lamely, "look at this." He pointed to his own, now fading bruise."

"Did you notice that this Peter Everton chap seems to have difficulty standing up straight?" she asked. "What would you do if you really disliked someone?"

"I think I really do dislike him."

"It's like dealing with a load of schoolboys," she said with exasperation. "Couldn't you all have a talk with your Professor or whatever you call him?"

"He's the worst of the lot," Eric said, grinning.

"It makes me wonder why this Everton chap came this evening", Eleanor observed reflectively.

Eric turned to see Peter talking to Clara in a corner of the hallway. Flashing lights were coming from the front room and the hall lamps had been switched off, so that Peter's face turned rapidly from red to blue and then green.

"I did wonder the same thing myself," Eric said uneasily.

"He surely must be able to work out that you were behind

his little fracas."

Eric had to admit this was a distinct possibility. Peter proving it was another matter. There was a loud crash from the front room and sounds of laughter. Eleanor moved forward and peered in.

"Somebody has fallen over," she reported. "Incidentally, did you lock your door?" Eric patted his pocket.

"Never fear. I had a feeling things would go on for a bit."

"Where do they go upstairs?"

He shrugged. "There are plenty of dark corners. I think there is even a box room somewhere off the second landing."

"As long as the loo is free," Eleanor said, "I'm desperate." She made her way along the crowded hall and Eric suddenly came face to face with Peter. He realised that he had yet to show curiosity about how Peter got his bruise.

"Are you feeling OK?" he ventured.

Peter nodded, his face close to Eric's in the crowded hallway. He grinned crookedly.

"Do you know," he said and continued to stare fixedly at Eric, "I'm quite enjoying myself."

"It's entertaining although I would prefer less noise. Anyway," Eric gestured at Peter, "isn't it all a bit uncomfortable for you?"

"This chap called Johnson?" Peter said. "Somehow, he found out that I was at Alan's place with......"

"He's her cousin, I believe," Eric put in hastily. "Eleanor's father seems to have some sort of business link with your girl friend's father."

Peter cut him short with a leer. "No point asking how he found us out so quickly I suppose."

"What about Alan?" Eric asked.

"He somehow managed to get out of the back door and

over the garden fence."

Eric successfully stifled laughter.

"Still, in an odd way I'm quite pleased now, "Peter continued. "Johnson seems to have lost all interest in me."

"So, this is by way of a relaxing night out for you and of course for Clara," was all Eric could think of saying. He glanced at the stairway but Eleanor was either still in the lavatory or waiting to get in. The bearded art college lecturer pushed past him, shoving him closer to Peter.

"By the way, Eric," Peter asked, "have you, er, have you seen the rationalisation proposals in full?"

"Do you mean the general statement on, what was it Friday?" Eric answered. Peter shook his head.

"No, the detailed profile. It has been leaked, comprehensively." Eric affected studied indifference.

"Nor," Peter added," the demotions panel procedure which has been proposed? No?" He paused, still grinning. "I can see you haven't. They're not supposed to be public knowledge for a few days yet. Clever timing, of course. Just before people disappear for the vacation."

"I have the impression," Eric said, "that you are trying to tell me something."

"Apparently," Peter said reflectively, "two members from our department will definitely have to go, either for re-training or out altogether, by way of a so-called golden handshake."

"When?" Eric asked.

"Oh, nothing too urgent. In about a year's time, as I understood it."

"Surely they can't give such definite statements yet. What about the union?" Even as he put the question Eric reminded himself of his lapsed subscriptions to the Association of University Teachers.

"There are difficulties," Peter agreed, "but my source is close to the Registrar's office and things are getting very tight indeed."

"I suppose a lot will depend on the attitude of the head of department."

If a grin could be said to become broader, then Peter managed the feat nicely. "Precisely," was all he said.

Gossip about a proposed demotions exercise, that much Eric knew, had been going on for days. Detailed lists of questions about teaching, research, the amount of university administration being done and so forth, were thought to exist. A committee, it was whispered, would then decide - like an aberrant promotions committee - who was to be asked to leave. Common room opinion had it that heads of departments would refuse to countersign the various statements. But then common room opinion had also had it, Eric remembered, that university tenure was of the strongest in the land. A recent briefing from an eminent QC had put paid to that idea. It might well, Eric saw all too clearly, depend entirely on Henry or Kingsly when it came to the crunch.

"Well," he ventured, "there are one or two near retirement age in our department."

Peter was silent for a few seconds and then spoke slowly. "One of the criteria, only one admittedly, is likely to be the number of teaching hours undertaken by a staff member, which of course is related to the actual number of students taught. It looks as though the idea of 'contact' hours has caught on as a rough and ready idea of measuring who is working harder than others. Well, the bureaucrats like the notion."

They would, Eric thought bitterly. He felt like someone watching a bus pulling away slowly with its door already closing. Not having the extra option classes looked set to be more

140

worrying than he had imagined. He began to see why Peter had dragged himself to the party.

"Yes," the latter mused, glancing idly at an attractive girl passing between them, "teaching hours will count and, of course, help in administration is a key factor. Working for the good of the institution, all that sort of stuff."

Eric mentally retraced his own distinguished non-participation in university affairs. As if from nowhere Clara reappeared and told Peter it was past midnight and time they were leaving. It cost Eric considerable effort to exchange small talk with the two of them for a few moments longer. As they left a West Indian girl approached him and insisted on showing him how they danced back home. The record of a steel band was going full pelt and the air in the front room was blue with smoke.

"Watch my knees!" she called, swirling and gyrating. Eric moved clumsily, pleased enough to watch the black dimpled knees. However, he was not sorry to be released with an affectionate pat on his bottom, at the very second Eleanor reappeared at his elbow.

"As soon as I turn my back!" She said. "Shall we get another drink?"

"What about sitting and watching for a while?"

They found two cushions near the fireplace. Eric sank down thankfully. The room had become emptier. Eleanor ran a hand across his head. "Another few years I think," she diagnosed.

"Days, at this rate," he snorted and briefly explained Peter's contribution to the evening.

"I see," she said, drawing out the vowels reflectively.

"Do you?"

"Well, in so far as I see any sense in your life. Still, lots of things could happen before this all becomes fact. People face unemployment with a lot less than you will get, you must admit."

141

"I've never really followed that line of reasoning," he said. "The fact that other people lose their jobs won't make me feel better if I lose mine."

Eleanor merely kissed him lightly on the cheek. "Well, this seems as good as any a time to tell you," she said, "that I shan't be staying tonight after all."

"But I thought..."

She shook her head. "Today was fun. I enjoyed it."

"Next week?" he asked tentatively.

"My 'German lessons' are probably on hold for the moment," she said briefly. Then, after a pause, she asked, "Albert, has he said anything to you lately?"

"I'm not sure what he gets up to." Eric discovered in himself no inclination to reveal what he had been told. Eleanor looked displeased. A thought abruptly occurred to him.

"You were checking up on me this weekend, right?"

She shrugged. "Not entirely. I had half thought of staying."

"And your mother's visit?"

"Now that I did not expect," she said with a flash of anger. Another facet of the situation surfaced in Eric's mind.

"Your father's project, has he, I mean, I imagine he's not so interested in exploring funding options now, if he ever was."

"Now that's more like the Eric I know."

She pulled herself up and straightened her dress. They went up past couples seated on the stairs to fetch Eleanor's things. On the top landing she paused.

"No, he's still thinking about the university," she said. "Maybe he just wants to leave his mark somehow. Whether you were ever likely to be a key figure for long, well. Actually, he has had a meeting with somebody else from your place."

They went into Eric's room. It was cold and he switched the electric fire on as she collected her few belongings.

142

"Who was his contact?" Eric asked.

"Not sure. He came out to dinner last week but I only saw him arriving as I left."

"I doubt your father ever really intended me to be involved at all," Eric said flatly.

"Well, be fair, you probably got him thinking about things more concretely, apart from being a sort of double check on what was possible. He doesn't want us, you and I, to become too friendly."

"So you've no idea about this other person your father met with from the university? What did he look like?" He watched her closely.

"For one thing he had a big nose. Mummy made a joke about him looking like a bird. Oh, and his hair was very black."

If it was possible to slump mentally Eric did so.

"My father seemed quite taken with him," she added, before kissing him briefly and going downstairs.

Eric decided not to re-join the party. Later, lying in the dark, he resolved among other things that he couldn't even be bothered to try to hold back Peter and Alan's proposed new course option. He would just take his chances, he thought, succumbing to a mildly pleasant fatalism.

Chapter Ten

Who would have, thought Eric asked himself, growing hotter as he stood in the body of the hall in his PhD gown and wanting more desperately with every passing minute to tear the floppy hat from his head, that so many of the dignitaries on the platform for the degree ceremony were employed in running the university as opposed to teaching in it.

"Those who can't, administrate," he muttered to himself.

He looked around. Students were examining the staff with undisguised interest, as well they might. Farther along Eric could see Henry standing solemnly as the procession wound down from the platform and past the two front rows reserved for gowned academics. Once the tail had gone by those seated here could attach themselves. The whole thing then shuffled out of the great swing doors at the far end.

Eric was reminded insistently of the conga. Face after academic face floated by, the unnaturally even plane of the heads determined by a concentrated effort to keep the largely rented mortar boards and caps in place. As it was Eric had only just recovered from a mild bout of hysteria at the confusion, during the award ceremony proper, when graduates invariably mixed up the arcane rules governing the doffing of hats. When his own turn came to join the moving queue he was paired with somebody he did not recognise.

Peter and Alan were walking side by side a few feet ahead of him. They were, he saw, of the horse-guards-on-parade variety of academic, opting not to run the risk of being drummed out of the service by returning the nods, timid waves and smiles from the common herd about them. Kingsly was of the same species, as was Margaret. Henry Helm, by contrast, moved amongst the tired and stiff-limbed throng dispensing regal glances to left and right. A few steps behind came Daniel, registering surprise at seeing students in the audience who could hardly have failed to be present to receive their pieces of paper.

By the time Eric got back to the dignified, wood-panelled room set aside for disrobing, the place resembled a self-service cafeteria at the height of the lunch hour. Despite the warmth many of those present were reluctant to throw off their gowns. The riot of coloured hoods did, he had to admit, look well with their scarlet, deep blues and fur trimmings set off by the dark walls. For all that his own borrowed gown and pink hood came off promptly, together with the pancake of a hat.

One or two academics, he noticed, were meticulously packing their gowns into personalised carrying cases. Daniel was one of them and Eric joined him, reluctant to stand alone.

"How can you afford that thing?" he asked, nodding at Daniel's case.

"Eric! Well, this has seen a lot of service. I bought it years ago."

"Are you staying for the buffet?" Eric asked, casually taking bearings to locate Alan and Peter.

"Never miss it!"

Kingsly materialised from somewhere, still begowned and perspiring freely.

"The mums and dads like to meet the staff, you know," he said. "Are you stopping, Eric?"

"But of course, Kingsly."

He could not help noticing that Kingsly was unusually subdued. The ceremony normally made him more garrulous than ever. Today he looked tired and appeared to lose interest almost at once in the general talk between Eric and Daniel. Jake joined them, to Eric's great surprise. Jake rarely attended

145

functions of any sort other than examining boards and the occasional staff meeting.

"Come for the lunch, Jake?" Eric asked.

He admired Jake, who had an abrasive quality. But Jake, like Daniel, Eric suddenly realised, was unduly respectful towards Kingsly. Indeed, both Daniel and Jake exchanged quick glances when Kingsly eventually drifted away.

"Am I missing something?" Eric asked.

Daniel beamed at one of the historians and promptly left Eric standing alone with Jake. The latter moved closer and lowered his voice.

"Do you ever wonder how grown men came to get like this?"

"Often," Eric replied. "I think they do it for the money. Why are you here?"

"Ah, Eric. Changes, changes. The important thing now is to be seen doing something. These are not times to be indoors."

"I gather," Eric said, grasping the nettle, "that home is precisely where some of us are going to be spending more of our time."

Jake glanced around. Then he said, "So you've heard about this panel thing?"

"I rather thought," Eric ventured," that I might be one of the superfluous two point whatever percentage it is of the staff leaving the German department."

Jake did not contradict him. Instead he wondered in a voice loud enough for Henry to hear why any sane person should want to stay in this madhouse.

"Could that, "Eric asked, "have anything to do with your constant globe trotting?"

In the past three years Jake had published two books and was in demand as an expert on regional linguistic and ethnic

146

problems in the European community.

"Off to Florence in a week," Jake said airily. "You'll survive Eric. Don't worry too much. Ignore all rumours."

"Difficult, Jake."

Jake shook his head. "It's partly bluff. Nobody knows what will happen. The government might decide not to make such drastic cut backs after all."

"The university," Eric confessed," is what really worries me. The government is too remote. Here I can see the knives coming out."

Jake nodded. "Still, it's a game. Step up pressures, hint. Enough people might panic and ask for premature retirement."

The expression always sounded to Eric like something the Mafia would undertake.

"Kingsly's the one I feel sorry for," Jake added, shaking his head.

Before Eric could ask what on earth he meant the movement towards the various centres of refreshment began in earnest. The German department had booked an upstairs room in which to entertain its current crop of graduates. These, together with proud but perspiring parents, trooped towards it. Eric fell in with Margaret, after leaving the gown in the cloak room.

"Margaret, what *is* the matter with Kingsly, do you know?"

She looked round anxiously and said in a lowered voice. "Henry is taking over the chairmanship of the department again, as from October."

"But I thought Kingsly was in for three years."

"Yes, it's unprecedented. Kingsly is most upset. He's talking about retirement."

"But why, for goodness sake?" Eric said.

Margaret surveyed him with a pitying look.

147

"I mean," Eric continued, "he still has his salary. And even if he does go, he should get a good deal. Not like me with my pittance."

"Frankly Eric, it's very worrying. It's unconstitutional for one thing."

"Do you mean there is no way that Henry can retake the chair constitutionally? I had no idea this place went in for electing chairpersons. Aren't they made in heaven?"

Margaret frowned and pursed her lips. "True, there is no specific provision to state that Henry cannot act so, but it certainly is, er, um, against the spirit of things."

"Henry was always a pragmatist," Eric said. "Couldn't the staff express displeasure?"

Again the look. The two of them helped themselves to sherry and Eric idly surveyed the more attractive mothers.

"As you are, um, aware, Eric," Margaret resumed, we all wanted a non-professorial head originally. Yes, yes, I er know that you didn't express any feelings one way or the other. Staff meetings have never been your cup of tea, have they? The trouble is that Kingsly is no more loved than Henry." Pause. "Daniel was the one most of us favoured."

It was with difficulty that Eric stopped himself from laughing out loud. He began to grasp the true depths of the crisis within the department. What a riot of non-commitment, he thought, would have attended Daniel's chairmanship. Kingsly was bad enough, with his congenital inability to reach decisions. Daniel's desire to please all and sundry amounted to a clinical condition. Henry would have none of that. Like the country, Eric thought, the department was about to get the leader it deserved.

"I suppose if Kingsly does go," he ventured, "some of the pressure will be taken off the rest of us."

"Not really."

148

"Oh, but surely, there must be some flexibility in the university's projected, what is the word, 'profile'?"

Margaret nodded emphatically. "Quite. But the give won't be here or anywhere on, what shall we say, er, the humanities side. The university is looking for a greater practical impact and that means science, business studies. More of the same."

Secretly, Eric was impressed by the vigour with which Margaret spoke. At the same time he was troubled by the advanced state of everybody else's knowledge of what was going on.

"But aren't languages 'useful', what with Europe and all that?" He ventured.

There was a tremendous crash from the other side of the room. He looked across to where a knot of parents were standing by the drinks table. Some of them in fact began to kneel. Eric put his own glass down and picked up a full one en route to whatever was happening. One of his students came away from the cluster of staff and parents.

"It's Dr White," he informed Eric. "I think perhaps he had too much to drink, or something. He doesn't look too good."

Indeed, Eric could now glimpse a pale and collapsed looking face slumped against the table leg. Somebody was offering it a glass of water. Without really wishing to, Eric thought that if Kingsly went and Daniel were ill, then....He hurriedly dismissed the thought.

"Didn't you know that Daniel is not a well man?" Alan asked as he joined Eric suddenly. "He has an ulcer. He's often a bit queasy but I must admit I haven't seen him as bad as this before."

Eric's initial reaction was, once more, that he knew less than his colleagues about pretty well everything around him. His next feeling was one of belligerence towards Alan.

"Congratulations," he said heavily, "on your new course option, by the way."

"Thanks," Alan replied blandly. "It should do well."

"You and Peter have suddenly found a mutual affinity then? Or is this just a disinterested pursuit of knowledge?"

"More or less what I expected from you, Eric. Actually, your proposal had no real chance, not at this stage. After all, you only put it up in the first place to make your own case look stronger, right? Well, we did the same. There's nothing personal. I like this job and I intend to stay in it."

He pushed his glasses up his nose firmly. Had Alan, Eric wondered, also acquired an untoward authority and purpose, or did the impression arise from his new suit, a dark grey outfit.

"Is Peter the ideal political running mate Alan?"

"He's all right. Everybody is entitled to the odd lapse. His work has been good and that's what counts, believe me."

"Publish or perish," Eric said.

He watched Daniel being escorted from the room by his wife, a pretty but tired looking woman with greying hair. Eric tried to imagine what it must be like having to live permanently with Daniel's wonderment.

"I suppose the university system will be producing a few more ulcers now," Eric said, adding unkindly, "mind yours."

Alan laughed. "No chance. I told you, I enjoy the work. Daniel has always been too worried by far. He'll be alright though. Henry is quite fond of him."

To Eric this sounded like implied criticism of himself. He was beginning to feel worn out by the sense of latent hostility surrounding him. Alan went on.

"There's nothing wrong with a bit of work. You could have made your own position much stronger, you know. Writing is part of our job, wouldn't you agree?"

150

"It depends what you mean by writing," Eric answered indifferently.

"It's no use," Alan said with exasperation. "You can't afford to be detached. Things are changing. You might as well get used to it."

"What makes you think I'm detached? Isn't there something a bit odd in churning out articles which hardly anybody bothers to read? It's a form of madness in itself."

"I'll go so far," Alan admitted. "I used to think that churning out stuff was the only thing that mattered. But it's that and being involved at every level. Yes, I do want a chair if I can get one."

Eric repressed the urge to say he would need one if Johnson caught up with him. Then he thought of Eleanor and, by association, Albert. He looked at his watch. He was due to be picked up at the main gate in about an hour. Alan was regarding him with a similar expression to the one on Margaret's face earlier.

"I *am* listening Alan." Eric said. "Even you have to admit that bets would not have been placed on the sort of deal that you've got with Peter now. Is he no sort of problem? I'm thinking of his letter to the 'Times' and his inane marking scheme."

"I'm not saying things are perfect," Alan said, with a touch of his former self, "but he won't be the same either, not after the last few weeks."

"But Henry? He'll have even more influence over us now."

"Haven't you heard? Henry has asked Peter to be his deputy."

No need to feel ashamed, Eric thought, at underestimating the workings of the Helm machine. Not only would Peter Everton now have to work harder than ever, but he would be so closely linked with the status quo that any pioneering urges he might feel would be well and truly buried.

"I can see you're wondering why Peter agreed," Alan went on, grinning. "For a start, Henry could have made life difficult for him over this student he's been seeing. After all, our leader is now tipped for chairing the committee distributing the proposed new research fund which the university is setting up. Peter is like the rest of us, he needs money for travel."

"Research fund?"

"Oh, it's been part of Henry's plan for a long time to get more research funding into this place. He seems to have persuaded the powers that be to put aside what he calls pump priming money. He intends, as I understand it, to get people looking all over the place, outside the system too."

"Won't all the universities be doing roughly the same thing?" Eric asked, recalling stories of British academics surfacing in far flung foreign cities looking for students to come to Britain, complete with fees. At that moment Jake rejoined them.

"This conversation is beginning to look serious," he said, "have you been on the same subject all this time?"

"I was trying to imagine some of our colleagues going cap in hand to Japan to pick up students," Eric said, picturing the impact Margaret might have on such a recruitment drive.

"It does make you cynical," Jake agreed. "We've spent the last decade or so running down our colleagues abroad and making fun of their students. Now we want to take them on any terms."

"Never mind your 'A' levels, how is your bank balance?" Eric offered.

"Or," from Jake, "just how long have you had an account with us?"

"Fine," Alan joined in, "but without money our jobs won't exist. If we need students who can pay, why not get them from

152

abroad? There's even a plan to get students from China."

"Christ!" Jake exclaimed, "this will cause havoc with our accounting system." They laughed together this time.

Mild hilarity seemed to have infected the room at large. By now there was little pretence of contact between staff and parents. Most of the latter had retreated with their platefuls of food to the chairs round the edge of the room. Some of them glanced resentfully as their sons and daughters fraternised in the centre of the room with assorted academics.

Out of the corner of his eye Eric had been observing Henry sidling between groups. He was having his normal effect, as each knot of people opened up to admit him, lost its previous coherence and reassembled only after the Professor had moved on. Eric guessed from the sudden smile on Alan's face a moment or so later that their turn had come.

"Must be off," Jake said. "Sorry Henry. Have a nice vacation Eric. Alan, bye."

Jake promptly joined a group of students near the buffet where he remained in full view, chatting and drinking.

"I really wanted a word with Eric," Henry informed Alan, giving him a brief glance. When Alan had gone Henry apologised for not having been available for the promotions exercise.

"I've been very busy, as you can imagine," he said, his dark head bobbing. "I gather you got by. There isn't much chance of extra increments at the moment, of course, but you've got a job at least, for the time being."

He laughed shortly then stared in silence. The gambit invariably made Eric lurch into a conversational opening without thinking properly. Today was no exception. He found himself expressing disappointment about the course option. Henry remained silent, his eyes dancing from side to side.

"Well, the time wasn't quite right," he said eventually.

"Alan and Peter can tie in some postgraduate work with their joint subject, whereas yours was well, a bit unformed."

No mention, Eric thought with silent fury, of Henry's original encouragement. In retrospect he now saw that this had been just one move in a larger scheme to stir everybody and everything up. If the cunning old bugger had come straight out with the idea of pushing Alan and Peter together it would never have been accepted.

"It leaves your teaching a bit light, of course," Henry said, looking at Eric from under his eyebrows, "but I was wondering if we could cover that with some more administration."

"Well," Eric began. Henry brushed his intervention aside.

"The admissions procedures need more personal attention now. It won't do just to take decisions on application forms any more. We need to sell the department. I've been thinking. What about," here he paused, "what about a scheme where we invite *all* promising applicants, I mean every single one, to come and see us next session? Say, for example, we set two or three afternoons a week aside and bring students here in groups of ten or so. Show them round the place, put on tea and so forth. Any use?"

So that, Eric thought, was that. Just as the price of Henry's tolerance of Peter Everton was the latter's involvement in the donkey work of the department, leaving the Professor engaged in high policy, so his own future lay in an unknown quantity of paperwork and commitment of time. The leisurely days of reading and teaching were dwindling at a rate he would never have believed possible.

"If you think that would help," was all he could say.

"Excellent!" Henry responded. "I've often felt that you had a certain facility for putting students at ease, getting them to talk and so on."

Eric comforted himself with the notion that it was still

154

some way to October and that, after all, a couple of afternoons strolling round the campus were not so intolerable. As the chink of light appeared, Henry closed it off.

"I think, perhaps, that our publicity material could be re-written. Our course brochure looks a trifle dated. Could you be thinking about this, getting some ideas together in the next few weeks? I think the printers will need the stuff fairly soon if they are to get it out for the beginning of term."

He pulled out his diary and waited expectantly for Eric to do the same. Eric took out his own notebook slowly but when he opened it the pages refused for a moment to come into focus. Then, as a date was mentioned four weeks ahead, Eric momentarily experienced a sense of calm. Its source lay in the idea of giving up his job. Instead of re-writing the wretched brochure he would explore the prospect of voluntary redundancy being touted by the university administration. He would say nothing to Henry until the very last moment, maximising inconvenience to the department. He was single, he thought as Henry rambled on, and unencumbered. So why not throw it all in? Why wait until he became like Kingsly? Almost as abruptly his mood changed. Income, future career offers? he asked himself.

At that precise moment, Henry started to talk about finance.

"I gather you, well, you've probably heard that I have taken over the research projects committee. Another thing, your man Varne is expressing interest in cooperating with the university."

"You must be very persuasive, Henry," Eric said. "I didn't have much success in getting any firm commitment out of him."

"Mm. He did seem a put out when your name came up, Eric. Of course it's all still up in the air. Varne is a forceful character, as you probably know. As long as he doesn't get upset," he ended, with what to Eric sounded as near a warning as anything could be.

Some ten minutes later, outside in the open air, Eric realised that the idea of resigning was still present, like a quiet, near dormant glow that could perhaps be fanned into life. If Aristotle was roughly right, Eric told himself, things in general could only get worse. As if to disprove this he was confronted by the sight of a familiar Jaguar drawing up at the front gate of the campus, Albert at the wheel. Seated in the rear was Suzi and next to her Eleanor.

Chapter Eleven

No sooner had Eric climbed into the car than Albert drove at speed through the university gates.

"Good meeting?" Eleanor asked.

Eric saw that Albert was watching him attentively in his rear view mirror.

"I thought," he said to Eleanor, "we had our big good-bye scene yesterday."

"Change of plan."

With tyres shrieking they negotiated a roundabout and joined the city's ring road system, almost immediately taking the left of a fork ahead. The coastal route again, Eric realised. He glanced back through the rear window. The road receded at an alarming rate but was empty. Suzi took out a packet of cigarettes from the dashboard and lit one for Albert.

"Why not," Eric muttered. "What next?"

Albert's eyes met his in the mirror. "Just relax," he commented.

"So where are we going?"

"Scarborough," Albert said shortly. He turned on the radio and conversation became impossible. Eric sank back feeling the delayed effects of the lunch time drink. He dozed off but Helm's face kept surfacing. An umpire, woolly-wrapped, prominent nose pointed, one finger in the air. "Out?" Eric murmured.

"What?" Eleanor said loudly. He sat up and looked out of the side window. They were passing an old Butlins resort on the right. It reminded Eric of former prisoner of war huts he had once been taken to visit. Even the people wandering in and out of the front gate of the holiday camp looked as if they belonged to another age. He half expected to see a sentry box and guard room alongside the railings. The perfect setting for the university of the future, he thought. All-inclusive, two-week degree courses plus fresh air and exercise.

Soon afterwards they drove past the imposing houses on the outskirts of Scarborough. Almost at once Albert turned off to the right between still larger residences. What was it, Eric wondered, that gave seaside houses the air of being seaside houses? A road parallel to the one they had just left took them to the sea front, the bay curving into the distance and the heights of the town on their left. It was bright but with the promise of rain. Albert stopped the car next to a public toilet.

"I'm bursting," he announced. Suzi turned towards him, frowning.

"I'll join you," Eric said.

The lavatory was set in ornamental gardens. A path going beyond the entrance to the grey stone building wound its way onwards and downwards steeply to the lower promenade. Eric stood a few paces away from Albert in keeping with the time honoured male ritual. The smell of disinfectant, stale cigarette smoke and general decay was diluted by cool air blowing through a rusted metal window. Albert finished first and splashed his hands briefly in the sink.

"Before we get back to the auto, be patient. You'll hear Eleanor's side of the story soon enough."

Glancing towards the car Eric saw Eleanor leaning back with her eyes closed.

"I've booked rooms for us in the hotel where we meet our German friends later," Albert said quietly. Only two rooms, by the way."

"Eleanor agreed?"

"Without a whisper. It has to be your PhD. What else is there?" He surveyed the road along the sea front and by no means for the first time Eric now realised.

"Are we expecting company," he asked, "only you're giving a passable imitation of a villain in one of those old gangster movies."

Albert swept his hand expansively to take in the sea front. Its white buildings and wrought iron work gave it grandeur.

"What a place!" was all he would say.

Suzi was replacing a small bottle of scent in her handbag as they got back into the car. Albert wound the window open a crack and they drove in silence towards the town centre, passing a cable car taking visitors down to the sea front and the joys of the Palm Court concert rooms. Some minutes later they came to a crescent of tall stone houses with porticoes and fine arched windows. They stopped in front of a double fronted building serving as a hotel.

Albert opened the boot of the car and fished out an expensive looking pair of suitcases. Eleanor, Eric observed, had a squashy, multi-coloured carpet bag, which could hardly hold an extensive wardrobe. It reminded him of his own absence of preparations. The three of them waited n the hotel entrance hall while Albert picked up the keys. They followed him up two flights of stairs, wide and carpeted with well worn fabric, before reaching a dark corridor lined with white doors, the numbers picked out in brass.

"Here you are, room 208," Albert said. He gave Eric a key with an enormous metal ball attached to it. "We are in 215. Tea in one hour?"

"Is there a shop open?" Eric asked.

Albert raised a case in the air. "You can use my razor and I have a spare toothbrush. See you later."

Inside the room it was warm, close even and Eric raised a heavy sash window a mere fraction of an inch. The net curtain rustled in the draft and he pulled the edge of the fabric aside.

159

Immediately opposite was a brick wall bearing proud testimony to the ingenuity of plumbers.

"As fine a piece of pipe work as I've seen in a long time," he said.

"We can always draw the curtains," Eleanor answered, and did so.

The room took on a greyish hue but was transformed into a passably cosy atmosphere once the wall lights had been snapped on. An open door led to a bathroom and shower. Twin beds were joined by a double wooden shelf in which a speaker was recessed. On the wall opposite was a mirror. A desk and chair stood beneath this with note paper at the ready. There was also an electric kettle, a collection of tea bags, tiny cartons of milk, a china pot and two cups. Eleanor sank into the only available armchair and threw off her shoes. There was something forlorn about these, Eric decided. He retrieved them without thinking and placed them neatly under the bed nearest the bathroom. Eleanor watched him closely.

"Tea?" he asked.

"Why not? On second thoughts, make it coffee. We can put some whisky in it. There's a flask in my bag."

Eric found two coffee bags on the tray and after filling the kettle sat down heavily on the bed facing Eleanor.

"What a bugger," she said after a long silence."

"Wait; let's have a cigarette shall we?" He lit one for her and then his own.

They smoked contentedly until Eric had made the coffee and added a generous measure from Eleanor's flask. After a few sips he said, "So, what about our long goodbye at the party?"

"You didn't really seem all that upset," she said, tapping her cigarette ash into a saucer.

Truthfully, Eric thought, he had barely had the time to feel anything, what with this, that and the other. She went on before he could respond.

"First, my father has been impossible for several days. He's been going on about Albert for a while and now that he's heard about him contacting one of the German visitors he's even more annoyed. That's part of it at least."

"Knowing what little I do about your father I should have thought that *was* it."

"Oh no. He's got the idea into his head that it's also your fault in some way or other."

Eric was puzzled and showed it. She waved a hand impatiently.

"Well, even I have to admit that Albert seems to be a lot cockier, shall we say, since he met you!"

"That's absurd. He gives me the distinct impression of being a free agent, to say the least."

"True, but he seems somehow to be more, how can I put it, directed?"

Eric considered this then said, "No, I'm the one being led by the nose. What am I doing here for a start?"

She shook her head in exasperation. "I'm sure there's *something* to it. Maybe you and Albert interact, or whatever, in some way or another," she finished lamely.

"Folie a deux, you mean?" Eric asked facetiously. Absurdly, he felt pleased by the thought.

"Stop smirking!" Eleanor reproved, holding up her cup for a refill.

Another thought occurred to Eric as he poured water on the used coffee bags and prodded them back to life with a plastic spoon, already bent by the heat.

"Are you honestly suggesting that your father is blaming me for Albert?" He still had no intention of revealing what he

161

knew of Albert's general plan. Eleanor shrugged.

"All I can safely say is that you are definitely no favourite at home."

"And here I am in the same hotel as Albert as well as Terry Varne's cherished daughter!"

"There's more. When I said I was leaving home he..."

"Wait a minute," Eric said, "you haven't explained why you *did* leave, I mean, in view of what you said at the party."

Eleanor took a deep breath.

"That was when I thought he would just drop you out of this scheme he's trying to hatch with the university. Well, he's done that of course but." she paused. "Then, you won't credit this, he told me yesterday that he was going to report you for assaulting his daughter. It was my turn then to lose my temper. I told him what rubbish that was but he said it wouldn't matter because," she came to a stop.

"For goodness, sake, Eleanor!" Eric stood up abruptly.

"He said that bothering students was just about all you 'idle sods' could be done for and he would enjoy dropping you in it, whatever happened."

As a child Eric had once run into the back of a lorry passing at a mercifully slow speed. It had been enough to knock the wind out of him and for a few moments he had flapped like a fish airlessly on the pavement. He experienced something like the sensation now.

"My theory is," Eleanor added, "that he got the idea from talking to your professor."

If so, Eric calculated, Henry must have known about all this before the graduation ceremony.

"In the end," Eleanor came to sit next to him, "I decided to leave, for the time being. Between you and me I can't see it being permanent. But I'm what he really cares about, perhaps the only

162

thing in some ways. You could say I've upped the stakes. Hopefully it should make him think twice about his daft idea. Besides," she added, "it won't do any harm for me to keep an eye on what Albert is up to."

"But Albert won't imagine that you might actually help him against your father's interests!"

"Perfectly true. To be honest I wouldn't even be here if it weren't for you. Suzi 'phoned me about this trip – I like her by the way– and I asked if Albert would let me come along so that you and I could meet up. Even then he insisted that Suzi and I could only join you when the business meeting was over. And one more thing." She stubbed out her cigarette. "My father has hired this Johnson chap to replace Albert."

Eric had to admire the economy of effort on Varne's part. In the same instant he conjured up the image of Albert scanning the horizon outside the public lavatories an hour or so earlier.

"Nearly there I hope."

Albert had dropped behind to speak to Eric in a low voice as they moved back towards the lounge bar for coffee and liqueurs. Suzi and Eleanor were several paces ahead, accompanied by Albert's contact and two other Germans. The lounge was shaped in the form of an enormous 'L' and large arched windows overlooked the road on the side where they sat on soft, straight backed chairs. One of the Germans, to Eric's disbelief named Hans, a man with a cherubic smile, balding head and glasses, leant forward.

"What you said earlier, Dr Farnham, that was a joke? That anybody who could write his name would soon be accepted in a British university?"

Eric briefly contemplated trying to explain but luckily

163

Albert interrupted to hand round cigars. A blue haze settled comfortably over the group. Suzi's polite smile, Eric could not help noticing, looked distinctly strained. Every so often a door on the opposite wall opened and a burst of music could be heard. Albert was talking inaudibly to his contact, a man wearing rimless glasses and with smooth, black hair.

"Well, Herr Farnham?" Hans asked.

"Sorry, do forgive me. No, this is a fine picture of your son. How old is he?"

He listened as Hans, the accountant apparently, talked about his family and house.

"Thank you. We have a pretty clear picture now, Albert," the German talking to Albert suddenly raised his voice.

Almost immediately his two companions finished their drinks and put out their cigars. Eric looked at his watch and saw that it was only 9.30. Eleanor and Suzi received slight bows from the trio while handshakes were dispensed to Albert and Eric.

"Aufwiedersehen!" Albert said, beaming and standing until the trio had left the room.

"Was it something we said?" Eric joked. Albert's smile vanished. He sat down promptly.

"Any luck then, with whatever it is you are hoping for?" Eleanor asked with a note of sarcasm.

Albert raised a hand and turned it from side to side. "My feeling is that they might prefer their own people to handle things at this end."

"Why bring us all the way out here?" asked Eric.

"Nothing to lose have they?" He sat brooding. "They're leaving tomorrow. If they were really interested they would still be sitting here. That's my take on it."

It struck Eric now that the prospect of an Albert-German partnership was about as likely as receiving a letter from Oxford begging one Eric Everton to take up a fellowship. "By the way," he asked, "where is the loo?"

Albert gestured towards the other end of the room where it made its right angled turn. Eric almost collided with a waiter as he went round the corner. There seemed to be far more people sitting here. He saw the signs to the lavatories at the far end. Just as he was about to move forward he recognized the back of a large head and a broad pair of shoulders. Johnson. A second man wearing an old leather jacket was seated to his left.

Albert looked up sharply when Eric re-joined them, jerking a thumb over his shoulder.

"Friend Johnson has arrived with another member of the Gestapo." He described the leather jacketed man. Albert's round eyes contracted.

"Time to leave, I think," he said, standing up.

Eleanor and Suzi did the same, picking up their bags. Albert beckoned to the waiter and pressed a few notes into his palm to pay for the drinks.

When they were standing in the entrance hall Albert spoke in a low voice. "They don't know Suzi, right? Let's assume they are by themselves."

"Can we be sure?" Eric queried.

"Any other suggestions? Right," Albert went on, "Suzi takes our keys, settles up and fetches the cases while we wait in the car."

A few minutes later, Albert, Eric and Eleanor were once more seated in the Jaguar. It was raining hard and they peered through the windscreen at the lighted hotel entrance.

"Keep your heads low, just in case," advised Albert.

Crouched uncomfortably in the rear seat, Eric whispered to Eleanor, "Did your father have anything to do with this?"

She grimaced. "My guess would be that Hans or one of the

others kept my father informed and he might well have tipped off Johnson," she answered, just as quietly.

"I was under the impression that relations between your father and the Germans were distinctly cool."

"No need to keep your voices down," Albert interjected. "My guess is that Hans and co know that Varne could still give them headaches in running anything in this part of the world. This way he owes them a favour. To be honest, I had my doubts but it was worth a try."

Eric peered apprehensively through the side window. Why had Johnson and friend not confronted them in the lounge. He put the question to Albert.

"They must have checked we were in," Albert said reflectively," then they sat having a quiet drink until the Germans gave them the nod. They probably had you pencilled in for a visit to your room. You can work the rest out." He laughed. "Good job you have a weak bladder."

"Now you mention it," Eric said. The rain on the car roof was not helping.

"Think of something else," Albert advised curtly.

At last Suzi appeared, hugging the cases. Albert got out to open the boot. The engine was damp and reluctant to start but when it sprang to life Albert reversed at speed. Eric's problem became more acute as the car moved. After a few yards Albert slammed on the brakes and got out. Eric watched him bending over a white Rover and letting air out of the two front tyres before climbing back into his driving seat.

"That should slow them down. You'll have time for a quick pee and I for one, my friend, will be joining you."

With the rain pounding on the car roof, the four of them slumped despondently, Eleanor broke the silence.

"You'll have to drop me off, Albert." She turned to Eric.

"He'll be calmer when I'm home," she said evasively.

Not much later relief arrived for Eric in the shape of the lavatories they had used on their way into the town. He enjoyed a moment of clarity as he stood in the dimly lit building, saying nothing to Albert, standing alongside him. Nor did the latter speak. Later they dropped Eleanor off and Eric tentatively arranged to meet her on the following Monday. He accepted Albert's invitation to use his couch and fell into a fitful sleep.

Chapter Twelve

Eric awoke the following morning feeling unexpectedly fresh. Albert and Suzi were not up. He stood outside their door wondering whether or not to take them a cup of tea. In the end he left the flat after writing a short note of thanks. Albert would appear sooner rather than later, he felt sure.

It was a bright day with dampness in the air from the previous night's rain. Strong sunlight made the leaves on the bushes shine as he walked down one of the long avenues parallel to Clara's road. It was tree-lined and elegant but like other streets in the city slipping slowly across a dividing line between comfortable shabbiness and decline. Numerous old cars in the street testified to the presence of a sizeable student population.

His spirits lifted as he reached the main road from the city centre before crossing the large park. The school holidays had yet to start so the ducks on the pond could move peacefully between their island and the banks. A narrow pathway ran from the water's edge to an ornate greenhouse containing tropical shrubs. With difficulty Eric resisted the urge to walk through and enjoy the steamy atmosphere inside. Gardeners could be glimpsed through the coloured glass attending to their rituals.

Soon he reached the road leading directly to his house and took some pleasure in moving along at a speed rivalling the traffic jamming the street. It was almost twenty minutes to nine. He marvelled at the way in which a city, scarred by decline and unemployment, could produce such chaos. Of course it had been planned, he thought. No random arrangement of roads and byways could have created such confusion. He barely squeezed through the level crossing gates before they closed, adding to the morning turmoil. Drivers glared at the train approaching the crossing.

When Eric finally got back to his room it felt stuffy. He threw open the arched window and traffic sounds came up instantly. It was comforting almost, from this angle at least, looking down on the scarred top of a blue bus. Picking up a towel he went downstairs for a wash and shave, the mean little room reflected in the cracked mirror. No sooner had he gone back upstairs than he sensed something amiss. His room door opened abruptly and Johnson stood there.

"Your friend not here today?" he asked, leering.

Beneath the sloping ceiling Johnson looked even bigger than Eric remembered. He tried to take comfort from the fact that his visitor had spoken rather than hitting him on sight.

"Not even a Scottish accent today?" Johnson asked, pulling Eric through the doorway.

Johnson's broken front tooth, Eric noticed, went well with the stubble on his chin but he kept the thought to himself.

"Look, I'm sorry about, well, what happened, but...," he stopped, noticing Johnson's massive hand curling by his side.

"This must be your lucky day." Johnson prodded Eric's shoulder to underline each word. "Mr Varne wants to see you again. You're to be to his house by 12.30."

He pushed Eric aside and turned to look at him as he left the room. "I enjoyed meeting your friends, by the way."

He laughed and shut the door with enough force to shake the walls. Loud footsteps going down the stairs were followed by a more distant crash signalling Johnson's departure. Eric quickly checked the window and saw the blue suited figure wheel to the right at the end of the garden path before disappearing from view behind the hedge of the neighbouring house.

He sat down on his bed wearily. The vacation had already begun but the annual conference of Germanists that he always

169

attended at this time of year seemed remote in the extreme. His watch told him that it was still only just after nine-thirty. Three hours before seeing Varne. He went into his cupboard and tidied up some clothing that had been left there for the best part of a week. Two pairs of underpants which he had thrust beneath a towel some time ago, roughly when he expected Eleanor to see a good deal more of him, he now discarded in a wastepaper bin beneath the mirror. Oh very good, he thought, half stooping and catching a glimmer of reflected light through the hair on top of his head. Then he heard more footsteps together with the sound of Suzi's voice. He opened his door to see her, followed by Albert, turning up the last flight of steps to his landing.

"Welcome," he called out. "I know I'm irresistible, or have you come to complain about not getting tea this morning?"

"Glad to see you in good form," Albert said briefly, squeezing past Eric and entering the room. He looked round and plumped up the cushion on the chair. Suzi immediately sat on it while Albert perched on the end of the bed.

"We came to see about giving you a lift," he said, "for the meeting with Varne? You'll have had your invitation by now. Varne telephoned and asked me to come too. It's like the song. We go together like a horse and carriage, at least as far as Varne is concerned. You know that song don't you, where you can't have one without the other?"

"Do you want tea or should it be coffee now? " Eric asked. "We can go down to the kitchen."

"Has it got more than the one chair?"

"Four, wooden and all still standing, Albert. In addition there is the view to the back yard."

"Come on," Albert said, rising heavily and pulling Suzi up from the armchair." She smiled, but not too warmly it seemed to Eric.

170

When they went into the kitchen he was relieved to see that he had done most of the washing up. He pulled out a chair for Suzi while Albert stood looking out of the window.

"Why do you think Varne wants us to see him?" Eric called from the small scullery off the kitchen, where he chose a selection of cups and emptied a few biscuits on a plate with a picture of Peter Rabbit on it. He had the sensation, as he often had these days, of taking part in a play. "Well?" he asked, as he took the things through.

Albert shrugged. Suzi fussed, making space on the table for the cups. One of these was also decorated with rabbits. Outside in the yard Eric suddenly noticed a dog squatting and he banged on the window.

"I think I'll take the cup that goes with the plate," Albert said. He munched a biscuit. "It's difficult to tell with Varne. He probably wants to give us a proper warning. Maybe Eleanor has something to do with it. We'll see soon enough."

He picked up an old copy of the *Times Higher Education Supplement.* "Shouldn't this be in that little room upstairs with the cracked mirror?" He guffawed.

"Alan used to read that thing from cover to cover," Suzi informed them. "He took ages over the jobs pages. Went through each one twice. He could never believe that there were so few openings for him."

Eric was familiar with the feeling. Albert snorted loudly.

"Here's one for you," he said. "In Australia." He read on for a few moments. "How do you keep going? This is pathetic. What about this north-south thing I keep hearing about. Can't you just move south?"

"Where the universities are concerned, Albert, the 'north' is all there is."

"How is it," Albert addressed the ceiling, "that lecturers

171

always get the conversation back to themselves?"

When they were finally sipping coffee Albert produced a small silver flask from his pocket and added whisky to his mug. Eric joined him but Suzi refused with a shake of her head.

"You should know me by now, young Eric," Albert said. "I like to look on the positive side. Varne can't do me much harm. I have rent from my flats and I've stashed a bit of money in various building societies. You could always join me, as I've suggested." He winked. "Take the handout you mentioned if you pack up early and invest!"

"I might have to," Eric said, giving them a brief review of what Eleanor had told him of Varne's intentions.

"Ah, but," Albert said, wagging a finger, "say she was misguided enough to leave home and shack up with you, would Varne really want to make it worse by causing more aggravation for you?"

"Those are very big ifs, Albert."

There was silence as the three of them gazed at the yard outside. Albert put his mug down and rummaged for a pack of cigarettes in his suit pocket. This time Eric refused and waited while Albert lit up. Why wasn't this man thinner, he wondered?

"We seem to get on, more or less, wouldn't you say?" Albert asked, staring up at his smoke rising to the ceiling.

"Where would I be without you?" Eric said.

"You'd have a few more bruises. Look, I know the German project didn't come off but would you be against helping me out more on other things?"

"Is he serious?" Eric asked Suzi. She said nothing and looked away.

"Well," Albert sounded irritated. "I have thought things through. I know this city pretty well now. What do you think this place is going to need for the next ten years or so?"

"Several million pounds injected by the government, a refurbished fishing fleet, a...." Eric stopped as Albert waved his hand imperiously.

"Listen, it's the same everywhere, all sorts of odd small firms are springing up. Shops, premises, services. There's always *some* cash about. As I see it, the best thing is to get involved, in all sorts of ways, quite small ways mostly, I admit but in lots of different projects."

Eric felt none the wiser.

"For instance, I might let some of my rooms out to small operations. Somebody at the Art College was banging on about my garage being just the place for a workshop. There's a trickle of cash for you. But," he paused, "above all I've got *contacts*. I'm not talking about anything outright illegal but I don't plan to work for the tax man either. I've started thinking of setting up some sort of agency."

"I still don't get it, Albert."

"Don't let me see you smirk," Albert warned, raising a finger. "People always need services. Packages to be delivered, not too many questions asked, people found, contacts arranged. I don't know, when you start thinking about it one thing leads to another. I could be at the centre of a network, yeah, that's the word. The beauty of it is I could put more money into it as things develop, when I see what line does best. I won't have to pay huge sums for premises up here and I could hire and fire for different jobs. Look at the labour pool sitting on its arse in this burgh!"

In spite of himself Eric found the idea plausible - a lot more so than the abortive German connection. "I suppose it could just work in a city like this, stuck up here on its own," he grudgingly admitted. Albert smiled broadly.

"Now you're talking. Look at Varne, that's roughly how he

got started. He's into just about everything, and I mean everything. True, even I'm not keen on some of his lines."

At the mention of Varne Eric saw one very obvious drawback to Albert's vision. Before he voiced his thought the latter nodded.

"I know what you're thinking. Varne won't be happy but he can't do all that much harm when it comes to it. He has bigger fish to fry."

"There is still the small matter of my job at the university Albert."

"I even thought about that," Albert said. He pointed to his cup. "Why don't we give Peter Rabbit another coffee?"

Eric went through to the scullery to rinse the cup clean. When he had refilled it Albert stood with it in the middle of the room. He reminded Eric of the Cheshire cat.

"If you had a little bit of extra work on the side," Albert went on, "you could see your university salary as a nice bonus. I mean, teaching must be a doddle for you by now. Why kill yourself there when the whole place is going to the dogs?"

"Is that it? I pick up my pay at the university, meanwhile popping into your, what is it, 'agency' between tutorials for a quick meeting or possibly nip across the city with a parcel?"

Eric stopped. It wasn't the fact that Albert was beginning to look annoyed. It was rather that his own fatuous questions struck him half way through their formulation as demanding affirmatives. What, he wondered, could Henry Helm offer? A rise in pressures of work? A spiralling series of odious tasks? Classes swollen in size? Increasingly tedious labour in the field of administration - the only one burgeoning in the world of education?

"Supposing," he said slowly, "just supposing I did fall in with your ideas. I mean, how would it benefit you? I can see that

174

extra money would be handy, but ...." He stopped at the sight of Albert gleefully making encouraging circular motions with his hand.

"I hope you might get round eventually to putting cash where your heart is. Why would you want to stand in a room talking to what I am told pass for students nowadays when you could be wandering about our fair city? Once you have the taste of freedom you won't look back."

He handed his cup back to Eric who put it with the others in the sink and covered them with water.

"I'm all in favour of moving off now," Albert called out. "We can take in a swift half on our way."

The expanse of gravel in front of Varne's house looked even bigger than Eric remembered. Varne opened the door himself before they had time to ring the bell. He nodded curtly and they followed him along the corridor to a room not yet seen by Eric. It was a small, luxuriously carpeted affair, with half a dozen comfortable chairs in a semi-circle facing a huge television screen. There was a video recorder beneath it. Varne pressed a button on a controller in his hand and a picture of a cricket field dwindled abruptly to a point of light.

"Useless bastards," he said. "They shouldn't stick to people who live in the county."

He pressed another button on the wall near the window and in a few moments Johnson came in. He was wearing black trousers and a short white coat.

"What'll you have to drink?" Varne barked.

"Whisky, please," Eric said promptly. Johnson's eyes briefly met his then flickered towards Albert who grinned broadly and asked for a Lager.

175

Suzi met Johnson's query about a drink with a frown but Eric imagined it was normal in the Varne house to take the men's orders first. Albert must have been thinking along similar lines and he directed a sheepish grin towards Suzi. She turned aside and perched on one of the chairs. He shrugged and sat down.

Varne lit a cigar before asking Suzi if she minded. He chose to stand with his back to the door, his short legs slightly apart. All that was missing, Eric thought, was a roaring fire to heat the master's backside. There was a brief silence during which the blank screen claimed every one's attention. When the drinks arrived Varne moved towards the window.

"Don't go," he said as Johnson was about to leave then turned to look at the others. "I don't mind saying, I'm pissed off with you lot."

"Hang on, the lady has nothing to do with anything, right?" Albert responded, raising a finger at Varne and gesturing to Suzi with the other hand.

Eric barely had time to fathom the look of irritation flitting across Suzi's face at Albert's words before becoming aware that Varne was sending a force nine shaft of dislike in his direction.

"Well," Eric began, "I'm not exactly happy. I had relied on what little you told me of your plans for funding. My position now is...."

"Your position!" Varne butted in. "Never mind that. And while I'm at it, keep clear of my daughter if you know what's good for you. Understand?"

Eric felt himself growing hotter. "Even assuming Eleanor would agree to make a formal complaint against me," he said, "which I suppose is what you're hinting at – what makes you think it would be taken seriously? You've been reading too many comics," he added. He felt sufficiently pleased with this to register a warning look from Albert only at the precise moment that he felt a stinging blow to the side of his face.

Varne stepped quickly towards Johnson, who looked set to strike again, and shouted at him to get out. "I can't say I'm surprised," Varne said to Eric, "he doesn't like you. Any road, I didn't tell him to do 'owt. Best take it as a warning though."

"Two can play at that game," Albert said.

Eric watched with disbelief as Albert and Varne bristled at each other like two bantam cocks. He glanced at Suzi who gave him a sympathetic look but otherwise seemed distracted.

"And you'd better be careful what you get up to in Inkers Lane," Varne said to Albert.

The latter raised his eyebrows. "So, there is truth to the rumours," was all he said.

Eric wondered what on earth the narrow, run-down road running behind the university playing fields had to do with anything but Varne chose not to answer Albert's last remark. At that point Mrs Varne came in carrying a tray. On it was a large pot with china cups, together with a plate of chocolate biscuits. Her cheerful smile turned into a look of puzzlement at the sight of the red mark on Eric's face. She put the tray down quickly and left without saying anything. Nobody seemed interested in the tea but after a few moments Suzi began pouring.

"Well," Albert said, "seems as though you are out to kill two birds with one stone, getting me here with our Dr Farnham. Warning noted but as it happens," he grinned cheekily, "I had my eyes on that run down little newspaper shop near the university end of the lane."

Varne glared but again said nothing. What next, Eric wondered. There were raised voices outside the door. It swung open giving Eric a glimpse of Mrs. Varne's pale face, a hand placed alongside it in worry. Eleanor stormed past her and slammed the door. She looked quickly at Eric then turned to her father.

"What did you think you would achieve by letting that moron Johnson loose in here? What *are* you trying to do?"

Varne looked apprehensive. "Now look, my girl…"

"Don't talk to me like that. I will say this now we are all here," she paused. "your idea of complaining to the university was stupid, yes, really stupid. Not to say embarrassing."

"I'm not saying I would have gone through with it," Varne said defensively. "You know there was more to it than that. Whatever happens, I'm not having him" - he pointed a finger at Eric - "around," he finished lamely.

"At this rate you won't have me around either," Eleanor said defiantly.

"Look, Eleanor, love I didn't tell Johnson to hit him."

"Can't we all calm down?" Albert suddenly asked the room at large. "Eric has had his lesson. I know roughly where I stand and Eleanor, well she's just a bit upset at the moment."

This remark was rewarded with a furious glance from Eleanor and yet another exasperated reaction from Suzi. Eric had the odd sensation of being a schoolboy whose fate was being decided by grown ups.

"Look," he said, "it might interest…."

"Shut up!" Varne and Eleanor both shouted to him at the same time then looked at each other in silence. Eleanor shrugged.

"Well, there's not much to be done right now. I'm moving out, for a while at least," She turned towards Eric. "Perhaps we can have a drink later, at Cottingly, seven 'ish?"

Eric agreed. Varne visibly fumed but remained stationary. Albert walked slowly towards Suzi, who ignored his proffered hand. Instead she spoke to Eleanor.

"Can I help you get a few things together? You're more

than welcome to put up with me for a few nights, if it helps."

Eleanor thanked her with a tight-lipped smile and Suzi got up to put an arm round her shoulders. Silence followed their departure until a door banged somewhere in the house. The sound appeared to deflate Varne in some curious way. Albert gripped Eric's elbow and pushed him towards the door.

"We'll let ourselves out, " he called over his shoulder.

Varne remained standing in the centre of the room like a general hearing bad news from the front. Eric watched the house recede through the rear window of Albert's car as it joined the traffic with its usual ease and the long bonnet pointed towards the city centre.

"Lunch," Albert said. "And, yes, we need to have a longer chat."

Eric was surprised when Albert parked the car in the narrow street leading to the *George Inn* then walked the quarter mile or so to the city's art gallery. It was pleasantly cool inside the spacious domed entrance hall and they wound their way up one of two marble stairways to a circular balcony. Seated at their table they could lean on the polished rail and glance down at the hall below. A reclining Henry Moore sculpture looked as good from above as it did on entering the gallery. The atmosphere was hushed. Two middle aged ladies came in and out of a door near one of the staircases carrying various items of food.

"I often come here, as a matter of fact," Albert said in response to a raised eyebrow and a hand gesture from Eric. "It's peaceful. And I like the tea."

"I imagine Suzi would be keen on it."

Albert shook his head. "I come here by myself. Only trouble is, no smoking allowed."

The solidity and coolness of the gallery relaxed Eric, although his cheek still stung. He explored the inside of it with his tongue and felt a small cut. Albert watched him.

"Probably feels worse than it looks," he said. "Johnson must be losing his touch. Er, a pot of tea please, for two. What sandwiches have you got today love?"

The last remark was addressed to a stout waitress in a black dress and a white apron wearing what looked to Eric like a cake band round her head. Albert chose ham and Eric did the same...

"White bread," Albert called out as the lady took the order off to the kitchen.

"Wait until Suzi hears about that," Eric grinned.

"Ah, Suzi." Albert paused. "What did you make of her today?"

Eric recalled her irritated glances. "Well," he began.

"Don't think she's too happy," Albert said, sounding distinctly unworried.

"You should have seen her in the old days!" Eric laughed. Come to that, he realised, he was often wary of Suzi himself. Maybe the strain was beginning to tell on Albert. "Don't tell me," he said, "she's monopolising the vacuum cleaner."

"You may jest." Albert sighed. "I've always looked after myself. Don't get me wrong. It's been fun. Suzi has her own sense of humour you know. Still," he shook his head, "I get the impression she is feeling roughly the same as me. She's been using her own flat most of the time."

He looked up expectantly as the tea and sandwiches arrived. There was a pot of mustard to go with the ham and the two of them bit into the thick crusty slices with enjoyment. The tea was strong.

"Right, Albert, Inkers Lane, what was Varne talking about

180

and why did everybody assume I knew what was going on?"

"No, no. All were aware that you did *not* know. Look, Inkers Lane is in Varne's sights, especially the stretch backing onto the playing fields at the bottom end of your campus."

Eric continued to look and feel puzzled.

"Shopping development, right? Mega store, as in out of town? Varne is about to submit applications for planning permission, that's why he was warning me off. I was winding him up."

Eric recalled the glass and chrome monstrosity that had sprung up near his parent's house, complete with fountains and piped music. He also remembered the traffic pouring in and out of its car parks.

"But the university can lodge objections at the planning office."

Albert signalled one of the ladies and asked for more hot water.

"True, your lot will certainly have a chance to object. But can you honestly see anybody in the city stopping the scheme?"

So, Eric thought bitterly, Varne's talk about funds had almost certainly only ever been aimed at pre-empting university objections to the plans he was drawing up. Ultimately, Varne had to get the ear of the Vice Chancellor so even Henry Helm, Eric guessed, was just another means to an end.

"Sounds about right," Albert grinned, when Eric told him what he was thinking. "Still, you can help yourself out a bit by letting this Helm man know more about what Varne is really up to. There's more on the subject of Inkers Lane, but," Albert waved a hand, "leave that for the moment. More anon."

"That means," Eric said flatly, "that Eleanor must also have known what was going on all this time."

Albert fixed Eric with a stare. "What do you think?" He

181

pushed a plate aside and put his elbows on the table. "Look, there was something else I wanted to ask you. This boyfriend of Suzi's, any chance of him taking up with her again?"

"When I last saw him he seemed pleased enough with what he had, but who knows? He and Suzi had been together for a good while before you worked your charms."

"I'd rather not just ask her to leave," Albert said, "unless I really have to. No, don't laugh. Could you sound out this, what's his name, Alan?"

Mentally reviewing Suzi's recent signs of displeasure Eric felt that Albert's worry about ending his short-lived affair might be ill founded. Why shouldn't Suzi revert to type as suddenly as she had deviated from it he asked himself?

"One thing," he said, "she's got Eleanor with her for a few days. You'll have some breathing space!"

It struck him that the same situation also precluded seeing much of Eleanor alone for the time being. The gallery was now filling up and he and Albert automatically lowered their voices. One of the ladies was looking pointedly in their direction. Albert noticed her, beamed and pointed to his teacup. When another pot of tea had been placed heavily on the table between them, without clean cups being offered, Albert shifted uneasily in his seat.

"There is something else," he hesitated. "I've been hearing about plans to enrol more mature students at the university."

"True, quite a few are taking part-time courses already. It's…"

Albert interrupted him imperiously. "Part-time, full-time, whatever. Would someone like me have a chance of enrolling?"

Oddly, Eric felt no great surprise at the question. He looked at Albert and said, truthfully, "I think you might go down rather well with the other students. What did you fancy

182

studying?"

Albert looked sheepish. "I'm quite interested in philosophy. Have been ever since I saw two gents arguing on television about whether the chairs they were sitting on existed. That was some years ago. Since then I've picked up the odd book. I still can't properly understand a lot of what I read but, well, I can't seem to keep away from it."

Eric, who had roughly the same relationship with books on theories of the universe, knew exactly what Albert meant and regarded him with genuine interest.

"Do you know," he said enthusiastically, "I can just see you getting stuck in at a seminar!"

Albert grinned. "It's hanging about with you, it must be catching, whatever it is."

A sudden thought struck Eric. "What was all that stuff about setting up some sort of small business."

"Don't get me wrong. I'm still looking into that. The money will be useful. But I keep thinking I want something else too. Know what I mean? Look at Varne. He's rolling in it but what about his private life? Nah, I used to admire him when I first started working up here. Definitely something missing there," he finished.

"Already sounding philosophical, Albert, well, how most people imagine philosophers ought to sound. As I understand it they aren't all that interested in the meaning of life, at least not in this country."

Soon afterwards they paid their bill and left the gallery. Albert insisted on crossing to the island in the middle of the road outside the art gallery. It housed the city's largest public lavatories. Here, in the tiled and brass splendour of the huge circular room, they stood side by side. While they were washing their hands at one of the heavy china hand basins Albert

183

suggested that they call in at Suzi's place just to make sure everything was ok.

Chapter Thirteen

"If they can write their names on the application form and pay the fees, they're as good as in. I am joking, of course. A few more years before we get to that stage I trust. But, seriously, commitment and some native intelligence get a mature student a lot of sympathy. As you know, Eric, the Vice Chancellor has quite a thing now about the university as a sort of supermarket."

Eric was startled to hear this under the circumstances. He had yet to inform Henry about the latest news from the Varne camp.

"Students from the town, indeed from the countryside around, will come with their, as it were, their, er, baskets, and see what modules they wish to take."

Eric had the distinct impression that Henry hadn't thought this one through, unusual in itself. Even so the professor continued to develop the parallel, to the point where students would be offered the utmost flexibility of choice and would be allowed to assemble their modules over a period of time suited to their work and lifestyle. Eric made a mental note to ask Alan for more information about 'modules.' Whatever they turned out to be he wondered whether dropping them into a basket could ever add up to anything like a degree as he knew, or thought he knew it.

"Interesting," was all he said.

"Where *has* that coffee got to?" Henry asked out loud.

He got up and went through to the outer office to find out. Eric heard him agreeing to take a telephone call in the secretary's office. Henry's desk showed its normal fearful symmetry. By association he recalled the neatness of Suzi's flat when he and Albert had arrived unannounced. It had taken a several minutes for Eric to realise why the flat felt strange. It was the absence of clarinet sounds. He had seen at once that there was little prospect of talking privately to Eleanor.

"I thought we'd seen the back of you for today," Suzi had remarked primly. Albert had opted for magisterial indifference and ignored the remark.

"The coffee will be with us any moment," Henry said, breezing back into the room. "Now, Eric, what exactly was it you wanted to see me about?"

Eric bluntly told Henry what he had heard of Varne's hopes for a shopping complex opposite the university. As he did so he couldn't escape the feeling that he appeared to be parodying Henry's earlier references to markets and education. Henry sat holding his spectacles to the side of his face, glancing up at the ceiling and giving the briefest trace of a smile from time to time.

"Thank you very much, Eric, for telling me this. Didn't you hear anything of this from your, from your, er, friend, I mean Varne's daughter?"

Eric shook his head.

"Mm. One supposes that our hopes for some sort of funding in that direction might be less rosy now," he mused.

"I'm not sure, Henry. I certainly won't be involved but you," he left the sentence unfinished for the simple reason that he could think of no way to end it. Henry smiled ruefully.

"I think we can take it that our mutual acquaintance had no more idea of advancing my career than he did yours."

Eric watched Henry open his desk drawer and take out a black notebook.

"No, we must assume that Varne was always after bigger fish. And with our Vice Chancellor," he mused softly, almost as though Eric were not present, "anything is possible. Not that development as such is bad," he added hastily. "Hm, but how to get some small influence over it. That would be nice."

He looked briefly through the pages of his notebook before reaching for the telephone.

"Angela. Could you try to set up an appointment for me with Donald West?" He read out a number. "See if he can make it for lunch tomorrow at the University. Thank you."

Henry put the telephone down and gave his thin lipped smile, joining his palms and resting his finger tips at a point between his chin and his lower lip. Eric, even with his limited knowledge of local affairs, knew that Donald West was a prominent figure on the city council and head of the much publicised Development Unit.

His mind wandered back again to the visit to Suzi's flat. At one point he had crossed Eleanor's path from the kitchen to the sitting room but his whispered query about the possible meeting she had herself mentioned earlier had come to nothing.

"We'll see, Eric. Best leave it for now, OK?"

"Shall I call you?"

"Better not. I'll try to get in touch with you at some point."

When they had re-joined Albert and Suzi in the kitchen Eric had formed the distinct impression of an argument interrupted. On the pavement outside Albert had said, "I think she's seeing that old boyfriend of hers." He rubbed his hands together vigorously. "That *would* be convenient."

"Well, Eric, what about you, I wonder." Henry's query brought Eric back to the present with a bump. "You've got yourself in a bit of a tight corner in the department. Not many friends at court, hm? Has Kingsly spoken to you lately?"

Eric looked and felt puzzled. "Kingsly? What should he have said to me? I don't think I've seen him since the degree day bash."

"What about Christopher Morton?"

Eric conjured up Morton's sparsely covered head and pendulous lower lip over near absent chin and felt even more perplexed.

"Something is going on there Eric. Not sure what yet. Ambitious man is our Christopher."

Now he came to think of it, Eric had overheard Jake making a dismissive reference to Christopher Morton preparing a paper on part time education. At the same time a recent image surfaced of Morton and Kingsly in earnest conversation in a corner of the Senior Common Room.

"About the admissions work," he began. Henry waved the remark aside.

I think we might hold on that for the moment, Eric. Perhaps your talents lie elsewhere. I'm still picking up the reins of the Department again. I have one or two ideas at the moment. I'll let you know but, in the meantime, don't worry too much, eh?"

The ensuing silence told Eric it was time to go. He slid quietly from the office leaving Henry already reading through the papers before him.

"Angela," Eric said quietly after shutting the adjoining door, "have you any idea at all what the Prof. is planning for me? I'm completely lost at the moment. One minute it's this, the next minute something else. What's going on?"

"Join the club, Eric. I do know he's been looking at Dr Morton's file. I've also had to arrange a meeting between Prof. Helm and Prof. Kingsly for later this week. Other than that, well, there isn't much to say. Your name did come up in something I was working on, but I can't say exactly what it is, can I?" She laughed.

"Why not?"

"OK," she immediately responded, dropping her voice.

"It's about new Masters courses that Prof. Helm is trying to draft out. If, ah, good morning Alan," she called over Eric's shoulder.

Alan Branch, who looked distinctly under the weather, placed a couple of sheets of paper on her desk and turned to Eric. "Do you feel like a coffee?" He asked.

The Senior Common Room wore the sleepy air that enveloped it at the start of the vacation. Within a few minutes of sitting down Alan launched into a meandering account of his plans for work over the next few weeks. Somehow his heart did not seem to be in it.

"You don't sound your usual cheerful self, Alan."

Alan took a couple more sips of coffee then put the cup down heavily on the table. "I've seen Suzi again, Eric. A couple of times, actually, for a quiet drink. Tell you the truth, I was really pleased to see her. Actually, I got the impression that she was quite keen herself."

"Why shouldn't she be?"

Alan looked embarrassed. "Am I mistaken, or is she not so enthused with this Albert character? I don't know what to think." Then, "she certainly looks different."

"Do you approve?"

"I do, as it happens. Do you know, we had quite a laugh. I don't think I've seen Suzi so relaxed."

"A change is as good as a rest," Eric said. "But what about you and, er," he began. Alan gave a wry laugh.

"You could say it was over as soon as it began," he said. "Perhaps I was just trying to get my own back. I can't say I was all that keen to start with."

"Well then, no harm in telling you that Albert seems a bit fed up too."

"You honestly think so?" Alan gave a broad grin. "Do you know, this other woman likes folk music! I must have blanked it

189

out. We went to a club somewhere out by the coast. It was a nightmare. People singing about docks and ropes. You wouldn't believe how many Aran sweaters there were to the square foot."

"I had the impression you found it easier to practise at least after you, er, after Suzi left."

"At first," Alan agreed, "but it didn't last. My reeds kept getting moved from the mantelpiece."

Literally, Eric could think of nothing to say.

"Eventually she asked me to turn that row off one morning at breakfast. It was the Goodman trio version of 'Sweet Sue.' I couldn't believe it. I went for a fast walk round the block. When I came back she was washing up and we had a bit of a chat. The thing is, she's also met an old boyfriend of hers."

"It'll all work out, Alan, I'm sure. I'm seeing Albert later. Perhaps I could find out a bit more for you."

"Could you, really?" Alan looked gratifyingly pleased

"No problem. By the way," Eric added as if an afterthought, "you don't happen to know if Kingsly and Morton are working on something at the moment?"

Alan looked over his glasses. "What do you know about modules?" he asked.

"Other than that they sound like something that might have to be removed surgically, not much."

"As I suspected, Eric, as I suspected. Well, modules and Morton look set to go together like a horse and carriage."

Please, not that song again, Eric thought.

"Briefly," Alan resumed, "our so-called colleague Christopher has as much chance of completing any decent academic research as I have of playing Carnegie Hall."

"Yes?" Eric prompted, as Alan appeared to drift off. Alan pushed his glasses further up his nose and resumed.

"So he's trying to get into administration. Even you, Eric,

must have noticed how keen he always is on the minutiae of staff and committee meetings."

Eric readily admitted as much.

"Well, he seems to think that he has found a university wide role to play in – pay attention – the process of modularisation."

"Can he?"

"Put it this way, he is the only person I know who has already mastered the lingo about single or double modules and who fully comprehends the distinction between a double module and two single 'linked' modules. There is much, much more, believe me!"

"You're saying that he who controls the modules has the power?"

"More or less. But the interesting bit comes next. You must have heard also that the university is looking into launching new taught postgraduate courses." He paused, looked at Eric and then said exasperatedly, "What planet are you on? Taught postgraduate courses bring income. As long as a student pays the fee, we can take as many of them as we can cram in. We won't be limited -unlike the undergraduate courses - by the number of grants that local education authorities can afford to pay out."

"Who is going to teach all the new courses?"

"Good question. No doubt we shall all be asked to come up with suggestions soon enough."

Eric revealed nothing of what Angela had barely hinted at but Alan's explanation made Henry's recent confidences the more intriguing. For the first time in many weeks Eric discovered that interest outweighed apprehension in his musings on university politics.

"If you thought departmental meetings were tedious wait until you've seen this lot in action, Jake muttered in Eric's ear.

Eric doubted his colleague not for one moment. Still, Henry had asked him to stand in for the department at the Board of Studies. He could hardly refuse. Each department sent two representatives- apart from the Professor- and Peter Everton was apparently unable to attend. Henry Helm could be glimpsed a flight of stairs up, talking to the chairman of the Board of Studies, a curly, grey-haired man with round glasses and a pinkish coat matching his complexion. Peering over the banister Eric saw Morton and Kingsly talking together as they came up towards the meeting.

"Now this, Eric, is what British universities are all about."

Jake waved his arm at their surroundings. Gone were the dreary cream coloured, chipped paintwork and scuffed linoleum enjoyed by most of the building's inhabitants. Beneath Eric's feet was a new, dark blue carpet. The walls were a soft pink colour at the top, grey at the bottom, while the doors lining the corridor were finished in polished wood. There were framed prints of indeterminate origin on the walls.

"Well, they like it," Jake announced loudly as they walked past the Registrar's office. More quietly, he said to Eric. "This is supposed to convey the corporate look. What does it say to you Eric?"

"Quite honestly, it reminds me of a minor hotel chain."

"It's all about *management*, Eric, but the sort that no self-respecting business would put up with for one moment. This is management circa late 1950s, them-and-us, don't-do-what-I do-but-what-I-say."

Indeed, as he entered the meeting room Eric experienced an acute sense of displacement. Following Jake, he sat at the far corner of a semi-circular arrangement of polished tables. These

192

faced a raised platform on which stood another expensive wooden bench. Behind this were three high-backed chairs, each with the new university logo engraved on them. Eric knew he was not alone in asking why the book, sword and Latin motto had been replaced by three triangles pointing inwards towards a circle, in the centre of which were engraved the words 'Education Aids Work.'

"Thank you," the Dean spoke from one of the chairs on the platform. Seated next to him was a large woman whose hard eyes were framed by huge glasses. She gave a token smile towards the Dean.

"Anne Mallinson," Jake anticipated Eric's question with a whisper. "Linguist comma manqué manager comma aspiring full stop."

The Mallinson woman's gaze swept the audience and she picked up a pencil with an air of expectation. A hasty glance of his own around the room revealed to Eric roughly the same quantity of unknown faces that he had glimpsed on 'Black Friday.' The Dean leaned forward and spoke.

"I think we can begin. We do have some important business to attend to. The first item on the agenda concerns the cuts in library funding."

Almost immediately Eric stopped listening and examined the back cover of a paperback he had bought at the university book shop. "When the battered corpse in the bicycle shed was discovered", he read with interest, "Denton School braced itself for the media onslaught. Edward Farnley found himself drawn into a moral maze as soon as...." Eric looked up as Jake nudged him, in time to see Helm slip out of the room.

"I've yet to be at a meeting like this without Henry disappearing and returning later," Jake explained.

Eric went back to his book, toying with the idea of writing

193

a thriller himself. Shouldn't be too difficult, he thought, he'd read enough of the bloody things. As usual he realised, after a few moments of idle speculation, that he would never have the patience to work out a sufficiently intricate plot. He turned to the potted biography at the front of the paperback. Barman, assistant to a cook in a hotel, courier for a travel firm and so on. Christ, the list of jobs took up a small paragraph. No mention of the chap ever having been a university lecturer. Eric looked up at the world he was actually living in just as Kingsly was being offered the floor.

"I hope colleagues will indulge me in a moment of reminiscence," he began. There was a general shuffling sound and knowing looks were exchanged.

"When I first came here," Kingsly went on blithely, "no student could finish the course without facing a huge wedge of finals papers. But of course, as we all know, everything changes. I remember that a previous vice-chancellor of this university once said ...."

Eric again stopped listening and instead thought of Eleanor. He imagined her leaning back in his armchair on the day of the party but it only served to remind him of the peripheral role he was now caste in as far as the Varne clan were concerned. Eric couldn't imagine Eleanor's tiff with her father lasting too long.

"Well, the historians are having nothing to do with modules, I can tell you that! They sound like something you dock with in space."

The speaker was the large, ruddy-faced man whom Eric had last seen on 'Black Friday.' He had on a check suit and in spite of his loud voice and resentful tone was enjoying the laughter that greeted his remarks. He continued to stand. Kingsly, too, was still on his feet, clearly thrown, Eric saw, by the interruption. Eric paid closer attention to the proceedings.

"Mr. Chairman, I must protest," Kingsly said, his facial hue notching up a degree, "but it was agreed that Dr Morton and I would present a general case for modularising."

"Present what you like!" The historian spoke again. "We don't have to listen."

There was more laughter. Eric watched Christopher Morton closely. Throughout the previous exchange he had embarked on a series of facial expressions meant to convey, as far as Eric could tell, that he, Dr. Morton, had no possible disagreement with anybody in the room or, rather, that he agreed with everybody present. Raised eyebrows alternated with mystified glances as his head turned slowly from side to side. Eric had seen this technique before and Morton had obviously been working hard to perfect it. Ms Mallinson whispered something in Morton's ear and then said loudly,

"Er, Mr Chairman, I believe Dr Morton would like to say something."

"He usually does" a voice called out. Mallinson rewarded the speaker with a glare.

"That was another historian," Jake explained to Eric.

"I would just like to thank my colleagues, Professor Kingsly and Fred Jackson, for giving me the floor." There was a pause while Morton directed a fixed smile to left and right. "It's a pity," he resumed, "that the temperature has gone up. I think we should try to maintain a reasonable tone at these meetings." Morton paused again. Eric noticed that he was keeping his voice deliberately low, so that all present had to strain to hear what was being said. He had seen that trick in staff meetings too.

"Speak up, Christopher," Eric called out. Ms Mallison's lenses swivelled in his direction.

"Thank you, Eric," Morton replied. "Well, if I could say a

few words first about modularisation generally. Perhaps then we might, er, have a discussion of some of the points raised. As you know, I am on the committee set up by the Vice Chancellor to examine the whole issue. It all starts with the need to be flexible. Well, we have a whole range of students approaching universities now without the normal educational background that we used to expect."

"As long as they can write their cheques," somebody called out to more laughter.

"I do think we should try to be serious," the Mallinson woman said, glowering.

"I am serious!" More laughter.

"Yes, yes," said Morton, "but we know we can't just stay the same as we were. It's not an option."

Eric sat back and gazed around the room, wondering what Albert would make of this lot. Morton had passed round sheets of paper with various flow charts on them and references to units instead of courses. Eric glanced at them briefly. There was more muttering as people worked out the details of what was being outlined.

"And of course we do need to get more mature students at the postgraduate level." Christopher Morton paused and Eric's interest was again reawakened. Had Helm discussed details with Morton or Kingsly? He decided not, on the whole, otherwise he would not be listening to what was clearly a bid for more influence from their camp. Eric had to admit that Morton's mastery of the jargon was impressive. There was a good chance of most listeners being as fatigued as he soon began to feel. At that point he saw Henry Helm sliding back into the room like a lizard emerging from a rock. Morton failed for the moment to notice his return.

"What the committee suggests," he droned on, "is that

further consideration be given to the whole issue of postgraduate modular courses, and perhaps a trial run, for example, could take place in my own department."

"Keep your eye on Helm," Jake whispered in Eric's ear.

Eric did as he was told. Helm was leaning back in his chair and, as ever, alternating an examination of the ceiling with swift, darting glances around the room. Somehow sensing one of these Morton turned to catch Helm smiling to himself.

"Er, we, er," Morton muttered, looking at his notes. "Yes, I think, the committee thinks, a trial run would be rewarding."

"Any views on this proposal?" The Dean looked helpfully in a number of directions.

"It could be, if I can suggest to the chair, it could be that since our department is offering to be the guinea pig, as it were, that we can take a quick show of hands." Morton spoke and duly waited.

There was a loud coughing from Helm. "If I may," he said, standing up and peering over his thick-rimmed glasses.

Eric, impressed in spite of himself, noticed that the room was now completely quiet. Morton looked distinctly put out and said quickly, "Mr Chairman, should we not take the vote? Is Professor Helm putting a point of order, or what?"

"Well, Professor Helm?" asked the Dean.

"I was simply going to advise caution, Dean. I'm sure, indeed we are all sure, that Dr Morton has the best interests of ," he paused, grimaced and adjusted his spectacles, "of the Department at heart. I would add, of the university."

"Why can't we just run the trial, so to speak," queried the Dean. Morton and Kingsly both signalled agreement.

"Technically we could, I agree. But I've been wondering if we ought not to pause for thought. Indeed, Dr Morton's point about mature students is relevant in a way. We simply can't afford to go off at half-cock. Of course, some here might suggest I am being too cautious."

Henry's eyes raked the room. Even the renegade historians said nothing. He continued.

"I certainly don't feel too confident as yet and, as some of you might be aware, I am heading my Department once more, for my sins, from next term. I would hope, simply, that all of you here will be tolerant and allow me the luxury of looking into matters before we start the pilot module Dr Morton referred to."

"Perhaps we could take a motion to that effect and then vote on it, Mr Chairman," Jake called out. "Look at Morton's expression," he whispered to Eric gleefully.

When the meeting ended some thirty minutes later and they were retracing their steps past the Registrar's office, Helm materialised at Eric's elbow.

"Eric, I wonder if you have a moment," he said, staring pointedly at Jake.

"Catch you later, Eric," Jake called out over his shoulder.

"Let's get a coffee in the Senior Common Room," Henry suggested.

As the two of them moved off Eric caught a furious look from Christopher Morton winging his way. It gave him a pleasurable sense of satisfaction. The feeling lasted as long as Henry's next remarks, delivered just outside the Senior Common Room door.

"Eric, I've arranged an initial meeting tomorrow with the Vice Chancellor and the City Planning Officer. A number of things are going to come up that might eventually be of concern to you if and when, you, er, well, come to my room at around eleven o'clock. We can walk over together."

He stopped talking as they entered the Senior Common Room and fished about in his coat pocket before producing one

198

of the departmental telephone message slips. "By the way, Angela asked me to give you this number. Apparently it's rather urgent."

On glancing down at the note Eric recognized Albert's handwriting.

"Same again, love", Albert leaned confidentially towards the blonde barmaid, "and have one yourself."

Eric watched Albert carrying the beer across the room. They were in the oldest pub in the city, once the domain of men only. To Eric the dark, wood panelled walls still conjured up images of pipe-smoking worthies. The huge inglenook fireplace and handsome stained glass windows looking out on the narrow passageway outside added to the air of complacent solidity that contrived to keep the clientele, still, predominantly male.

"I tell you Eric, it's a relief."

"It was certainly quick!" Eric grinned.

"It's not that my old mate, it's the *type*," Albert grimaced. "Honest, your honour, I dunno what came over me."

"If it's any consolation you've probably done them both a good turn. Maybe they won't be so complacent now."

"Maybe she will get to like his clarinet," Albert replied. "I can't see it though. She had quite a thing about his music. Well, onwards and upwards." He raised his beer glass. "It was interesting, in its own way. She's a bit of an exhibitionist you know."

"Don't say it! You were captivated by that combination of prim exterior and passion! No wonder the male is so disadvantaged."

Albert grinned sheepishly.

Once more Eric thought back to Alan, barely a few weeks ago, perched alongside Suzi on the sofa in her flat. Studying

Albert's round face he understood the whole recent episode even less.

Albert leaned forward and dropped his voice. "The reason I left the message for you to ring was because I have a bit of information you might just be interested in."

Eric suppressed a slight anxiety while Albert slowly sipped his drink. "First," he said, "I've got some news too." He told Albert about the next day's meeting.

Albert raised an eyebrow and thought for a moment before resuming. "Interesting, yeah, very interesting. Did your Professor what's his name give you any more information?"

"Only to be in his office at 11. New management style. What time did you say Eleanor was coming here?"

"Don't worry; we've got a few more minutes yet. Is anybody going to be there from the City Council at tomorrow's meeting?"

"Yes, apparently."

"One last question. Is the man from the council a friend of Helm's."

"That seems likely," Eric said, remembering the telephone call he had heard Varne initiating. "Henry is quite well connected with the city authorities I would say. So?"

Albert's brow cleared. "Come on, you're the thinker. If Helm can play a part in getting the university round the table with the Council before Varne has actually submitted detailed plans there'll be much more room for bargaining." He stopped and stroked his chin.

"What?" Eric eventually asked.

"I'm still not quite sure why you should be at this meeting."

Eric, reflecting on the personnel being assembled for the following day, had asked himself the same question. He picked up his beer.

Albert stood up. "I'll go for a short stroll, say about twenty minutes or so, before I rejoin you. I've a few 'phone calls to make. Eleanor should be here any second."

Eric watched Albert take his glass back to the bar, where he was rewarded with a smile from the barmaid that went beyond the call of duty.

"I'll be back," Albert called over his shoulder. He winked at her as he left.

Just as Albert had predicted, Eleanor came in moments later. She would have to have the stunning black suit on, he thought. When they were settled in the corner with a gin and tonic she gave him a small peck on the cheek.

"By the way," she said, "Suzi should be dropping in for a last drink."

"Now she can concentrate on keeping Alan in line," Eric said.

"Actually, Eric, I like Suzi. She's been kind to me. If you want my opinion, Alan would be lucky to have her."

She placed a hand on his arm and squeezed it. He felt as he imagined a faithful old dog might, when patted on the head after fetching the ball. For a few moments they observed the barmaid dealing with a couple of pinstripe suited customers.

"At least you won't be hearing anything more about what my father calls your conduct. I made it very clear to him that it was *our* conduct."

"I can't say it's not a relief. I would have thought he'd had more than enough of the university by now."

"Ah, business is business, Eric. He soon rises above the personal when he needs to. Here they are."

The last remark was coupled with a gesture to the doorway. Suzi came towards their table and Albert veered off to

201

the bar abruptly, bringing to Eric's mind something he had read concerning the behaviour of differently charged neutrons. When Suzi sat down she barely glanced at Eric before fixing Eleanor with a knowing smile. It was returned with equal warmth. "Won't be long now," she said.

"No," Eleanor replied.

Albert was laughing at the bar but when he turned with the tray of drinks he composed his features into something resembling thoughtfulness. He sat next but not near to Suzi. For a moment or two they all drank quietly.

"So what are your plans now, Albert?" Eleanor asked.

Albert looked quickly at Eric who gave a slight shake of the head.

"I think I shall make ends meet. I've got the odd idea or two."

Eleanor nodded. "Sorry about you and Suzi by the way. Well, no harm done."

Ask Alan, Eric wanted to say but did not.

Albert waved an arm. "On that subject", he said, "I have promised Suzi to drop her off. I trust you two will be able to manage without me. First, I must nip out to the boy's room. Anybody care to join me?"

"As it happens," Eric said, putting his drink down carefully.

The lavatory was in a dark narrow outbuilding at the back of the pub. Albert snorted with laughter.

"This is for your ears only," he said, shaking his right hand vigorously before standing back to zip up his trousers, "but when you are at that meeting tomorrow keep in mind one little point."

He splashed his hands in the cold water and then spoke over his shoulder to Eric. "You must have guessed there was a bit more to come on the Inkers affair? Well, I managed to push through the mortgage on a second house on Inkers lane a few days ago."

Eric joined Albert at the hand-drier. "And?"

"Well, I could be reluctant to sell my two houses couldn't I? Poor tenants, thrown out of their house to make room for another greedy developer's schemes."

"I seem to remember reading something in the local paper about residents wanting to leave those old houses."

"Oh, I think I could come up with tenants who wouldn't want to move," Albert pointed out and smoothed back his hair. "And," he turned towards Eric, "this could be useful for your position. I might be persuaded by you, if you see what I mean, to withdraw any objections I have to any plans put forward, whatever they turn out to be."

Never in his entire career, Eric thought, had he come across such a generous offer. "I do see!" he said, smiling ridiculously.

"Whoa, don't put too much weight on it," Albert said.

When they got back Suzi looked pointedly at her watch. She gave Eleanor a hug, said goodbye to Eric and followed Albert out. He nodded to Eric just before leaving.

"Talk tomorrow night? I'll call by at about six?"

"Look forward to that, Albert. We can have a bite to eat."

Eleanor regarded Eric with a mixture of irritation and undisguised interest as he sat down.

"It's nothing," he lied. "We often have the odd drink together."

When they finally left the sky was darkening and the lights from the windows highlighted faces sitting under the ivy-covered area across the pub's courtyard. There was a heavy scent from the window boxes. Eric followed Eleanor along the lane leading to the car. When they reached it Eleanor turned round and threw him the keys.

"You can drive."

"And how do I get back?"

"I'll call a taxi. Of course, you don't have to come with me."

Eric opened the passenger door first and stood there for the pleasure of watching her skirt ride above her knees when she swung into the seat. After he started the engine and switched the lights on Eleanor pressed the cassette recorder. The sound of a piano and violin filled the car.

"We'll go the long way round through the villages," she stated.

Eric nosed the car into the main street and then turned north of the city to follow a back road towards the market town en route to Eleanor's home. Within a few minutes Eleanor began fumbling with the zip to her skirt.

"Let's see how good your self-control is," she said leaning towards him.

If only they could see, he thought, as other traffic passed. He swung the car along the winding road. Ahead he saw the signpost to a village that he knew for certain had several remote corners.

Chapter Fourteen

Eric glanced down at his suit. It looked less than impressive. Supposedly black, in the brightly lit ante-room to the Vice Chancellor's the fabric looked grey and shiny. He sniffed at the material again. It was too late to do much about the musty aroma from the garment's lengthy imprisonment in his wardrobe. In any case the strong scent being given off by the new carpet neutralised that of his jacket.

Without thinking he brushed his hair and removed a strand from his lapel. On the wall immediately opposite the row of chairs on which he was sitting was a large framed print. It showed a fishing boat battling its way into the port, or what the port must have looked like before it became a 'Marina Complex.' A small plaque alongside the frame testified to the mutual good will of the city and the university.

We'll soon see about that, Eric thought.

He examined his finger nails and then extended first one leg then the other to check on the state of his shoes. His watch showed the planned meeting was already ten minutes late. There was no sign of anybody else. He was beginning to feel like a schoolboy in the waiting room at the clinic. It made him recall his misplaced optimism years ago, when answering with an emphatic 'no' the school dentist's query as to whether there had been any problems over the past week. His heartfelt denial had never spared him the ensuing discomfort.

On an impulse he pulled out the combined brush and mirror once given to him as a present. It was then that he caught sight for the first time of the small remote camera in the corner of the ceiling. To his dismay he now saw a second camera in the other corner facing him. A loud burst of laughter came from the closed door on his right. Eric tried not to think it was prompted by his actions. The door opened and a small, neat woman with hair pulled back from her forehead invited him to come through. He wondered how a secretary in a university could afford the expensive collection of gold festooning her neck and hands.

Briefly surveying her small office he took in the view of the seat he had just vacated on a screen standing alongside a computer on one of the desks. He was taken through a second door and into a large room with windows along the left hand wall. These looked out over the main entrance to the campus. He registered the extreme thickness of the carpet and the highly polished oval table in the right hand half of the room.

The table was surrounded by blue leather chairs with the university logo on the backs that he could actually see. Most of the seats were already taken. He was offered a place in the middle of the table facing away from the window and towards an expensive looking bookcase fronted by heavy glass doors.

"Good morning, Dr. Farnham, you probably know who I am" - a brief round of chuckling from the assembled greeted this remark - "but let me just clue you in on the others here. On your right is the planning officer of the university, Mr Black."

Eric glanced at the cadaver-like face of Mr Black and said hello. He did much the same for Professor Clam, chairman of some research group or other, who presently sat bolt upright in a dark blue suit and beamed at Eric. He knew by sight the next three figures, namely Dr Ranger, the expert on armed warfare (what other sort of warfare was there, Eric always wanted to ask), Professor Carpenter, the biochemist and, of course, Helm. The latter beamed encouragingly at Eric.

"Last but not least, the Vice Chancellor went on, "the most important people here this morning."

There were protests of, "By no means, Vice Chancellor" and, "not at all, not at all," from two men and a woman facing

Eric.

"Credit where it is due," insisted the Vice Chancellor. "Immediately opposite you Dr Farnham is Donald West, head of the city's Growth and Development Unit. On his right is Philip Wilson, one of the council's economic advisers. Next to him is Betty Liston, who is the assistant to Donald West."

Eric smiled in turn at a ruddy faced and friendly man in his forties, a younger and much thinner individual with a straggling beard and, finally, a woman with thick black hair and round glasses whose age Eric placed at anywhere between twenty-five and thirty-five.

"No point beating about the bush," said the Vice Chancellor, and invited Donald West to give a brief account of planning applications that one Terry Varne was preparing with respect to land behind the university playing fields. "Of course, the Vice Chancellor added, "only those in the room are privy to this er, preliminary consultation."

Plot, Eric wanted to say but did not. While West succinctly outlined the state of play Eric studied the chief of his university at close quarters for the first time. He was physically bulky with a large head topped by thick ginger hair. More such hair curled out from his shirt cuffs. These were of brilliant whiteness and contrasted with brown hands, the colour roughly matching the Vice Chancellor's face. Serious sun worship had taken place at some point. Eric's examination was interrupted by Henry Helm's monotone taking over from West.

"It is the combination of new facilities and interesting new courses which will, we believe, attract students," he began, "which is partly why I invited Dr Farnham to attend, in so far as he might well be engaged in our, er, possible postgraduate schemes, which of course will need new premises."

Relief and expectancy hit Eric in equal measures.

"What about this man, Verne, Varne?" The VC asked.

"Yes, he is a player of importance," Helm agreed. "But we, that is to say I, had another exchange with him only last night, after I had talked with Donald, of course. I can't say Mr Varne was exactly over the moon about my, our, initiative in setting up this session today. But, well, it does look as though he sees the benefits if we can pull off a, um, marriage of business and academia in respect of developing Inkers Lane. That is when, I should say if, the City Council also grants planning permission for some sort of shopping complex but, and this is crucial to our agreement, which also allows extensive new, university-related buildings."

The Vice Chancellor beamed at the assembled guests once more.

"Also, as I understand the wider situation in the City Council, it seems desirable that during further discussions between Varne and the university," Helm continued, "we make the case for including some affordable housing units in any final scheme."

Eric guessed that the cost of any such 'units' would be far beyond the means of the residents in the houses currently designated for destruction.

"Well, I think we can proceed to setting up some sort of joint liaison between Varne's organization and ourselves," The Vice Chancellor pronounced. "Professor Helm is the obvious man from our side, all agreed?" He looked towards Donald West.

"Fine, fine," the latter responded, "no problems at our end, I suspect. It will be difficult to stop planning for the sort of joint venture that Prof Helm has just outlined, union of business and university and all that. Of course, one can never be absolutely sure of the outcome to planning committees. Even so, on this one, I can't believe...."

Donald West's precise tones were interrupted by those of the thin man, Wilson, who had been looking restless throughout the preceding discussion. He spoke with a pronounced local dialect.

"I think we should definitely *not* jump the gun here. I take Donald's *general* point." Eric heard the word as "genwal" but Wilson's speech traits were clearly familiar to his colleagues. "As some of us are aware, there is also a lot of enthusiasm on the council for a full-scale housing development with a very much smaller shopping complex. As someone partly responsible for wider economic strategy I have an interest in increasing our housing stock."

"The logical outcome of that," Helm responded immediately, would be rather less space to develop purely university related building."

He removed his glasses and chewed them gently. Betty Liston, Eric discovered, was watching him closely. He smiled briefly and was rewarded with a wide grin. Surreptitiously, he studied her more attentively, noting again the thickness of her hair and what looked to be full breasts beneath the suit jacket.

"But with all due respect for Mr Wilson's admirable sentiments," Henry went on, "I think he underestimates the economic good that would come to the city from the educational dimension of the project. I believe all of us on this side of the table, as it were, take the community approach seriously. And of course," he gave a sly look, "increased income from a large retail centre would also boost council spending in areas less directly favoured in the, er, present climate."

Henry stopped for a moment and glanced down at the piece of paper in front of him. The cheek by jowl of student and supermarkets was a logical outcome of current educational trends, Eric felt like calling out. He could almost hear the university public relations staff whirring into gear. "A first for the city! Get your degree and new furniture under the same roof."

Henry's tone when he resumed resembled that of a parent talking to a young child. "Of course," he finished, "more jobs as well as more students coming into the city must also be to the general good."

Eric watched Philip Wilson's colour deepen.

"Not all of the city's inhabitants would necessarily agree that more students coming into the city, as you put it, are an unqualified good, and...."

"Point taken, Mr. Wilson," the Vice Chancellor's voice boomed, "but we ought to keep our personal feelings aside on this one and try to take an objective view. This is the 'can do' university, as we have taken to marketing ourselves recently."

Eric had heard this odious phrase coming on several occasions from the beak like mouth of Christopher Morton. His feelings sank another notch or two at the additional evidence that the man was gaining in influence.

"There is one point," Eric said tentatively.

The Vice Chancellor's head turned in his direction like a radar scanner locating a hostile aircraft.

"I understand that a third party has a substantial interest in the Inkers Lane site," Eric continued. "I am referring to", he named Albert, "who owns two of the existing terraced houses on the site."

"Compulsory purchase, Dr Farnham, compulsory purchase," the VC said loftily. "The man will be given a good price, I understand." He looked in Donald West's direction, who confirmed this. Philip Wilson shifted his seat. Helm smirked.

"It is my information, with all due respect," Eric relished using one of Helm's favoured phrases, "that the person in

210

question has no intention of going quietly. He tells me he is ready to stir up protest against any threat to the character of that area. As you know, there was quite a fuss over the demolition of terraces on the other side of the city."

"If I may say so, Dr. Farnham, you seem remarkably well informed about this man's intentions."

"Well, to be honest, Vice Chancellor, the person in question specifically asked me to mention his interests at this meeting. He has no formal status here."

"But I'm sure," Helm interjected, "that Dr. Farnham could use his, er, influence with his man? Hm?"

He looked pointedly and directly at Eric having put on his glasses to do precisely this. Eric detected a flicker of excitement somewhere in the region of his upper abdomen.

"I'm sorry, Henry, I'm just the messenger," he said, affecting a modest glance at those assembled. Both Betty Liston and Philip Wilson were looking distinctly pleased. Donald the planner was not.

"Perhaps we ought to arrange a separate meeting with Dr Farnham's client," he said, with no trace of humour.

"Well," Henry began, "Mr. Varne surely would not be without some influence on this, this Albert fellow." His voice rose at the end of the sentence and he looked again at Eric, who in turn expressed surprise.

"Oh, I *am* sorry, Henry, I assumed that you must have known that Varne, or rather Mr. Varne, parted company with my contact recently. Indeed," he hurried on as Henry prepared for a follow up, "I gather the parting has made him more determined to oppose Mr Varne's plans."

There was utter silence, finally broken by the Vice Chancellor. "I propose that we continue our general discussions but that we pencil in an urgent date when we can see Dr.

211

Farnham's contact, if I may put it like that."

"Perfectly acceptable, "Helm said, "but we really will have to move quickly Vice Chancellor if we are to have any reasonable prospect of advertising future possibilities for prospective students and sponsors."

"Right. Dr. Farnham, do please contact your man and get back to my secretary, if possible later today. And you, Donald, your people will be available for another meeting, either later today or early tomorrow?"

"Yes," from Donald West, "the time scale is rather tight on the planning approval side. I think we have to go with your suggestion."

After a brief flurry of diaries the chairs were scraped back and a general move towards the outer office took place. Eric found Betty Liston at his side.

"Time for a quick coffee, Dr Farnham? Philip is keen too."

The invitation was issued in an undertone and Eric accepted. When the main party went into the corridor the three of them splintered off towards the stairs leading to the refectory. Eric had time to register looks of varying degrees of hostility, puzzlement and resentment from both West and Helm before the pair drifted towards Henry's part of the building.

Betty Liston sat next to Eric in the staff common room at a table near the window while Philip Wilson fetched coffees from the machine.

"I did enjoy that Eric," she said. "I can call you that can't I?"

"By all means, er, Betty. But I can't really see what can come of all this. No matter what I said just now I don't see Albert holding up the council steam roller for long."

"With a little bit of help from the engine room he might."

At that point Philip Wilson joined them and put three

cups of coffee on the table from a tray. Small plastic milk containers and wrapped sugar lumps cascaded beside them.

"I need to put on weight," he shrugged, grinning. He seemed to be constantly perspiring. Eric wondered if that had anything to do with his weight loss.

"Eric," said Betty, "while your friend Albert is clearly not fond of Varne I'm assuming that he won't really try to arrest *any* development, no matter what?"

"Getting back at Varne is probably the major consideration as far as Albert is concerned." Eric agreed, far from certain that this was the whole case.

"There are other people on the council opposed to the super store idea," Philip chipped in, "and there is also pressure for developing a site where a whole range of small businesses can start up. There could be lower rates for the early stages of any enterprise. And," his face shone with fresh perspiration, "it would make much more sense to have a campus input in that sort of environment. You know, links with research at the university."

Where, Eric wondered, would linguists fit in. He rather thought that, historians, say, and philosophers at the university would ask themselves something similar. That would apply in triplicate and underlined for the classics department. It cheered him up in some obscure way to imagine the reaction of the distinguished professor of Greek studies to the idea sketched out by Philip Wilson.

"All I can do is to have a word with Albert," Eric said. "I promised to see him this evening."

"So, nothing much can be decided today," Betty Liston stated with satisfaction. "We can let the Vice Chancellor's secretary know that the additional meeting will have to be tomorrow, preferably in the afternoon. Even so," she beamed at Eric, "perhaps we could join you and your man for a drink this evening, after you've talked to him?"

"Why not?" was all that Eric could manage to say.

The station hotel had seemed the most convenient place to convene with the council people.

"Yes indeed," Albert said with relish after Eric had reported on the meeting at the university, "I begin to see more profit than I thought in this venture."

He sipped his beer and sat back in his chair.

"You say that this Wilson character and the woman were definitely against the supermarket idea? Of course," he frowned, "we don't know how important the two of them are, do we?"

Eric was only half listening. Much of his mind was re-running his conversation with Henry Helm not long after he had finished having coffee with Wilson and Liston in the university staff club.

"You have to consider your own, er, interests very carefully," Henry had observed.

"Quite honestly Henry, I don't think I personally have much interest either way in what sort of development there is."

"Perhaps you ought to view this from another, shall we say, er, angle?" Henry had put his hands together on his desk while his head shifted forward imperceptibly.

"We can't," he asked rhetorically, "separate what happens on the proposed site from our, what, our general conditions of *work*, can we?"

"Do you mean better offices?" Eric queried.

Henry shook his head sorrowfully.

"That is one consideration, but rather a small one. I was thinking more perhaps of your long term career prospects." He

214

paused. "Of course, if the proposed graduate school takes off, I should say *when* it takes off, it would be housed in new building on the Inkers Lane site under our proposals. I was wondering generally about your possible role in that set up. This could certainly bring a bigger office, but more importantly would open up, perhaps, other avenues to er, to promotion?"

And the price, Eric wondered but said nothing.

"As you know," Henry went on ruminatively, "the Vice Chancellor is a key figure in any promotions exercise. And nowadays", he went on, "qualities other than research are very much taken into account in deciding who is promoted."

Was this, Eric wondered, a less than obscure thrust at his own sparse record of academic achievement? Probably nothing personal he decided. Several emphatically even less distinguished lecturers than he had already joined the be-suited numbers trotting into the management bunker. The image made him acutely aware that he had no desire to leave the rank and file.

"Not that I am suggesting for one moment, Eric, that you are not a respected figure in your own academic field."

Nobody, Eric thought resentfully, could better convey the exact opposite of what he was saying than Helm.

"Anyway, Henry, as I say, I can't really do all that much to influence events. Of course," he added, "I will put the various points to my friend when I see him later."

"Please do, Eric," Henry had finished dryly.

"One last drink before they arrive?" Albert asked, bringing Eric's attention back to the lounge and its abundant ferns. When the two full glasses eventually arrived Albert shuffled uncomfortably in his chair.

"Look, I've been thinking things through. Would you mind if I see these two council characters by myself?"

"Whatever you think best, Albert," Eric said, feeling and probably looking put out.

Albert did not notice or affected not to notice anything. Fatigue suddenly washed through Eric. He left the lounge in time to see Betty Liston and Wilson making their way through the station concourse towards the back entrance of the hotel.

Chapter Fifteen

At four the following afternoon Eric sat once more in the ante-room to the Vice Chancellor's office. Helm had gone through ten minutes earlier, barely glancing in Eric's direction as he passed by. From the sound of muffled voices within, the meeting would soon be underway. In the event, Betty Liston and Wilson proved to be absent when Eric joined the others. Donald West, on the other hand, was seated at the very centre of the table. He looked worryingly relaxed. Next to him was Henry, who at the moment Eric entered finished murmuring something to West. Both men smiled their greetings.

Eric was placed next to the skeletal Mr Black, who also gave what could be taken for a friendly grin. "Yes, you'll notice that we've got rid of a bit of dead weight," he said...

"I did wonder," Eric responded.

"The Liston woman," Black lowered his voice almost to a whisper and leaned towards Eric, "just too ambitious for her own good apparently."

He gave a guarded look in the direction of Donald West, who was again talking quietly with Henry. The Vice Chancellor stood near the doorway next to Ranger and Carpenter.

"She's been after West's job for a quite while now," Black said. "Looks as though she's got her come-uppance."

Before Eric could put any questions a woman he recognized from the refectory came in pushing a trolley with jugs of coffee and biscuits on it.

"Help yourselves while we are waiting for our late arrivals gentlemen," the Vice Chancellor's confident tones rang out. "Shouldn't be long now, my secretary tells me."

He too, Eric noticed, looked inordinately pleased. Before

he had time to worry about what this could mean two more people entered the room.

"Good morning," the Vice Chancellor gushed, "good morning. Do help yourself to a coffee."

"Don't look so surprised," Eleanor said quietly to Eric as she settled into the vacant seat next to him. Her father had gone to sit on the other side of Helm. Varne was wearing a dark blue suit with a snow white shirt. From the collar of this sprouted a large and colourful tie. Varne glanced at Eric and inclined his head a fraction.

"What are you doing here?" Eric whispered to Eleanor.

"As PA to Varne Enterprises, or something like that. Well, it was only a matter of time really. Where else could I make so much money?"

With Black giving an unconvincing appearance of not trying to listen to this exchange Eric said nothing further. He discovered a strong urge to stroke Eleanor's silk-suited form. Instead, he picked up his cup and took a few mouthfuls of coffee.

"If we are ready then, we might make a start." The Vice Chancellor's raised voice was just audible over the rattling of cups and saucers. "I think it perhaps best if we let Donald West open the proceedings with a short report on what has happened since yesterday. Donald?"

"Thank you, Vice Chancellor. Well," West began cheerfully, "most of the, um, obstacles that came up yesterday have more or less been disposed of, if I can put it like that."

Black smirked at Eric.

"Yes," West continued, "internal council sessions yesterday quickly clarified our overall priorities and preferences. In the end, as I have always maintained of course, the regeneration of the city and the prospect of extra jobs were the deciding factors for most of us. There were naturally healthy

218

differences of opinion. These are now, as I say, resolved."

There were murmurs of appreciation and general assent.

"There are therefore no serious objections at least to going ahead to plan for a combination of a large shopping complex and new buildings dedicated to the university, including additional student accommodation. I understand Vice Chancellor that this will be chiefly for your planned postgraduate expansion."

The Vice Chancellor nodded sagely. Without rubbing his hands together he managed to convey the impression of having done so. Questions whirled inside Eric's head. He had the feeling they would soon find answers.

"Perhaps Mr. Varne, you would also like to say a few words. As most of you know," the Vice Chancellor's gaze quickly circled the table, "Mr. Varne is seen as central to the process of putting together significant private finance for our, well, I suppose joint venture is indeed now the appropriate and of course fashionable phrase. Mr. Varne?"

Eric had not seen Varne in a formal public situation before. Against his will he was impressed. Like a famous but short labour politician, who had once addressed an audience in which Eric happened to be present a few years earlier, Varne seemed physically to grow in stature as he spoke. All listened raptly.

"I know all about the usual objections to large shopping complexes," Varne began, "but the fact is that in this city it would inject a healthy dose of competition. We've all grown up with the rows of shops; we even love some of them. But they charge what they like and to my mind at least the service is not what it was." He paused, looking about him defiantly for any disagreement.

"What's more," he went on, "the Inkers Lane site is a complete mess at the moment. It's an eyesore and I know for a

219

fact that many agree with me. I see only a win, win situation by redeveloping."

"I'm not sure that those still living in the area would see it quite like that, would they?" Eric blurted out. Varne turned towards him.

"Have you looked closely at those houses lad? Some of them have no inside toilets, they're riddled with damp. They smell. I can tell you, there'll not be many objecting to moving, not when they start adding up what they've got to gain from it."

In a moment, Eric thought, Varne would say you can't make an omelette without breaking eggs. Instead, he continued brusquely, "In any case, compulsory purchase schemes are already being drawn up. As far as I know from my last chat with West here, no real difficulties are expected now."

Eric noticed that both Helm and the Vice Chancellor, not to mention West and Varne, were examining him in a way he imagined a stoat might weigh up a rabbit's next move.

"It's just that yesterday", Eric began, "there seemed some doubt that all the present residents would be willing to move. As I remember there were other concerns expressed, for example about helping small businesses and possibly providing affordable houses."

If knowing looks could be said to ripple round a table they did so now.

"I understand Dr Farnham," said the Vice Chancellor, "that your, um, your contact, belatedly agreed yesterday to back the plans now being put forward. That is to say, he will raise no serious objections to having the properties he owns purchased compulsorily."

"Nor should, he," Varne snorted, "at the price he's been offered. If I'd had my way," he began to say.

"Yes, yes Mr Varne," the V.C. interrupted him, "but all's

well that ends well, wouldn't you agree?"

Outside in the corridor as the meeting broke up Eleanor barely had time to suggest they meet later for a drink before her father clasped her elbow and, with a hostile glance at Eric, moved towards the stairway.

It was almost six by the time Eric managed to turn up at the pub in town, having arranged a prior meeting with Albert. The latter was leaning on the bar talking to the same barmaid who had been there on Eric's previous visit. He looked over his shoulder at Eric and grinned.

"Better make it a double, darling," he said, indicating the malt whiskies on display at the back, "and another of the same for me," he added.

Albert carried both drinks to a corner table near the fireplace.

"Yes, I know, I know," he said, holding both hands up after they had seated themselves opposite one another. "But don't forget, I had most of my loot tied up in that set-up, you didn't." He sipped his drink. "How could I not take the best deal when it came to the crunch?"

"Was it really necessary to drop me right in it this afternoon. I felt and probably looked like a complete idiot," Eric protested, almost blushing at the memory.

"Thought of letting you know what was going on, but, well, I only made up my mind at the very last minute. Honestly, I did. When I met that Liston woman I could see right off she had no chance of bringing in any scheme she might have had. Talk about ambitious, she makes you lot look kind-hearted."

"Go on," said Eric.

"OK. I admit I covered myself with a few telephone calls to that Donald West bloke. Of course I did. How can I put it, he

221

came up with an offer, well several offers really, that I couldn't refuse." He smiled. "And of course that meant he had to screw more out of Varne to cover my end of things. Upshot is, satisfaction all round. Well, I can't speak for you...."

Eric shrugged. "I'm wondering how I ever imagined I would benefit from any scheme Henry Helm has his fingers in."

"He won't have it all his own way, though, not now Varne's lot are in with the university," Albert said cheerfully.

"There'll be something in it for Henry," Eric responded, "you can bet on that."

"Still, your Prof can't be all that much against you can he? If it hadn't been for you and Eleanor hitting it off in the first place he might never even have had a foothold, eh?"

"I doubt if he'll see it like that."

"He might," Albert winked. "At any rate, I can't see you not keeping your job, if that's what you really want."

"I thought at one point Albert I was supposed to pack in my work to join you!"

"What makes you think I've given the idea up? When I do get something going at least Varne won't be an obstacle now. His Inkers Lane project is taking up his time and energy. Besides, the money from this compulsory purchase deal gives me a few more options. I still might yet become a mature student!" He laughed.

"You could have to wait a bit, Albert. The university is only just starting to tip toe towards taking more mature students, at least those without formal qualifications."

"Ah, but your Prof. thinks it might be a good idea to have a guinea pig or so in the meantime." Albert held his hands up again. "OK, I had words with him too after talking with West. This Helm bloke thinks he might, what is it, kick-start the process? Naturally," he added, emptying his glass, "I hinted strongly that you would be an ideal course tutor for a small class of oldies like me."

"I'll make damn sure you have to work for whatever it is you think you're getting." Eric said, grinning in spite of himself.

"Never been afraid of hard work, my son," was Albert's riposte. "You won't find it's as easy as you think, teaching somebody like me. Another?"

Eric agreed with both propositions.

"One or two more of these and things will look even better," Albert said, putting what looked to Eric two double shots of whisky on the table.

Eric shook his head. "This is definitely my final one for the moment."

"Fair enough." Albert knew that Eric was going on to see Eleanor.

Eric glanced at his watch. He still had almost an hour before that meeting at Cottingly but what with bus timetables, oh, sod it, he thought, deciding to take a taxi. As if reading his thoughts, Albert said,

"I could drop you off if you don't mind being ten minutes or so early. I'm having supper with the warden of that very nice hall of residence at the bottom of the village."

"You don't mean to say that you are planning to live in the hall? Isn't that taking the student thing a bit too far?"

Albert smirked. He pulled out a packet of cigarettes and lit one before offering them to Eric.

"I shall probably make a bit more cash letting out my own place for a year, maybe two if I like it. I can see me settling in very nicely with the students, can't you? What with my natural charm and all."

Despite himself, Eric had to smile again.

"I suppose," he said, inhaling deeply and then finishing his own glass, "with all this emphasis on students and their needs, who knows, you could be a useful ally."

"There you are. I knew you would see it my way. Now let's hit the road to Cottingly."

After being dropped off Eric watched Albert drive away, his hand waving from the window. Inside the pub Eric turned to his right to enter the small bar, the one with neither fruit machine nor music playing. Eleanor was already sitting in the corner by the window.

"Not late, am I?" He asked, "another drink?"

She shook her head, indicating what looked like a gin and tonic on the table before her.

"I haven't got all that much time, Eric."

Eric thought about her reply as he waited for his beer to be pulled. It more or less perfectly summed up not only their public meetings but their fleeting and decidedly intermittent physical contacts. For almost a full minute after sitting opposite Eleanor there was silence.

"Your turn, I think." Eric finally said. The brief flash of irritation in her eyes depressed him.

"What can I say about today? I never planned to be part of any conspiracy. What would you do if the boot was on the other foot and your father wanted help with his business?" She asked.

"Do I have to answer that?"

"The lofty moral tone is a big help, Eric. I take it you took the same line with Albert?"

The note of exasperation with which Eleanor put this last question stung Eric.

"Your old man didn't exactly leave him all that much room to manoeuvre did he?"

"All's fair in business, Eric." Another sip of gin. "Anyway, for what it's worth, I did feel awkward about the meeting in your VC's office this morning. And don't forget, I didn't know the full details of what Albert had fixed up with the council people until the last minute. What good would it have done to let you know at that stage?"

Eric conceded the point. There was another silence. A couple came into the bar but sat on the far side of the room talking in low voices. Eleanor dropped hers to a whisper and her hand squeezed his wrist.

"Of course, I shall have to work closely with your lot as the project develops. My father is keen on that. So there won't be anything to stop us having coffee now and then, even the odd meal, or," she nudged Eric's arm, "something."

Eric felt like the class dunce being given a special award for trying hard after the other prizes had been handed out. So? He asked himself.

"Did you come in your car?"

Eleanor nodded, finishing her drink at the same time.

"Do you think you could, er, give me a lift back to my place?"

"Oh, I think that can be arranged."

Eric paused momentarily outside the staffroom door listening to the scraping of chairs and coughing as everybody settled down. Just as he was about to turn the handle he saw Jake coming along the corridor with a coffee cup in his hand.

"Thought coffee and all that had been banned from meetings in this room now," Eric whispered.

"You mean since they started referring to it as the Board Room? But that's *why* I'm bringing this," Jake grinned in reply, "and I've got a crumbly biscuit in my pocket."

When the two of them entered the room Henry Helm acknowledged their arrival and they sat together almost directly beneath one of the windows. Jake promptly opened it, giving a disarming smile at the same time.

"As I was explaining," Henry continued with mild irritation, "the Dean of what will become the School of Humanities – of which of course the Languages Department will be a member – will say more about budget models in due course."

A white faced, thin man in a brown suit seated opposite to Henry nodded his large head in response to this, briefly smiling as he did so. Next to him was a statuesque woman with obviously dyed blond hair, who turned out to be one of three secretarial staff present. Another, with thick horn rimmed glasses, was from personnel and introduced as Karen Spender. The third was older than her colleagues, somewhere around fifty Eric guessed, and introduced as Brenda Langton from Registry.

"Can I just ask, Mr Chairman," Kingsly piped up, his face shining above a collar of brilliant whiteness, "whether it is really appropriate to talk about budget models at what I understood to be a general meeting to plan our strategy for the next few years."

"Which he might not be here to see," Jake whispered in Eric's ear.

The Dean, a Professor Easton it turned out, a geologist, gave Kingsly the sort of look he might have devoted to his more disappointing rock specimens. Eric watched while the three ladies from administration all faced in the same direction as the Dean, as if in a synchronised dance movement.

"Er, Wallace," said Henry Helm to Kingsly, "we had agreed I think that we can hardly consider our general strategy without taking on board the, um, implications of the budget model that will be implemented, indeed is already in the process of being implemented."

"Implemented?" Kingsly persisted.

"Well, in the sense that figures are already in play which

indicate the likely deficit, or not as the case may be, for each Department, or as will be, each section of the new School."

"But surely," Kingsly went on, looking decidedly hotter, "you can't just switch to departmental or sectional or whatever budgets overnight, can you? There has to be some warning, some sort of chance to plan beforehand."

"Right," Jake called out. "What happened to the budget model that assumes a central pool of n pounds to be shared between departments, and that if for some reason one part of the institution has problems, funds are diverted to help it over a difficult patch?"

"Oh, you mean like in a university," Eric interjected.

The academic staff members present adopted various facial expressions registering either neutrality or agreement; all except Henry, who looked exasperated.

"This is not the place to tackle the government's Higher Education policy," Henry said, "what we have to concentrate on is…"

"Where is the place then?" Daniel White suddenly asked.

Eric looked at his colleague with genuine interest. Daniel's face was set in a grim frown and his body was rigid, as though taken over by an outside force. Others in the room looked surprised too.

"I mean," Daniel went on, "just how much more are we supposed to take from the so-called administration of this place? It's like a, like a, a virus," he said triumphantly. "It used to be the case that the centre" - this enunciated in italics - "more or less tried to help the academics carry out their work. And let's be clear about this, only the academics can teach students."

"Hear, hear," said Jake. Encouraged, Daniel's voice went up a notch or two.

"All this talk about budgets and *board* rooms for pity's

sake. How are we supposed to be concentrating on education like this," he gestured around the room with disgust. "And all this talk of a business," he went on, "well, we keep hearing the language of private enterprise but I don't believe the people purporting to manage this institution would last five minutes in the market place."

Eric was now transfixed. Henry's eyes roamed the ceiling and walls while Kingsly nodded furiously at Daniel's words. The Dean simply stared ahead at the wall opposite. The three secretaries made notes.

"Daniel," Henry said at last, "I think...."

"Henry!" Daniel almost screeched in reply. He stood up abruptly. "I've had enough. I've got better things to do than to sit here all day."

He picked up his papers and left the room to a stunned silence.

"Who would have thought," Jake muttered in Eric's ear. "Good old Daniel."

"As I've said elsewhere, I don't think it helps very much when the temperature goes up like this," Christopher Morton said, making a placatory hand gesture towards the Dean. "I suggest we hear in a bit more detail exactly what the university has in mind."

"I rather thought Daniel's point was that we *are* the university," Jake interjected. "And we don't seem to have very much idea at all of what is going on."

"That's why I suggested that the Dean should tell us more," Morton replied smoothly, wincing as if in pain at the speaker's inability to understand his point. Eric managed with difficulty not to ask Morton where he was hurting. All eyes swivelled towards the archaeologist with the large head.

"Thank you," he said. "Well, whatever we might think

228

about what is happening, accountability is here to stay. That is the first point to make. Budgets are just a way of showing that we are accountable, or at least are being asked to be accountable. By the way, Sandra," he turned to the blonde woman, "I assume you are keeping the main record of the meeting. As I was saying," he went on in response to an affirmative from Sandra, "the university management group has worked out from a careful examination of income and expenditure by different departments, sections, whatever we might call them, which of us are in balance and which are, um, in the red. And, well, to cut a long story short, languages fall into the latter category."

"One moment, please," Margaret interrupted, "I don't understand."

"I think," the Dean continued, "it is easier to grasp it all if you think of students for the moment purely in terms of units of income. Each undergraduate student entering a course here accounts for a proportion of your income. Basically, the more bottoms you can get on the seats of your lecture room, the more money you have at your disposal - after of course a percentage is deducted for the university's administrative cost. There is, as you know, income from grants, whether from government or private institutions and, as you are perhaps aware, fees for postgraduate courses are much higher, so there is potential there for sucking in more money."

Eric watched Margaret's face registering mounting anger in the course of the Dean's remarks.

"I am not," she informed the room magisterially, "some sort of retarded child - which was the level at which you aimed your explanation. I think you can safely assume that most of us in this room are aware of our dependency on student income. What I want to know," she paused for some seconds, "is what it means, for practical purposes, for languages to be as you put it in the red?"

The Dean looked icily at Margaret. "It means," he said quietly, "that your books have to be balanced - I am sorry if this sounds too simple - either by getting more students, more grants or by spending less."

"You mean by staff leaving?" Jake called out.

"Bluntly, yes," said the Dean.

"And the administration?" Jake continued, standing his coffee on the floor. "The 'centre', the entity that survives by - what is it called now, ah, yes, top slicing any income we earn with our hard labour - is that going to have to balance its books?"

Growls of agreement came from various points of the room.

"I was only asking, "Jake went on, "because the Dean seems to have brought three secretaries with him for this meeting, all necessary I'm sure."

At that moment the door opened and Daniel reappeared. He sat down just behind Margaret. His reappearance made the Dean lose concentration for a moment.

"Running a modern university demands very different qualities from those with which many of us here were familiar in our early days in education," he eventually resumed. "A university is a corporation, a major employer in the region, a multi-million pound set up, it can't be managed just by academics taking their reluctant turns of duty. Not," he added hastily, "that academics can fail to have key roles in the administration, but they do need the aid of highly specialised support staff."

"A lot more of them, you mean," said Jake. "You only have to look at the notice board in the entrance to the main building. It's three times the size it used to be and it's mostly devoted to telling you how to find different parts of the administration."

"I recall," Kingsly began.

"This is not getting us far," Helm interjected.

Daniel spoke up again, brushing Helm's remark aside with a wave of his hand.

"And why are so many people employed to produce that monthly rag, 'University Scene'?" He asked the room at large.

"More to the point," Jake interjected, "why is it full of pictures of the admin staff? Hardly a month passes without a full frontal of the Vice Chancellor, holding up a cheque or standing next to a prominent somebody or other or even," he grimaced, "wearing a helmet on a push bike."

Laughter rippled round the table, notably missing the Dean and his retinue. Even Henry failed to suppress a brief smile.

"Look," he said, "we may not like what is happening in education, well, some of you have made only too clear that you certainly don't like it. As it happens, I have much sympathy with what Daniel and Jake have said but we live in the real world. We have to compete for students now. That is a fact. If we can come up with a strategy to recruit more language students then the prospect of staff cuts will recede."

"Yes, I would underline, "the Dean chipped in, "that the calculation of your current deficit is precisely so that you can, um, so that you can address the problem. I think Professor Helm's thinking is that," he paused for a moment, before dabbing his forehead with a handkerchief, "this is the first of a series of meetings where staff can come together to identify possible er, ways forward." He loosened his tie and then ran his hand across his balding head. "This still, that is to say, the university still cannot entirely rule out cuts…"

Until this point, Eric suddenly realised, Peter Everton had uttered not one word. Now Peter leaned forward at the end of the table.

"As I understand it, the present figures suggest that in any event we might only have to lose three members of staff, at the very worst."

But which three, Eric asked himself.

"That is true, Dr. Everton," the Dean said, "and the university is working on a relatively generous compensation scheme for anybody considering voluntarily leaving."

"Voluntarily!" Jake exclaimed. "I wonder," he went on, "if one can 'chose' to do what one does not actually *want* to do."

The Dean appeared ready to tackle the point but although his mouth opened no words issued from it. The three secretaries rose as one, all turning towards him but not quickly enough to prevent him slumping forward. The sound of his head striking the table would stay with Eric for some considerable time.

Chapter Sixteen

"Not exactly a stroke, apparently, so Helm reported after he got back from the hospital. The doctors were referring to the Dean having some sort of cerebral 'incident'."

"Nearest he's got to thinking for some time," Jake muttered in response to Eric's account of the day's events to Albert. The latter raised his eyebrows in mock horror. By chance he had come across Eric and a few colleagues, sufficiently united by the dramatic turn of events to make a rare visit to the small pub almost opposite the university gates. The proximity to the main buildings that encouraged students to drink there generally deterred academic staff , with some exceptions, from doing the same.

"A sign for the Dean to slow down, if nothing else," Eric went on. "He'll be out of action for some time. Needs at least a couple of month's complete rest, according to Helm."

"This will be Henry's big chance, mark my words," Alan Branch put in. He looked reflectively at the weak coffee he was nursing. "Watch this space, you heard it here first. Henry will take over as acting Dean. No chance of *him* having a sudden turn."

"It could be worse," said Margaret from one of the more comfortable chairs grouped around the marble topped table.

To Eric's surprise Margaret was on her second gin and tonic. Nor was she showing signs of impatience to be gone. Not without reluctance he mentally replaced his image of Margaret at home surrounded by musty books and relics with one of her comfortably seated before the television, bottle conveniently to hand.

"What do you mean, Margaret?" Eric asked, thinking how

rarely he actually used her Christian name.

"Well, Eric," Margaret answered, resting her glass on the table for a moment and leaning forward, "Henry is good at getting his own way. We all, er, we all know that. If he does take over as Dean I believe he will do his best to see that the language department or, um, section does not get too harshly treated."

"Can I get you another one, Margaret," Albert suddenly chipped in. "After all, it's not every day that you have a shock like this."

"Do you know, I'm sorry?"

"Albert," said Albert smiling.

"Well, Albert, I think you have a point there. I will have the last one if I may."

Eric declined an offer of an extra pint but Alan and Jake happily held out their glasses.

"Student of yours, Eric?" Margaret asked when Albert went to buy the drinks.

"He seems to think he might be," said Eric. "Mature student and all that."

"One without any formal qualifications, you mean," Alan piped up. "I mean, there have always been mature students but usually because their education was interrupted in the first place, like all those poor sods who had to do National Service. No, this is definitely something new."

"Well, I think I rather like Albert," Margaret informed the room.

"Anybody who buys me a pint deserves the benefit of the doubt," Alan said, glancing quickly at Eric.

Jake grinned. "Getting back to Henry for a moment, will he want to pull out of his new role as, what is it, research overlord? He can't do that and act as Dean, or can he?"

Eric personally would bet on it and said so.

234

Albert returned with the drinks and promptly sat between Jake and Margaret after pulling up a chair from a nearby table.

Eric realised with surprise that he was thinking about the coming term with interest, a turn of events he would not have credited even a few days earlier. It wasn't just Albert's robustness, much as the idea of others like him in a seminar group should cheer things up. Rather, the sheer pace of events in the past week had dispelled the anxiety he had felt about losing his job. If asked to put his thoughts as succinctly as possible he would have come up with something like, Professors appear to be safe come what may, therefore to be supported by one is certainly better than to be opposed by one. Not that support was quite the word to describe Henry's relationship to him, Eric had to concede. He saw Albert standing up and coming towards him.

"I took the liberty of glancing in your pigeon hole on the way over. Recognized the handwriting. Thought you might want it sooner rather than later."

Eric recognized Eleanor's handwriting on the expensive looking envelope addressed to him c/o of the Dept of Modern Languages. He was aware of colleagues looking at him closely.

"It's just a note from one of my students. Can't be urgent. I'll look at it later."

Later turned out to be sooner than he had imagined, in that he could not resist peeking at the letter during his next visit to the lavatory. Eleanor suggested a night away during the following week in a nearby market town. That much was apparent from the opening sentences and he hastily pushed the letter back into his pocket as he heard the outer door to the lavatory pushed open. He was not that surprised to see Albert's moon like face appear at the inner glass door.

"Well, d' you know, I suddenly thought I'd just about had

enough. As Muriel said, I don't need the hassle at my age."

Kingsly paused as he rummaged through his desk drawer before triumphantly brandishing a key. Eric thought, another one bites the dust….It was almost a week since the Dean had collapsed and Kingsly had announced later that day that he was taking the offer of early retirement with enhanced pension payments. Shortly, the department was to assemble in the Senior Common Room for a goodbye ceremony, hurriedly arranged by Helm.

"And it's not as though we really need the money," Kingsly resumed, "Muriel has her teacher's pension from next year."

He unlocked the top draw of his filing cabinet. Out came a half empty bottle of malt whisky. It was joined on his desk by two dusty glasses, also from the depths of the cabinet. Kingsly wiped them with a tissue before half filling each one.

"Well, it is almost twelve," he announced, handing a glass to Eric.

"Cheers," Eric said.

Kingsly had pulled him into his office when Eric was about to check his mail, his mind still half on his meeting with Helm earlier that morning. Alan had been spot on. Henry would indeed 'soldier on' for the time being as acting Dean, as well as developing his new brief as IC research. Had it been his imagination, Eric wondered, or had Helm been even more energetic than usual? Certainly, he had never seen Henry pacing his office quite as much.

"Did, er, did Henry say anything about my decision to go?"

"Not really, Kingsly," Eric lied.

He looked guiltily around Kingsly's domain, soon, according to Henry, to be the temporary home of whoever took on the task of running the proposed new Masters' course.

"I imagine I'll keep the use of my room and it is normal to be offered an honorary title of some sort, Kingsly remarked. "Besides, I think Dr. Morton has plans for me to work on some joint project with him next year."

If only, Eric thought with mild regret, Kingsly were not so insufferably complacent. From what Helm had intimated the said Morton was aiming for a spell in university management and had received some encouragement from the Vice Chancellor. There was only one major concern of Morton's, Eric reflected, namely Morton.

"Well, thanks for the warm up drink, Wallace. I'll leave you to be getting on with things. See you shortly at the party."

Eric did not in truth relish the prospect of the leaving do. He shut the door on an image of Kingsly looking vacantly at a calendar above his desk and felt a pang of self-loathing. The university pole was as greasy as any other but what puzzled him was how he appeared to be sliding up it without trying, or at least actively wanting to, whereas poor old Kingsly.... But was he being honest with himself? If he wanted to keep his job then feeling even faintly sorry for Kingsly was nothing short of hypocrisy.

"Penny for them, Eric," Angela called out as she passed by carrying a folder.

"Oh, hello Angela, just thinking." He smiled warmly and followed her into her office on her beckoning.

"Well then, young Eric, who would have thought," she said teasingly as she held up the folder. "Next term's duties, timetables and what not. You seem to figure quite prominently, I must say."

"So it's official, now, is it?"

"M.A. coordinator for you it is," Angela said, laughing. "Let's hope you can persuade enough students to come to this place."

"Well, the course doesn't get off the ground for another year Angela."

She shook her head wonderingly. "But Eric, you'll have to oversee the course construction - persuade your colleagues to come up with suitable course modules", she emphasised the last word, "and then there will be the brochure to put together. It all takes time."

"Not to mention piloting the whole scheme through the university course approval procedures," Alan, who had just entered the room, added. He shook his head in mock sorrow. "Can't see much of a vacation for Eric, can you Angela?"

They both laughed. Eric left them together discussing how much wine should go across to the Senior Common Room from the departmental stock. To his surprise he found Albert waiting outside his office.

"Got a moment squire?"

"Come for some reading tips?

Albert raised his eyebrows. Inside his office Eric opened the window, pushed aside a pile of folders on his desk and placed an ashtray on it. The two of them lit up, contravening the latest circular from the Vice Chancellor's office about smoking in the buildings.

"You won't believe this," Albert said. "Varne has asked me if I would be willing to work for him again, I should say work *with* him."

He surveyed the tip of his cigarette before raising his head and looking directly at Eric.

"I take it the 'with' has some significance? Wait a minute," he added, "was this something you had in mind all along?"

"It most definitely was not." Albert inhaled deeply and blew a series of smoke rings towards the ceiling. Not for the first time Eric wondered how many times a day Albert shaved. "I told you, knocking about with you and yours has given me a taste for a change."

"So you won't be reverting to being Varne's driver, not even," Eric asked caustically, "his better educated driver?"

"Security consultant – that's how Varne sees it. "Well may you chortle young Eric but what's in a name? What will you be now, what is it your clarinet playing friend said, ah yes, MA co-ordinator. What's that? And you're not listening, I haven't given Varne my answer yet."

"Fair point, Albert," Eric admitted, trying in vain to emulate his companion's smoke rings. "That means, I take it, that Johnson will no longer be part of the Varne team."

"No way," Albert agreed. "This university partnership is really going to Varne's head. I think he's looking for respect in the city. That'll be a first, believe me. Well, he's about at the change of life stage, right?" He inhaled deeply. "Maybe his missus is behind it. She can see herself hosting really big meals, yeah?" He chuckled.

"That *does* make sense," Eric responded, thinking back to his one and only dinner at the Varne ranch.

"And there's Eleanor." Albert stubbed his cigarette on a saucer and looked expectantly at Eric.

"Meaning?"

"She's keen on the Uni link. Believe me, well, you've seen for yourself, Varne's real commitment is to his daughter. She's one of the few people he can get upset about. He still won't love you but he can't start cuddling up to the establishment *and* get in the way of Eleanor."

Bigger and more obviously criminal types than Varne, Eric was thinking, had managed to become civic figures.

"And another thing," Albert went on, "Eleanor has got her old man to cough up some extra money after all for a

239

postgraduate fellowship, whatever that might be. I'm sure she'll tell all in due course. Now then," he looked at his watch. "Isn't it time we went to the party? That Margaret woman said I ought to drop in for a glass or two."

Anything was possible, Eric thought, following Albert out of the office, not forgetting to lock his door as instructed by a recent circular from the university administration. He scanned the corridor for the sort of figure who might be expected to break into his room, as also advised in said circular, but saw only Peter emerging in the near distance.

Caught in a shaft of sunlight from one of the arched windows, his colleague looked distinctly well, better than he, Eric, currently felt. Peter waved a hand in their direction before moving towards the stairway. Down below people were drifting along the corridor leading from the mock Tudor timbered entrance hall towards a distant babble of voices. Eric was surprised on entering the room to see so many people from other departments. The historians were predictably in evidence, if grouped loosely together at the far end of the room and all holding glasses in their hands. He caught sight of another lecturer from geography and several more from the English department.

Kingsly was smiling radiantly at the centre of a knot of people from the administration, mostly secretaries as far as Eric could tell. He looked around for Helm and saw him lurking at the edge of the gathering, drinking a glass of orange juice. Naturally, Eric told himself, at the same time lifting a large goblet of red wine from a table along the wall. It held besides the drinks an array of dishes with various sandwiches and rolls. There were also some brightly coloured cakes. Daniel was already eating one of them.

"Eric!" he called out, "congratulations on the M.A thing.

240

Do you think it will take off?"

"Hope so, Daniel, hope so."

"Nothing like optimism," a voice spoke behind Eric when Daniel had drifted off to look for other surprise guests. Eric turned to find Morton peering at him over a glass of what looked like water. In his other hand he held a paper bag.

"Quietly confident, you know," Eric answered, taking a gulp of his red wine. Morton gave his wolfish smile. Eric confirmed with satisfaction that his colleague's hair was receding at a far greater rate than his own. "Anyway," he added, "I had the impression you were moving up in the world." When Morton looked quizzically at him, Eric added, "up as in further up the chain. Administration, management, whatever it's called now?"

"Oh, nothing official yet Eric. Well," he relented, "it's looks likely that I shall be in the Academic Registrar's office, as it happens."

He observed Eric closely, as if waiting for an answer to a question in a tutorial.

"Academic Registrar's office," Eric repeated, searching in his mind for some significance. "So?"

"So we'll probably have a lot more contact in future. M.A., quality control and all that?" Morton grinned again. Was it his imagination, Eric wondered, or was Morton's tone threatening?

"Look forward to it," was all he said. "Must have a word with Margaret," he added, leaving Morton with his water and paper bag.

"You know what's in the bag, don't you?" Jake asked, appearing at Eric's elbow. His colleague also carried a large glass of red wine. "Sandwiches!" Jake exclaimed before Eric could answer. "All made by his fiancée's fair hand." To Eric's puzzled look Jake added, "Our young Morton doesn't believe in eating at the university's expense. Matter of principle, do you see?"

"No," Eric answered.

"Nor does anybody else," Jake said.

In response Eric told Jake the gist of the short conversation he had just had with Morton. Jake shook his head in mocking admonition.

"Well, you *are* in for a change of life. Remember, his favourite technique is to try to get his colleagues tied up with as much paper work as possible. God knows what he'll be like when he's not confined to departmental meetings." He shook his head again. "Can't say I envy you Eric, even though you are going up in the world. Oh, must just say hello to Kate over there."

This last remark was occasioned by the arrival of Helm, who had slid alongside the two of them.

"I've been thinking about the M.A. Eric, any ideas yourself yet?" Helm asked after an awkward silence.

"Not really, to be honest. I suppose I shall have to see first what colleagues can offer."

"In other departments as well, I assume," Helm said.

"Other departments?"

"Well, if we are to offer a convincing interdisciplinary M.A. - and I believe thinking is moving towards something in the European Studies line, given that we are foreign languages - then it will be imperative to bring in, say, historians, geographers and so forth."

Eric almost laughed insanely at the notion of asking the historians to collaborate with the language department but the sensation did nothing to lessen his trepidation. He was beginning to see the M.A as an animate creature, spreading tentacles and shutting off any free time he might have expected in the next months. More like years, he thought pessimistically. Varne's next words confirmed his fears.

"Perhaps we ought to schedule a meeting fairly soon. You

had no other plans I assume? Good, an initial brainstorming in my room should help. I'll round up a few suitable people. If you could just prepare a short working paper, nothing elaborate. Title of proposed degree, short summary of possible course modules, statement of general aims for each one, you know the sort of thing. Academic Registry can give you an idea of what is needed," he added, almost as an afterthought. "I believe they are planning some sort of template and hope to have a draft by the end of next week. Now that Christopher Morton is joining them things might speed up, extra pair of hands and so on."

Little wonder, Eric reflected, that Morton had been so pleased with himself. At that moment the sound of raised voices made him and Henry turn round abruptly. Alan and Peter looked as though they were trying to placate Kingsly, who was glaring at Morton. The latter had put his glass of water down but was holding his paper bag in front of him. His posture reminded Eric of a priest he had seen in a film, waving a cross at a suspected demon. With a thrill he watched the bag fly sideways after a quick movement from Kingsly's right arm.

"Round one," Jake whispered as conversation in the room was reduced to a few murmuring voices. The volume picked up again as Kingsly was persuaded to sit in one of the armchairs, leaving Morton standing by himself. He shrugged his shoulders before moving towards the door and out of the room.

"Well, well," said Albert, who had been talking to Margaret but who now joined them. "So this is the modern university is it? More like the Dog and Partridge on a Saturday night."

"Did you hear what that was all about?" Eric asked. "I mean, you and Margaret were standing right behind them."

"Something about dropping a joint project now that, what's his name, the one with the missing chin?"

243

"Dr. Morton," Eric said.

"Yeah, Morton. But I'm not sure that was the main problem. It was when the two of them started talking about accommodation that it heated up. When the red faced old gent heard something about having to give up his room, that was when he lost it. Dear, oh dear," Albert shook his head, "you academics."

At least, Eric reassured himself, Kingsly was unaware of who would in fact be taking over his quarters. He glanced anxiously in his soon-to-be-former-colleague's direction. Helm had now joined the huddle around the chair. Eric drifted to within hearing distance. He arrived in time to hear Henry trying to placate Kingsly with a reference to a thorough review of staff rooms once the new building plans were underway.

Another lie, Eric thought savagely. Henry had specifically told him about the Vice Chancellor's aversion to giving space to retired staff. He was apparently in favour of something called 'hot' desks. Eric was reasonably sure that whatever these were they would not turn out to be as intriguing as they sounded.

Henry managed to suggest a date for the initial 'brainstorming' on the M.A for the following Wednesday morning, at the very time Eric had arranged to drive off with Eleanor.

"Is there a problem Eric?" Henry had asked a couple of days earlier, when first suggesting the time and date. Eric hadn't quite been able to conceal his annoyance.

"Er, no Henry, that is, I would have preferred a bit more notice."

Henry had peered over his glasses, pencil poised. "Well, this is only a very preliminary phase. Bring whatever you've

244

managed to put together for the meeting and we'll thrash out a few problems together, Mm?"

Eric thought briefly of his study at home, strewn with templates, or whatever the wretched things were called. At first glance the pattern for registering new modules had looked merely complicated. Now, after wrestling with the purported distinction between aims and objectives, not to mention learning outcomes, Eric saw the documents as the product of a person or persons unknown with a serious personality disorder. He had asked Jake about it in the newly opened *Campus Coffee Corner* in the entrance hall to the main building.

"Say no more, Eric," Jake had remarked, glancing down at the name of Doreen Barker, inscribed at the bottom of the letter accompanying the templates and other materials. His voice suddenly dropped. "In fact here she comes now, look. The one with the blue suit."

A short, plump woman, somewhere in her fifties Eric would have guessed, was moving towards the counter, where she asked for a large latte. Her hair was of the frizzled variety, rebelling against the odd, strategically placed hair grip, and of pale brown hue. There were two younger man with her, one also short as well as bald wearing round glasses, the other a nervous, tall character with a desiccated air.

"Yes," Jake muttered, "our Doreen is rising faster than skin on warm milk. Not held back by scholarship you see, Eric. Have you noticed," he said in louder voice, "that the only relaxed looking people coming here for coffee are all either secretaries or administrators?"

Eric had noticed just that. "And they all seem to be dressed as though they are on an outing," he ventured.

"Yes, sit here long enough and you will observe an impressive array of suited and folder bearing persons. Good that we are being so well looked after," Jake had added, his voice rising once more as Doreen Barker passed by.

Eric came back to the present with a rush, staring at his own folder on the round table before him. In it were the results of frantic last minute cobbling together of sentences, aims, objectives, delivery targets and much more besides. He looked at his watch again. Only an hour and a half before he was due to meet Eleanor and still no sign of Henry, who had promised to join him for a coffee prior to the meeting.

Fifteen more long minutes passed before Eric caught sight of his professor coming through the door. He was accompanied by the Vice Chancellor and a well dressed woman. Instead of leaving this group and joining Eric, Helm waved in his direction before moving up the stairs towards the administration block.

"Thank you so much, Henry," Eric said under his breath. He looked once more at his watch. After another ten minutes he stood up abruptly, gathering the papers together. Moving to the internal phone near the coffee counter he got through to his department. Angela answered.

"Look, will you give my apologies to Henry, Angela, and tell him that I've been called away urgently."

"Is that wise, Eric?"

"I don't know but he's left me sitting here for forty minutes and I have to go."

"Shall I say where to?"

"Better not," Eric answered.

He left the building with a mixture of exhilaration and trepidation akin to that he had experienced years ago, on deciding on the spur of the moment not to go to the office of the London lawyer to whom he had been all too briefly articled. The sight and sound of the tube train leaving as he climbed the steps to his local station came back to him. He had turned on his heel, walked back home and collected his bicycle for a trip to the open air swimming pool. A few months later, after finishing at the office and enduring a brief spell as a librarian, he had been offered a university place.

Outside the sun was shining brightly and Eric started to walk to the pub where he had arranged to meet Eleanor. The trees were a brilliant green while the clarity of the light made the surrounding buildings look as though outlined in pencil. He slowed down abruptly on seeing no more than thirty feet or so in front of him the unmistakable head of Kingsly. To avoid overtaking him Eric went into a paper shop and bought the *Guardian.* Pavlovian response, he told himself, barely glancing at the paper he had in reality come to dislike. No news, all opinions. Well, he had been given quite enough of those from just about everybody around him. The paper went into a waste bin outside the shop. Kingsly was no longer to be seen. It was only after entering the familiar smoky atmosphere of the pub that he saw his colleague once more, sitting in the far corner. Kingsly looked up suddenly, leaving Eric no option but to say hello.

"Won't you join me, Eric?"

He could think of no excuse not to and asked Kingsly what he wanted. To his surprise the latter gestured at the drink he was in the process of finishing and asked for another.

"Whisky?"

"A single malt, please Eric. Just a drop of ice in it."

Standing at the long bar Eric caught sight of a computer generated poster advertising a group called the Varsity five, listing among others the name of Alan on clarinet, and scheduled to play on Friday evenings and Sunday lunchtimes.

"What can I get you love, you seem happy!"

Eric looked at the dark haired, well rounded girl behind the bar and smiled at her while ordering drinks.

"What's the food today?" he asked. She passed him a menu.

"Have what you like, love." She winked at him. He suppressed what would certainly have been an ill-advised riposte. Instead he thanked her and ordered a cheese and pickle sandwich. He carried the drinks towards Kingsly's table in a passably good mood.

"Your very good health, Eric," Kingsly said and lifted his glass.

"Not your usual haunt, this place, is it Kingsly?"

"Ay, well, I needed a drink and this is on my way into town."

"You look a bit subdued, I would have thought celebration was in order now that you can get out of this madhouse."

"True, I'll not be sorry to leave the job. But to be honest, I was hoping for a better deal, you know with rooms, library membership and so on." He sat in reflective silence. "Do you know," he picked up again, "it's as though I've disappeared. I checked a few books into the library this morning and I was told that they had already taken my name off the system, whatever that is."

He picked up his glass again and almost emptied it.

"Yes, but all you need to do is register as retired staff and you should be able to carry on using the library as normal," Eric told him.

Whatever normal might be, he reflected, thinking of his most recent visit to the periodicals room, where he had been forced to listen to a gaggle of students talking at one of the tables. Above their heads hung a large notice informing those present that this was a quiet area. At least two librarians had passed through the room without a word of rebuke.

"What was that spot of bother at your farewell do last

week, Kingsly, if you don't mind my asking."

By now Eric had a fairly good idea from departmental gossip but he could think of little else to say. He looked at his watch and noted that Eleanor would be arriving within half an hour.

"I suppose it was making mountains out of molehills really, but, you know, I just saw red when Morton told me that the project I was supposed to be involved with was off for the foreseeable future, at my own leaving party too. I suppose he has his career to think of but even so..." Kingsly's voice tailed away and he gazed at the table. "Well, what with that and then hearing about not even having my room from the week after next, I, well I just hit out. Silly thing to do, I know."

Inspired, thought Eric, treasuring the memory once more of the fleeting shock on Morton's face as his bag of sandwiches flew off to the side.

"Another drink, Kingsly?"

His colleague pushed his chair back and leant down to pick up his case.

"Better not, I'll catch the next bus, it's due in a couple of minutes. Thanks, Eric, it was good to see you. Perhaps we can have another session sometime."

He rested his hand briefly on Eric's shoulder then went out through the revolving door. For the first time, Eric realised, he was not feeling irritated at the sight of Kingsly's head from the rear. Instead, he found himself thinking seriously once more of what it would be like to escape from his own job.

He looked at his watch again. No sign of Eleanor. His sandwich turned out to have more than enough cheese and pickle in when it came. Predictably enough, he was halfway through the last part of his food, simultaneously chewing and dabbing at a small splash of pickle that had attacked his jacket, when Eleanor slid into the chair opposite.

"Just as well I'm a bit early," she grinned, nodding at his lapel.

Eric half rose for his customary kiss of greeting but Eleanor held out two fingers in the form of a cross. Eric sat down again.

"How did the meeting with your Prof go this morning?"

"It didn't, as a matter of fact."

She scowled. "But I had the impression that you were getting together to discuss your module thingies."

Eric said nothing for a moment or two.

"Well?" She asked.

"I did wait for him but he turned up incredibly late with a visitor and just went directly upstairs. I sat around for a while and then decided enough was enough."

Eleanor's frown deepened. "Was the visitor a well dressed woman of about fifty?"

Eric nodded.

"That happens to have been the local M.P. Eric! My father is due to meet with her this evening, along with the Vice Chancellor and a few local worthies. There's quite a head of steam building up behind the building project now."

"And?" Eric asked.

"Bloody hell, Eric, this is not really the time to annoy your Professor. You can't have that many friends and supporters in this place surely?"

"Look, don't let this interfere with our plans," he said, placing a hand on her arm. To his dismay her cross look remained. "If I had gone to the meeting I probably would never have been able to get here in time," he finished lamely.

In response Eleanor took her mobile phone from her pocket and pointed at it.

"Right, right. But I got really fed up sitting around at Henry's beck and call. And I'm heartily sick of messing around with bits of bloody paper and modular structures."

He pushed his briefcase irritably from the chair as he spoke

"To be honest," he went on, "I'm beginning to think I want nothing to do with *any* of Henry's schemes."

Eleanor shook her head. "Not really an option, Eric. Who is going to come to the rescue if you pack in your job?"

Eric thought with some bitterness of the years he had devoted to what expertise he had managed to acquire. "I've probably got better prospects as a former modern language lecturer than as, say, a former historian."

"True but you're not going to get a call from the United Nations to beef up their interpreting team are you? I'm not belittling your skills Eric, but how much could you stand of the sort of routine you would have if you left the university?"

The thought had long since struck Eric. Hearing it articulated rubbed the point home nicely.

"Don't look so glum," Eleanor added, reaching across and patting his hand. "Look, let's get on our way. You'll have to think up a really good excuse for not going to the meeting but we might as well make the most of your free time while you have it."

"What would your father say about this, this jaunt?"

"Probably not so much now, if he knew of it. Not that he would be happy but I'm working alongside him and he is getting less and less anti- university by the day since he started hob-knobbing with your Vice Chancellor and his sidekicks."

"Do you think he would want an extra hand?" Eric asked, only half in jest.

An explosive snort came from Eleanor as they came out in the sunlit street.

"I'm afraid it's likely to be more of the same for you my dear. There'll be no sudden summons to a wonderful job in London!" She paused and rummaged in her bag before handing over a piece of paper. "Talking of calls, Albert asked you to ring him. Use the phone box over there while I get the car round. Don't be too long. We still have to pick up your things."

Eric watched her moving elegantly away and felt the usual stirring. He looked down at the crumpled note and then took it into the telephone box nearby. He kept the door open a crack with his foot once he had taken a lungful of the stale air inside.

"Hello?" A voice said abruptly.

"Albert? It's me, Eric."

"Eric. Now, listen, I haven't got much time. Firstly, I'm not taking up the Varne option. Had enough of that sod in the past few weeks. I think I preferred him as a straightforward crook before he got this, what do you call it, town and gown thing. Two, reverting to plan one, I *am* going to start up some sort of business. Varne's new toy will mean that he'll be even less bothered by me. He won't find it hard to find a new dogsbody in this place."

"I thought you said you were working *with* Varne," Eric ventured.

"Shut up. Three, do you want to risk putting your miserable severance hand-out into my little scheme? Not straight away of course. But at least keep the general idea in mind?"

Eric felt a rush of blood to his head.

"What else would I have to live on? I mean, I can't see your idea making much just yet."

"That's where you could be wrong. You types always underestimate people like me. I've already got several things lined up, let alone the compensation I will be getting for releasing my houses on Inkers Lane. Then," he paused, "there are a couple of other properties I'm about to get hold of out on the coast. Might need a bit of help managing those. Might be a, what do you call it, a share option for you in due course."

Eric saw Eleanor's car pull up outside and waved briefly to her, holding up a couple of fingers.

"Nice to know that you see me as a sort of messenger cum rent collector, or perhaps emptying out machines from some little dive of yours in Bridlington. I suppose I could work up to being a full time office boy."

"Yeah, yeah," Albert interrupted. "And what are your prospects now that Henry wotsis-name and Varne have got your balls in their hands." There was a pause. "And how long do you think you've got screwing Eleanor? Like father, like daughter. I can't see your ambition matching hers for long, but you should know." He chortled.

During the past few minutes Eric had begun to feel an unstoppable sense of excitement seeping through him. Conjuring up the tightly reined-in persona of Helm, the meaningless good cheer of the Vice Chancellor, the faintly demented churning out of modular descriptors for-the-filling-in-of, the prospect of having Morton bearing down on him, let alone the tone of rampant self-advertisement now apparently demanded of and all too happily exhibited by so many of his fellow lecturers, Eric could find no good reason to stay put. Albert must have sensed something.

"Come on Eric, you *are* thinking of jumping ship. Come along my son, leap!

An insistent honking came from Eleanor's car and Eric turned away from it.

"Look Albert, I've got Eleanor waiting outside so I'll have to go but..."

"You're tempted?" Albert interrupted.

253

"Albert, I think I am, I really do!" Eric shouted gleefully.

"Your brawn and my brains, Eric. What have we got to lose? Tomorrow night, when you get back from your jaunt. Station Hotel again. We'll drink to it."

"Station Hotel it is!" Eric said.

He clambered into the car and Eleanor let the clutch in. They picked a case up at his flat and in no time the bonnet was pushing its way along the road leading towards the distant coast. As the houses on the outskirts of the city passed by Eric realised with pleasure that the problem was not and had never been the place itself. It was and always had been the university at the root of his unease."It was and always had been the university at the root of his unease. On an impulse he almost poured out his thoughts to Eleanor. Then, glancing down at her legs he decided otherwise. What her reaction would be to his new plans he could only guess but it decidedly would not, he told himself, help his love life. He reached across and placed a hand on her knee. It was not removed and he settled back to relish the prospect of the coming weekend.

You're learning, my son, he pictured Albert saying over his shoulder. And by God he was.